SHOW ME THE HONEY

A Sweet & Dirty BBW Romance

Cathryn Cade

Copyright

Show Me the Honey
Sweet & Dirty BBW Romance Series. Book 1
Cathryn Cade. -- 1st ed.
ISBN 9781944973322

Dedication

To
Good friend & fellow author
Debra Elise
for her fabulous story suggestions,
including more of Jack.

Summary

***When a small town cafe owner is grabbed by a rambling
biker looking for nearly a million in stolen cash, she must
convince him to let her go. But finding out he has the wrong
woman only makes him more determined to hang onto her
... this time for all the right reasons.***

*Lindi Carson has no time for romance in her life--not when
she's scrambling to make a success of her Coeur d'Alene Lake
shore café. She's barely keeping her head above water when
biker Jack Moran hits town, sure she knows where to find
nearly a million in stolen cash. When Jack grabs her, Lindi
must convince him he has the wrong woman.*

*But Jack's not the only one after the money, and someone is
willing to kill to get it. With murder lurking in this idyllic resort town and a dangerous MC on the prowl, Jack must
persuade Lindi she belongs not only under his protection ...
but in his arms. He'll use every ounce of his rough charm to
get her, but he may have to battle old ghosts to keep her
there.*

Can he convince her that love's sweetness is worth the sting?

A Sweet & Dirty BBW Romance

Chapter One

Monday

Lindi Carson steered her bicycle off the lake road and into the parking lot of the BeeHive Café. Gravel crunched under her tires as she coasted toward the small, white building hunched in the early morning shade of the mountain. Her breath steamed in the chilly air.

She scanned the evergreens on the far edge of the lot and then sighed with relief, her tight shoulders relaxing. No beefed-up vintage Chevy Blazer idled in the shadows this morning. And if Darrell wasn't here by now, he was off somewhere on business. Which meant that for once she could begin her day without her creepy nemesis glowering at her from the corner table, freaking her out and making her so nervous she sometimes forgot parts of breakfast orders and nearly burned others, thereby threatening the burgeoning reputation of the BeeHive Café as serving the best breakfasts on the north shore of Coeur d'Alene Lake.

After wheeling around to the back of the café, Lindi switched off her bike safety lights and leaned it against the cinderblock wall behind the dumpster. She fished the keys from her pocket, unlocked the back door and stepped into the warm quiet of the tiny back hallway, lit by an emergency nightlight high on the wall.

She inhaled the familiar odors of cooking and cleaner as she stripped off her gloves and flexed her cold fingers. Riding a bicycle at dawn in early April could be a chilly endeavor. An unseasonably warm spell had melted the remains of a late snow off the North Idaho roads, and the weather report called for a warm afternoon, but this morning the thermometer on her kitchen window had read only forty-seven degrees. And just looking at the snowbanks still lying in the shadows of the evergreens along the lake road had made her feel colder as she pedaled.

Cycling was great exercise, she reminded herself. Since deciding to walk or ride her bike whenever she could instead of driving her ailing Caprice, she'd lost nearly five pounds. She'd hoped to lose more, but evidently she'd have to give up eating for that to happen. She enjoyed food way too much to do that. She also ate when stressed, and lately her life qualified as stressful with a capital 'S'.

Luckily, she enjoyed feeding other people even more. Loved watching their faces light up when they saw her offerings, loved watching them take that first bite and then close their eyes in bliss. And not in some fancy cordon bleu restaurant, but right here.

Anticipation fired with each one of the bank of lights she stopped to flick on. First the kitchen, merciless fluorescent that showed every flaw and crumb, then the warmer yellow lights in the café proper.

Unzipping her windbreaker and the fleece jacket underneath, she tossed them onto her office chair as she passed the tiny cubicle that held a desk and file cabinet opposite the big upright freezer. Her bicycle helmet joined the jacket.

In the narrow galley kitchen, she pulled a clean, black apron from the pantry and tied it on over her white tee and black yoga pants. With black trainers, this comprised her work uniform.

Next, she uncovered the fryers, checked the oil levels and then powered them up along with the grill. She set the two ovens to warm, made sure the smoke detectors were working, and hurried around the other side of the high service counter to get the first pots of coffee going.

Since she left the coffee machine set up every afternoon before she went home, all she had to do now was power it on. She waited to hear the familiar sounds of hot water burbling through the pipes, then reached up to flip the boombox on to a local country station. As Blake Shelton crooned about riding in his pickup truck, she turned to survey her domain.

The BeeHive's signature yellow Formica counters gleamed. Six matching tables lined the front window and arced around the corner toward the restroom.

Outside, the spring dawn lightened the eastern sky over the mountains and the parking lot in a wash of cool green and gray. She glanced at the clock on the wall over the glassed-in front door. Five minutes to six o'clock.

Just time to step into the bathroom for a quick glance in the mirror over the sink. Her face was still pink from the chill, but that would soon be replaced by the flush of heat from the grill. Mascara and a dusting of taupe shadow emphasized her brown eyes. Peach lip gloss moistened her lips. Blusher defined the underside of her cheekbones in her rounded face.

She bundled her shoulder-length dark blonde hair up on the back of her head and pulled a black scrunchie from her pocket to hold it in a ponytail, then fluffed her long bangs. Thank goodness her hair was wavy and full of body, so she didn't have to do much with it on these early mornings. It needed highlights, but not happening on her current budget.

She tugged her tee down over her rounded hips, with a last look in the mirror to confirm that the snug black yoga pants looked at least okay on her round ass. Fortunately she had long legs to balance the extra weight she carried. And her boobs were nice.

As an older customer had once told her with a twinkle in his eyes, a well-padded cook was a sign of good cooking.

Anyhoo, time to get to work. With a bounce in her step, Lindi hurried back to the hallway, and snapped another switch. Outside, the neon sign flickered to life, the yellow arcs of an old-fashioned beehive framed by the words BeeHive Café. That done, she crossed to the front door and unlocked it.

A single headlight appeared as if summoned around the curve in the narrow, winding road along the lake. A big, gleaming black and silver Harley rolled into the parking lot and pulled to a stop before the café.

Lindi tensed, but when the lone rider was not followed by others, she relaxed. Not a rowdy crowd of Spokane or Silver Valley bikers coming back from a night's revelry and mayhem. Just one man.

He kicked down the stand of his big bike and lifted one long leg over it, rolling to his feet with easy grace. In his leather jacket, faded jeans and boots, he was an imposing figure. He pulled off his dark stocking hat and stuffed it in a pocket, then raised one gloved hand to push back his sandy blond hair.

Lindi sighed. With those broad shoulders and cocky stance, and that sexy-messy hair, he could model for Harley cycles or men's cologne

Their eyes met through the glass door. Slowly, his square face crinkled in a smile, his white teeth gleaming.

Realizing she was gawking from a lighted window, Lindi stepped back abruptly, her face flaming. She was a business owner, not a star-struck teenager. Time to act like it.

By the time the biker pushed the door open and walked in, bringing with him a waft of cool, piney morning air, Lindi was behind the counter, busying herself with the coffee service.

"Morning," she called over her shoulder. "Coffee to start your day?"

When he didn't answer immediately, she turned. Standing just inside the door, her customer stood, booted feet apart, slowly stripping off his gloves as he cast an encompassing look around the small space and back at her. He stuffed the gloves in a pocket of his black leather jacket. Only then did he move forward the few steps to the seat nearest the open end of the counter.

He straddled the stool and sat, gaze intent on her in a way that made her feel as if the two bees embroidered on her apron had escaped and were buzzing around in her middle, a sensation that wavered between delicious and unnerving.

His eyes were light hazel under thick lashes and heavy brows a few shades darker than his hair. His skin was tanned, with creases that said he smiled or squinted into the sun a lot. His wide jaw and the pugnacious set of his mouth said he was not a man to be messed with.

Finally, he lifted his chin in acknowledgement, his gaze never leaving her face.

"Yeah, coffee sounds good." His voice was deep and rough in a way that sent pleasure prickling along her nerve endings. Darn, was there anything about the man that wasn't sexy?

"Right," she chirped. "Coffee, comin' up."

She filled one of her sturdy mugs and set it before him with a napkin and a spoon. She turned, squatted to pull a saucer of cream packets from the small refrigerator under the back counter—because bending over just emphasized her big ass—and set it near his place setting.

Not like he was here to look at her, anyway. She moved a few steps away, pulled the tray of plastic honey bears that were a signature of the BeeHive from a lower shelf and began to set them out along the counter, one for every two places.

"Need a menu?" she asked.

He picked up one of the creamer pods and flicked it open with a thumbnail. His hands were as big as the rest of him, and calloused but clean.

"You give good breakfast?" he asked.

Lindi met his gaze, her cheeks warm. He'd managed to invest the question with a nearly sexual innuendo. And his sparkling eyes seemed to miss nothing, including her reaction. Well, it took more than a mouthy biker to rattle her.

"The best you ever ate," she retorted.

His wide mouth twitched in the hint of a smile as he stirred the cream into his mug. "Just coffee for now, Lindi."

He knew her name? Duh, right. Her name was spelled out in yellow thread, with the bees buzzing around it, on her black apron. "That's me. And you are?"

He tilted his head in the ghost of a courtly bow. "I'm Jack."

Her cheeks heated even more. "Okay, Jack. You, um, let me know if you want anything to eat." And anything else, like maybe picking her up and pulling her right over the counter for a long, hot kiss.

The plastic bear in her hand spurted honey. No wonder, she'd been squeezing it. As honey dripped over her fingers, Jack's grin widened, his eyes twinkling. God, she was such a dork. Lindi grabbed the tray of bears and turned away to dip her hand and the sticky bear under a stream of warm water, carefully avoiding that knowing gaze.

"You get many customers out here?" he asked.

"I do," she answered with satisfaction. "The warm weekend we just had brought lots of cyclists and walkers out to the trail along the lake. Also, wild turkey season just opened, so I expect a lot of turkey hunters to make it a three-day weekend. And there'll be fishermen headed out onto Coeur d'Alene Lake for spring kokanee."

"Sounds good for business."

"Uh-huh, sure is."

As she set the rest of the bears out on the tables, a pickup truck with two men swung into the lot outside, followed by a red Honda SUV. Lindi breathed a sigh of relief. Her day was about to get busy. That was excellent—money in the till and no time to continue this semi-flirtation or whatever it was.

Anyway, Jack probably flirted this way with every woman he met. And they would certainly flirt back—he was a lot of man, and he had a way of focusing on a woman that made her feel special—not threatened in a nasty way, like that creep Darrell.

By ten-fifteen, the breakfast rush at the BeeHive was over. The last vehicle of outdoor sports enthusiasts had rolled out of her parking area, leaving Lindi with a comfortably full till, a dishwasher and sink loaded with dirty dishes ... and Jack.

He'd remained, drinking coffee and watching her cook and carry out platter after platter of pancakes, cinnamon rolls, eggs, bacon, sausage and hash-browns, along with a few orders of granola and one bowl of oatmeal.

Finally at eight o'clock he'd ordered the Fisherman's Special— three whole-grain huckleberry pancakes, two eggs and a rasher of crisp bacon. She'd watched with satisfaction as he ate with relish, noting that he was a honey man—he drizzled that over his pancakes instead of the maple syrup favored by many. Having put away every bite, he thanked her with a nod of appreciation and resumed drinking coffee.

She'd nibbled a few bites here and there herself between customers—a broken fried egg, a piece of bacon and a ruined pancake with honey and huckleberry syrup. She'd love to chow down big plates of food like her customers, but she was already self-conscious about her weight, so she tried to watch her intake. Dave had loved her breasts and her ass, calling it heart-shaped and perfect for a man to get a good grip on, but for herself, she'd love to be a couple of sizes smaller.

Nevertheless, cooking and waitressing was hard work. She'd take time for a solitary lunch before she rode her bike back to her apartment in the older part of downtown Coeur d'Alene.

Now Lindi watched the last SUV full of satisfied customers disappear up the road, and looked at Jack over her soapy cleaning rag. Why was he still here? Unless he wanted to ask her out, and didn't want an audience. Right—like this man would mind onlookers. He'd expect success. Still, a thrill of heat ran through her at the possibility.

"You waiting for someone?" she asked, wiping syrup and coffee off the far end of the counter. "Because I close at eleven. I'm not open for lunch on weekdays." She'd like to be, but only the weekends and holidays brought enough mid-day traffic out here along the lake. Someday she intended to be a destination worth driving a little extra for, but that hadn't happened yet.

Jack took a last drink of coffee and set his mug down. He turned, his torso twisting as he surveyed the empty café and parking lot. He'd taken off his jacket at some point and tossed it across the stool next to him. His snug white tee shirt bore the logo of a California brewery. The thin knit lovingly outlined the heavy muscle in his shoulders, torso and upper arms. A leather belt adorned his waist, with a Harley buckle and sheath holding a large folding knife.

"You could say that," he said, turning back to her.

Lindi paused, wet rag poised between counter and sink, a rivulet of warm, soapy water trickling down her forearm and splatting on the floor. For the first time since he'd rolled into her parking lot, a frisson of alarm ghosted over her skin. The way he watched her now, those light eyes like a hawk's watching his prey, did nothing to allay her wariness.

God, she hoped he wasn't some crooked associate of Darrell's. He could be a hit man or a serial killer for all she knew. Just because he was hot didn't mean anything. Look at Ted Bundy—he'd gotten all his victims to go with him willingly.

"Well," she said, "hope they get here soon. I'll, um, I'll just be in the back if you want anything else."

Her mother had always told her and Cissie to obey their instincts, saying God gave women an extra dose for good reason. And belatedly, Lindi's instincts drowned out her hormones, screaming *danger*!

Dropping the rag in the sink, she wiped her wet hands on her apron as she strolled back through the short hallway to her office. She palmed her cellphone from her desk, thumbed the button to bring it to life, then gave a huff of nervous disgust. No service, as usual. Something about the cinderblocks used in the café's construction blocked most calls, unless one stood just by the plate glass windows up front.

And she could hardly dial 911 in front of the man of whom she was suspicious, now could she? There were no other phone numbers that required only three digits, and he seemed to notice everything she did.

Keeping her back to the café area, Lindi slipped from the open office door and then glided the several steps to the back door. It opened with a squeak, and she winced. Nothing like advertising her getaway.

Inspired, she shoved her phone into her pocket and hurried back to the trash can just inside the kitchen. Without looking at Jack, she yanked the bag shut and pulled it up out of the barrel.

She turned to carry it along the passageway to the back door, and stopped with gasp as a large body blocked the light. Jack loomed at the corner of the counter. His gaze flicked from the garbage bag to her face.

"You usually take out the trash before you finish scraping dishes?" he asked.

Her heart pounding, Lindi shrugged. Darn, he really did notice everything. She backed up, keeping the garbage between them like a shield.

"Sometimes," she said, her gaze locked on him as he moved forward. "Wh-what's it to you?"

"Put it down, honey," he ordered, taking another step toward her with the smooth, prowling gait of a predator.

Lindi's heart stopped. Oh, God. She'd been right. He was here for a lot more than breakfast.

As he moved closer, Lindi heaved the trash bag at him, whirled and dashed for the back door.

She nearly made it.

Chapter Two

The BeeHive's back door slammed open, Lindi leapt from the narrow stoop onto the ground—and was yanked to a halt by a hard grip on her arm.

She cried out in shock and fear as her captor swung her around, then yelped in pain as her cheek banged against his collarbone. For a second she saw stars.

Her free hand to her face, Lindi pulled away from his long, hard body, eyeing him through a haze of terror. "No," she protested. "No, *don't*."

Jack—if that was even his name—frowned as he surveyed her face. "Ah, hell. Sorry about that. Listen, I'm not gonna hurt you, just need you to give me what I want."

What he wanted? Lindi's meager breakfast roiled in her stomach, and she clapped her hand over her mouth as she fought the urge to vomit. "G-give you what you want?" she repeated, hoping against hope it wasn't her body.

"Yeah," he said. "Just tell me where it is, honey."

Wait, *what*?

"Tell you where what is?" He was after something else—not her. He wasn't going to rape her. Relief swamped her, so intensely his next words didn't register at first.

"You know what I mean. Where's the money?"

Lindi stared up at him. "Money?" He was a common thief? Boy, had she read him wrong. "I—I have maybe three hundred in the till. Take it. You can have it all. I won't say anything to anyone, I swear."

Many of her customers paid with credit cards, so at least he couldn't take that too.

He snorted. "Nice try, Lindi. I'm talkin' about the real money."

"What real money? I don't know what you're talking about. I don't have any money."

This was true—so far she barely made enough to keep this place open, buy groceries and pay her utilities. The bank owned more of the BeeHive than she did. And they were not happy about the pace of her repayment of her loan—a letter a few days ago had demanded politely that she make an appointment with her loan officer to discuss concerns. Concerns, such a bland word for the panic the notice had loosed inside her.

If she didn't step up her payments, she could lose it all. And she had no one to turn to, no one to depend on but herself. Her mother, after raising two girls on menial jobs, had no savings at all, and while Lindi's brother-in-law had a very well-paying job, he and Cissie had two little girls and their own bills to pay, which for the last year had included hefty medical bills.

Dave had been helping Lindi make loan payments, his way of telling her he was behind her one hundred percent, when he died a year ago last winter, his motorcycle skidding on an icy patch of the lake road one night. But when he died, so did the extra payments. Since then she'd just been keeping ahead of her debt by the skin of her teeth. If this biker stole today's take, she'd be in the hole even deeper.

Jack sighed, and his gaze hardened. "All right. If that's the way you want to play this."

Straightening, he hauled her around the corner of the building.

Lindi gave a gasp of sheer terror when she saw that a dusty, late-model black SUV now waited near the front of the café, the engine running. A lean man in jeans, boots and leather vest over a dark Henley vaulted out and held open the back door, surveying Lindi with a cold gaze. "She tell you where it is?"

"Nope." Lindi's captor smacked her on her ass. "Not yet. Up, woman."

There was a third man driving. Jack had cohorts? That meant this was organized, planned. This was *big*. Oh, God, they were part of a biker gang.

Lindi shook her head so hard her ponytail flipped back and forth, and dug her heels into the gravel. "No! I won't go with you."

Big hands closed on her waist, and she found herself lifted through the air, and tossed into the back seat as easily as if she weighed next to nothing. She landed on her hands and one knee on soft leather, then the vehicle rocked as the other two men jumped in after her.

Lindi scrambled across the seats, got one hand on the far door handle, only to be captured again with a powerful arm around her waist.

"Drive!" ordered Jack.

The vehicle leapt forward. The momentum threw Lindi back onto her captor's lap. She squirmed frantically, kicking and clawing at his encircling arm with her short fingernails.

"*No!*" she gritted, defiance her only weapon, although her heart was pounding so fast and hard she felt faint. "You can't do this! I don't have any money, and I don't know where any is."

Kidnapped by a group of men who thought she had access to a lot of money—this was bad, really bad. She could imagine how they'd try to make her talk. Her heart pounded faster, and her head whirled. Escape became her only goal.

"Ow!" Jack grabbed both her wrists in an iron grip. "Jesus Christ, stop clawing me. Told you, we're not gonna hurt you."

"At least, as long as you cooperate." The driver smirked in the rearview mirror, steering one-handed up the narrow road away from the lake. He looked to be in his early twenties, with tattoos, a greasy faux-hawk and piercings in places on his face that made Lindi wince. He wore no shirt under his leather vest, and she was pretty sure the stench of stale booze and sweat in the SUV was mostly coming from him.

As his hot, leering gaze met Lindi's, a whimper worked its way out of her throat. She stopped trying to get away from Jack, instead shrinking backward into his embrace. The driver reminded her of someone ... Darrell. He had the same spark of twisted obsession in his eyes.

Yup, these men were mixed up with Darrell somehow. She just knew it. Or maybe he'd even sicced them on her for spite—telling them she would be payment for some debt he owed them.

The third man, who had a silver ponytail spilling down the back of his leather vest, turned sharply, giving her a narrow-eyed look around the back of the captain's chair. His tanned but unlined face contrasted with his hair color, as he couldn't be more than thirty-something.

"Shut up, Twig," he ordered the driver. "She thinks you mean we got somethin' in mind other than talk."

Jack peered into her face. "Aw, hell." He loosed her wrists to pat her thigh, and his grip on her waist eased. "You can put that out of your head right now, honey. No one is gonna lay a hand on you, not that way. We want information, pure and simple. You give us that and you're free to go, no blowback."

Lindi struggled to slow her panicked breathing enough to speak. Not that she believed they wouldn't hurt her—the kind of men who'd grab her right out of her café wouldn't shrink from doing more. She was in big trouble.

With the perfect clarity of hind-sight, she saw that instead of trying to dial 911, she should've stood in the front window of the café and smiled at Jack while she phoned one of her two best friends, Sara or Kit. Then she could've chatted about their favorite restaurant or something while passing them a coded message to call the cops ... Except that she'd been too scared to think up any kind of a secret coded message, and Jack might not have let her make a phone call to anyone at all.

Okay, so she wasn't exactly a kick-ass heroine with lightning fast reflexes and super skills in thinking on her feet. But if she could just get through the next moments, maybe she could survive this intact.

And she still had her phone in the pocket of her apron—she'd use it the instant she got the chance.

"Wh-what do you want to know?" she asked. "I already told you, the only money I have is in my till." And as little as she could afford to lose that, if it would keep her alive, they could have it all. Heck, they could have the equipment in her café kitchen too.

"Right. Like you don't know, bitch," the driver sneered as he wrestled the big vehicle wide around a curve.

An old pickup coming the other way swerved to miss them, horn blaring. The sound faded in the distance as the faux-hawked Twig gunned the engine harder, making the SUV skid sideways on the gravel. Lindi let out a cry of distress, voicing the tumult of fear inside her, which his crazy driving amplified.

"Watch it!" Jack ordered. "Jesus, Keys, why'd you let him drive?"

Lindi nearly slid from Jack's lap when the SUV rocked from side to side, and she grabbed his big forearm. His flesh was hot, corded with muscle and tendon, and rigid under her grip.

His arm tightened again, holding her snug against his hard body. At least he was warm—despite the growing warmth of the sunny day, she was shivering, nervous sweat leaving her skin cold and clammy under her clothing. A trickle ran down her cleavage to pool in her bra. She was gonna smell as bad as Twig if they held her very long.

"I'll be drivin' from now on," Ponytail said, giving the driver a hard look.

"Yeah, fuck both o' you," the younger man muttered. "I ain't your mule. Anyways, I said we shoulda come on our bikes, didn't I?"

Jack's grip on Lindi's thigh loosened, his thumb stroking over it, oddly soothing through her knit yoga pants. "We wanna know what Gaspard did with the money," he said in her ear. "All you have to do is tell us where it is, and like I said, you're done. Free to buzz on back to your little café."

Lindi twisted her head far enough to gape at him in bewilderment.

"David Gaspard?" she said. "Dave never had any money." He'd worked at a local auto-body shop and spent his paychecks pretty much as soon as he earned them—some on his motorcycle, but a lot on her, bless his big heart.

And after he died, she'd not only had to deal with her grief at losing the man who loved her, but with her guilt for holding back with him, refusing to commit totally to their relationship. She'd told herself it was because he wasn't 'the one', but a small, shamed part of her knew that maybe he had been, if she could just bring herself to trust any man unconditionally.

But it seemed impossible, after watching her father break her mother's heart over and over. Cissie had managed the leap of faith, and was happily married, but Lindi had held back, and now it was too late for her and Dave.

"Who the hell's Dave? I'm talkin' about Darrell Gaspard," Jack corrected.

Okay, this was just getting weirder and weirder, although she'd been right in the first place. "Darrell? Why would I know what he did with his money?"

Dave's older brother had a legitimate business, a shop up this very mountain where he rebuilt cars, SUVs and pickup trucks, turning them into souped-up custom street-rods. Dave had pointed out some of Darrell's work the summer before in the classic car and street-rod show on the streets of downtown Coeur d'Alene. The annual gathering was a real tourist draw for their little resort town.

But also according to Dave, Darrell had his hands in a few other businesses, too—the kind that were best left unmentioned. Dave would never tell her what they were, and having met Darrell, Lindi was happier not knowing.

Since Dave himself had hung around the fringes of a local MC, the Devil's Flyers, doing the club favors now and then, although he'd never patched in, she knew his brother's dealings must be deep for Dave to disapprove. Dave had come home smelling of weed once in a while, but he'd made clear his disapproval of stronger drugs, and assured her the Flyers did not run or sell drugs. That didn't mean Darrell didn't do so.

She just wished she had some way to prove her worst suspicions of Darrell—that he'd had something to do with his own brother's death.

Jack sighed. "All right, let's cut through the shit. You'd know 'cause you're his woman."

"What?" Oh, my God. That explained a lot. This was all a big mistake. Lindi huffed out a breathless laugh.

Ponytail turned to give her a strange look.

Lindi smiled at him, dizzy with utter relief. "Darrell? I've never had anything to do with that lowlife. No, see, I was with his brother, David. Only he—he died last winter And God knows Dave never had any extra money. Hoo, boy, I see it now. You have the wrong girl."

Chapter Three

Lindi wasn't entirely sure there was a right girl—for Darrell, that is. She'd never seen him with a woman. Who'd be stupid enough to go with him?

Although of course the answer to that was, plenty of women. Just look at those who married prison inmates because they were good-looking, despite whatever horrendous crime had landed them in maximum security. That's the kind of woman Darrell would attract.

She'd worried when she first met Dave about the wisdom of dating a guy who hung out with bikers, but he'd won her over with his easy-going nature and big heart. He hadn't been the best looking guy in town, but the way he'd treated her had made her feel beautiful and sexy. He was completely different from his skanky brother.

There was a short, charged silence, as the vehicle rumbled along the winding road. Ponytail exchanged a look with Jack over Lindi's head, and shook his head, as if to say 'women', or maybe just 'this one's a nut-job'.

"Damn, bitch," the driver swore, "you really think you can shine us on, don'tcha? You don't cut this shit out, all that sweet talk about not touchin' you don't mean a thing. We know you're Darrell Gaspard's pussy."

"What?" Lindi gasped. "I most certainly am not." Her stomach twisted in revulsion.

"Twig, pay fuckin' attention," Jack's deep voice over-rode hers as he gestured to the left. "Here's the turn."

The SUV swung to the left onto a narrow, rutted lane up through the trees. Lindi had been this way only once with Dave, but she remembered the lane led to Darrell's place. As the vehicle lunged upward over rocks and through deep ruts, all she could do was hope the man holding her wouldn't drop her. His big, muscular frame cushioned her from the worst of the jolts, but she clung to his forearm just in case he let go.

He was protecting her from the bumps, but that didn't mean he would protect her from other things—far worse things—when they reached the cabin and shop where Darrell worked on custom cars. Her stomach twisted again.

"I really don't—" she began, over the whine of the big engine.

The arm around her squeezed, pulling her more tightly back against Jack's hard torso.

"Shut it," he growled. "No more talk, unless I tell you. You're just stirrin' shit."

Lindi hunched her shoulder as his warm breath tickled her ear. In contrast, his voice held a note of cold menace. She shivered again with the chilling realization that he wasn't so much protecting her as keeping his information source safe.

The SUV cleared the bare-limbed vine maples lining the road, and emerged into a flat clearing. They slowed to a stop in a sweep of gravel. The old cabin hunched to their right. Lindi knew Dave and his brother had both grown up here, and Dave had told her that when their parents were alive it was clean and well-kept, but it certainly wasn't now. A filthy gas grill and one chair stood on the sagging porch, the dirty remnants of snow still drifted on the north end of the worn boards. Oddly, the front door was open.

In contrast to the squalor of the cabin, Darrell's big custom shop loomed to the left, with a neat gray metal exterior and closed doors. All the snow had been plowed away from the two massive vehicle doors, and piled back in the shelter of the tall evergreens that surrounded the lot.

"Sure is a nice shop for the middle of the woods in Bumfuck, Idaho," Twig commented as he turned off the ignition.

"Custom rides are worth big money, done right," Ponytail said. "And Gaspard's good."

"Maybe we'll find some cash from that end of his business too," Twig said, and leapt out of the vehicle.

"C'mon," Jack said. He slid out of the back seat, bearing Lindi with him like a child. He set her feet on the ground, but kept his arm around her.

Ponytail looked them over. "You got 'er?"

"I've got her." Jack's voice was hard, determined.

Determined to do what? To somehow use her to rob Darrell? Lindi's legs shook under her. She stumbled on the uneven ground, and Jack's arm tightened again—in support or captivity, she didn't know. Either way, it had the same effect.

Willy-nilly, her feet carried her across the graveled sweep—Darrell did not consider a lawn a necessary accoutrement of country living—and up onto the porch. It creaked ominously under their feet, and the dim interior of the cabin yawned like open jaws.

"Do we have to go in there?" she asked, digging in her heels. "You better be careful. Dave said Darrell shot at a guy once, just for showing up on his porch and surprising him."

She wasn't sure, at this point, which would be worse—Darrell shooting her captors, or vice versa. No matter who won, she'd still be between a rock and hard place.

"Oh, I don't think he'll be surprised to see us," Ponytail said dryly, but he moved ahead of them into the dim interior of the house.

Lindi peered around the small living room anxiously, then grimaced in disgust. The place smelled of dirty laundry, cigarettes and stale booze. "What a pit-hole," she mumbled.

Jack grunted. "Yeah, surprised you don't do a little housework around here for your man."

"*Me*?" She was getting really tired of being lumped with her worst enemy. "I told you, I am not with Darrell. I hate him and I hate this place."

And she hated Jack too, with a passion that burned deep and hot. How dare he show up at her café, convince her he was a nice guy and then turn on her like this?

"Really?" he said. He didn't sound as if he believed her. "Wanna try that again, sweetheart? 'Cause this little shrine to your loveliness says different."

Ahead of them, Ponytail pushed open an interior door. Jack walked Lindi through it, snapping on an overhead light as they entered.

The smell was worse in here, with strange floral overtones, as if someone had tried to mask the stench. At first, Lindi looked at the furniture, trying to understand why they were here. There was nothing in the room but an old flowered sofa, the once rust and cream fabric dingy with age, a rickety end table, and the castoffs of a messy bachelor strewn about—an empty liquor bottle, an old shirt, a dirty towel.

Until she looked up, and saw the wall on the far side of the small room.

Footsteps shuffled as the other two men came in behind them. One of them bumped the door and it thumped on the wall. The sounds registered vaguely, along with the pounding of her heart, the lightness in her head, and the prickle of black pin-dots at the edge of her vision.

No longer breathing, unable to do anything but gape, Lindi stared ... at herself. Over and over again. Laughing, smiling, serious. Outdoors, indoors. Clothed and naked.

The entire wall of the room opposite the sofa was covered with photos of her, tacked to the paneling in an enormous collage. And while some of them were of her smiling from in front of the BeeHive, and behind the counter, some of them were extremely intimate. Photos that only a lover could have taken.

"Nice pussy shot," Twig said, moving to reach out and grab one large print. "Not bad for a fat chick."

Lindi stared at it in horror. She lay in tumbled sheets, smiling sleepily at the camera, everything from breasts to crotch on full view.

"*No*!" She shook her head, and pushed back against Jack, working her feet in the carpet, trying to worm her way back through him, into him, anything to get away from the horrific invasion of her private moments. All the parts of her body about which she was most self-conscious were displayed for these men to see. "No, *no*. He had no *right*."

"Aw, c'mon," Twig leered at her. "You didn't mind then. You spread for the camera all smiles. And there's a lot of you to spread."

Her outrage flamed into fury—at him, at Darrell, at all of them for being here, for forcing her to be here. She glared ferociously at him.

"Not for *him*!" she shouted, her voice breaking. "Never for him—and not for you either! Get out, all of you. *Don't look*."

She tore from Jack's grasp, and surprisingly, he let her go. Lindi yanked the photo from Twig's hand, then flew at the wall, clawing at the photos, ripping them down. They fell like tattered snowflakes around her feet. She leapt to scrabble for the highest, then snatched more down.

"Crazy bitch." Twig gave a cackle. "Jesus, she's fuckin' nuts."

"Let her be," Jack ordered.

Lindi didn't stop until the images lay around her in tattered heaps. Her fingers hurt. She noted distantly that her left index finger was bleeding, and stuck the digit in her mouth to suck away the blood.

She dropped to her knees, scraping the photos into a pile with shaking hands. She needed a trash bag, but her apron would work—anything to hide these private images. Reaching behind her, she untied the apron, and yanked it off over her head. Her ponytail holder slipped free, her hair sliding down around her shoulders.

Ignoring the men watching her, she began to pile the tattered photos onto the fabric. A can of floral scented room spray lay discarded on the floor. Her rage and pain coalescing, she hurled it at the wall, but it only thudded off and bounced on the filthy carpet, rolling back to where it had begun. Figured.

Surprisingly, Jack and Ponytail squatted to help her gather up the pictures.

"Who took these, honey?" Jack asked, his voice so gentle she answered without thought.

"David," she said, accepting a crumpled handful from him. Her voice cracked on a sudden burst of regret and sorrow. "M-my boyfriend, like I told you. He was always taking pictures with his phone. He—he promised me no one else would ever s-see the—the nude ones."

The goof-ball had driven her half-crazy, surprising her with candid shots. He'd emailed her the photos of her at the café. She'd been so proud the day it re-opened, and he'd been right there, grinning from his place at the end of the counter as customers came through the doors.

She hadn't liked him taking the nude shots of her, but he'd told her how pretty and sexy she was, and made her laugh, and she'd always ended up rolling her eyes and making him swear never to let anyone else see the photos.

She'd trusted Dave to keep his word in this, if not to give her forever. And when she was around his friends, she'd paid close attention, but none of them had ever given her looks that said they knew what she looked like naked. So he'd kept the pictures to himself—until Darrell had pirated them.

"Wh-when he died, his phone disappeared. Darrell must have found it." She'd believed it must have flown out of Dave's pocket and into the underbrush, lost forever when his motor-cycle skidded off the road.

Instead, all this time Darrell had had the phone, and he'd been printing these photos out and hanging them up here to look at—and probably doing more. She eyed the dirty towel lying nearby with renewed disgust.

Shame and hatred jumbled in her mind in a noxious brew. She just hoped the creep hadn't gotten around to posting any of these on the internet. Were her images gracing some X-rated chat room?

Her stomach lurched again, and she forced her attention back to the task at hand. She couldn't think about that now—she'd think about it later.

* * *

"So, Darrell had a thing for you, huh?" Jack asked Lindi Carson.

He held the apron as Keys stuffed the last of the photos into it. Jack wrapped the apron strings around it and tied it in a bundle, then looked at her, hoping the disgust and anger burning in his chest didn't show on his face.

Jesus, he wished Gaspard was here right now. Jack would slam his fist into the slime-ball's face so hard Gaspard would swallow his own teeth. Then he'd kick his balls up into his throat to join them.

What kind of a sick fuck perved over his own brother's woman? Gaspard had created an X-rated gallery, all of a woman Jack should've known was too sweet and wholesome to look twice at Gaspard. If that weasel had a woman, she'd be a hard-eyed, chain-smoking club whore, not a pretty, friendly blonde whose smile lit up her little café, and who blushed when a man flirted with her, even casually.

When he, Keys and Twig had come up here the evening before, intent on getting their money back from Gaspard if they had to beat it out of him, they'd found no sign of the money. But they had seen these pictures and they'd assumed the woman in them had to be Gaspard's pussy, who could talk even if he couldn't.

Since some of the pictures featured her at the little café they'd driven by at the foot of the hill, they'd known right where to find her. And Jack had volunteered to run point, for reasons he hadn't examined too closely, but which he now admitted had a lot to do with one of the pictures on Gaspard's wall.

He kinda wished he could've kept that one. She'd been laid out in rumpled sheets in the prettiest pose a man could hope to see—her legs crooked open to reveal the dark blonde curls on her mons, one heel hiding most of her pussy, her arms raised to shield her full breasts but succeeding only in plumping them together, hair tumbling over the pillow in just-fucked disarray, and a soft, sleepy smile on her face for whoever had taken the picture.

She was one helluva curvy armful, just right for a big man like him. He didn't like holding a woman and feeling like he had nothin' but bird bones in his grasp. Plus, she had a pretty face and a sweet smile.

So yeah, he'd wanted in there. Figured if she was Gaspard's, she sure as hell wasn't choosy. Hadn't occurred to him she wasn't really Gaspard's, that the fuckwad was a stalker, on top of being a liar who'd tried to cheat them out of their share of the profits on a certain shipment.

Now the blonde café owner pressed the back of her hand to her mouth and swallowed hard. Her face was pale too, her rosy glow gone, her soft peach-tinted mouth quivering. Jack hoped she wasn't gonna puke in here—the place smelled bad enough as it was.

"Well, I knew he ... he was always saying things," she told him, her voice shaking, "even when Dave was alive. Telling me he knew I put out for Dave, so why not him, why should his little brother have all the fun. But I thought that was just nasty, mean talk, because that's how he was. I didn't know—" she flapped one of her capable hands at the now empty walls, "that there was this."

Jack and Keys rose, Jack with the apron bundle clenched in his fist. If he didn't get to punch something or someone pretty soon, he was gonna explode. The whole trip had been one cluster-fuck after another, and this piece was partly on him. Maybe he should punch his own damn face.

He'd scared the shit out of an innocent woman, all for nothing. And if she decided to call the cops on them, they'd have to disappear faster than cold beer at a club barbecue. Because he was *not* holding her against her will just to keep her quiet. That would lead to trouble he didn't even want to think about, and it wasn't how he and Keys rolled.

Instead of rising with them, Lindi slumped sideways against the wall, back on her heels, looking played out with emotion. Her hair had fallen out of her ponytail, and curled around her face, one silky strand clinging to the corner of her lips.

"I don't understand any of this," she said, her voice shaking. "Why don't you just tell me what you really want, so you can get it, and go back wherever you came from?"

"All right, enough of this bullshit," Twig said, exploding into action.

Before Jack had a chance to react, Key's nephew grabbed the blonde by one wrist and yanked her up to her knees. He drew back his free hand and smacked her viciously across the side of her face. "Tell us where the money is, bitch, or this is just the beginning!"

Lindi Carson's head snapped to one side, her mouth open, eyes glazed with shock, hair flying.

"No!" Jack roared, fury roaring through him so hot he was across the room before he knew it. "Leave her alone!"

He grabbed the skinny younger man by the arm, forcing him to release Lindi. Then he showed the little fucker what it felt like to be hit in the face by someone bigger and stronger. His partly open hand thwacked Twig's face so hard his mohawked head snapped back, mouth open, eyes glazing—just like Lindi, only worse.

Jack let him go, and the kid slammed into the wall. Something cracked, the cheap paneling or Twig's head, Jack did not fuckin' care.

Chapter Four

The crack of Twig's hand echoed sharply in Lindi's head, followed by pain exploding in her temple, and the dizzying whirl of the room around her. She heard his words only distantly, followed by a hollow thud as she fell against the wall. Dizzy and lost, she slid down the slick paneling, letting gravity take over.

Jack roared something, his deep voice booming like distant thunder. Twig's lean body flew past her, slamming into the wall so hard it cracked under his weight.

Huddled protectively, one hand up to ward off further abuse, Lindi watched dazedly as her tormentor fell to the floor and lay still, eyes closed, mouth open, blood seeping from his nose and the corner of his lip.

Jack stood over him, fists clenched, face livid.

"One o' these days I'm gonna kill you, you little prick," he swore. "I don't care if he is your nephew, Keys. A man *don't hit women!*"

"May do him myself," Ponytail said, his voice hard. "Stupid piece of shit. Jack, see to her. I'll dump his ass out in the cage."

When Jack crouched before her, Lindi shrank away, shaking her head even though the motion sent renewed pain through her head. "No, no. Leave me 'lone. I don't know anything. I don't, I swear." Tears flooded her eyes and thickened her voice, but she was past caring.

"Fuck me if I don't believe you," he said, his voice gentle. "C'mon, let's get you out of here."

"No, no." She tried to scramble away, but he caught her as she got her legs under herself.

Ignoring her protests, he pulled her carefully the rest of the way to her feet, then lifted her high into his arms, and bore her out of the room. Lindi cried out in alarm and grabbed at his shirt, sure he'd drop her. She couldn't remember the last time a man had carried her anywhere—maybe never. Jack made it seem effortless.

"Ssh-hh, settle, honey," he said as he carried her into the galley kitchen. "I need to see to your bruises."

He shoved aside something that fell off the other side of the counter with a clang and rattle, and set her on the bared surface, then turned her face to the small west window, and pushed her hair back to look her over. His face hardened, his eyes blazing, although his big hands remained gentle.

"Swear to God, lifting a hand to you was never part of the deal," he said. "And it won't happen again."

Lindi watched him warily. Finally she realized he was waiting for her to say something. "And I should trust you, why?"

"'Cause I mean it." He lifted a hand. "How many fingers?"

"Two."

He nodded. "Thank fuck, no concussion then."

Moving a few steps away, he yanked open the door of the freezer above the refrigerator. He grunted in satisfaction. "Good. Least he's got ice."

He reached into his back pocket, pulled out a bandanna, and dumped the ice tray into it with sharp crack that made Lindi jump. She put a hand to her aching head, wondering dizzily if she could just lie down on the counter before she fell off of it. But when she braced her free hand on it, her palm landed in something sticky. She shuddered—if she did lie down, she'd probably be stuck like a fly on fly-paper, and they'd have to call the EMTs to cut her free.

Keys strode past, Twig over his shoulder in a fireman's carry. Lindi flinched away from the sight. Keys' heavy footsteps thumped across the front room and faded outside.

"Here," Jack said, moving close. "Hold this on there. It'll help till we can get you some painkiller."

The ice pack was pressed gently to her temple and cheek, her hand over it.

"Hang on, honey." His hands slid under her, and once again she found herself borne high against his broad chest. "Let's get you out of here. You're right, this place is a pithole."

Outside, Lindi was vaguely surprised to see it was still the same sunny, peaceful spring day. Sunlight slanted through the evergreens, limning the big, mud-splattered black SUV. The air in the clearing had warmed even more. A flock of robins twittered cheerfully in the trees.

Ponytail stalked forward to meet them, his expression dark. "He's in the back," he told Jack. "When he comes to, we'll have us another chat about the consequences of mistreating women."

He looked down at Lindi. "I'm sorry, babe, about the way he talked to you, and even more that he hit you. That should not have fuckin' happened. I'm ashamed the kid's my nephew. You want, you can beat on him yourself, while I hold him for you."

Jack set Lindi on her feet but left one hand on the small of her back.

She ducked her head self-consciously, hiding behind her hair and the ice pack. Apologies aside, she didn't know these two, and she sure as heck didn't trust them because of a few words of regret. What if they now decided she was a liability? Maybe when they were through with her, they'd dump her in the back of the SUV with the horrid Twig.

She took a cautious step back, away from their booted feet, then another.

"Whoa. No you don't." Jack's hand pressed on the small of her back, holding her next to him. Okay, darn. That wasn't going to work.

"What now?" Ponytail asked.

"Well," Jack said. "Now we talk. See if the three of us can figure this situation out in a way that's advantageous to all of us."

Lindi peered up at him around the ice pack. She found him watching her, the suspicion of a smile crinkling the corners of his eyes.

"Advantageous would be you taking me back to my café," she blurted, welcome anger kindling under the pain of her throbbing head.

He raised his brows approvingly. "See, now you're talkin'. Although I'm thinkin', you help us, we may be able to sweeten the deal a good bit more than that."

"Help you? How? And why should I?" They weren't back to her knowing where Darrell hid his ill-gotten gains again, were they?

Ponytail chuckled. "Suspicious, and I don't blame her."

Jack crooked a finger. "Let's go sit down, and we'll tell you all about it."

"Think we've still got some o' that beer from last night," Ponytail said. "I'll get us each one."

"I don't want a beer," Lindi said, revolted. She hadn't even had lunch yet. Although the way her stomach felt she wouldn't be eating anytime soon.

Ponytail soon returned with two beers. He held up a red can for Lindi. "Found a Coke rollin' around back there. It ain't cold, but it also ain't beer."

Jack took the Coke can, wiped it off on his tee and opened it for her.

And so it was that Lindi found herself seated like an honored guest of sorts in Darrell's one plastic lawn chair, now placed in the sun on the cement apron before his workshop, Jack's leather jacket heavy and warm around her shoulders, a warm Coke in her hand, ice bag in the other.

Jack squatted at her side, and Ponytail leaned against the wall a short distance away.

"Drink," Jack ordered. "You're shocky and need the sugar and the caffeine."

Deciding she really didn't want to argue with the adamant set of his jaw, Lindi drank. Screw calories, the Coke was sweet and she was thirsty. Also, after the past few hours, he was right, she needed a caloric boost. When the can was empty, she crumpled it in her hand. The thin aluminum bent inward with a crackling sound. She'd like to do that to both of their thick heads.

She muffled a burp from the carbonation behind her hand. "May I go home now?"

"Soon," Jack said. He cocked his head and gave her that look he'd given her at the café, the one that said she was pretty and fascinating and he was glad to be looking at her. Lying bastard.

She glared at him and looked away, sniffing hard to deny the tears that flooded her eyes. "I have to get back," she said. "My—my grill is still on."

"No, it's not," he said calmly. "I watched you turn it off. And I locked the front door and turned off the lights while you were pretending to get your garbage out."

"Well, aren't you thoughtful?" She was still reporting him to the sheriff. And the FBI. And whoever else she could think of.

"Yeah," he said dryly. "I usually am, when it comes to a pretty woman."

Right. He was so full of it.

She sniffled again, and then wiped her runny nose with the back of her hand, staring at her knees. She had a streak of dust across the right knee of her black yoga pants, and a wet smear across the other.

Brushing at it, she stared at the red staining her fingertips.

It was blood.

Chapter Five

Great, now she was bleeding and no wonder, the way she'd been tossed around.

Lindi set her ice pack in her lap and leaned over to pull up her capri leg. The soft knit revealed her bare calf and the curve of her knee. However, her fair skin was clean, no marks save a few faint freckles.

Wait a minute. If she wasn't bleeding, that meant the blood on her pants wasn't hers.

Lindi flicked a wary glance up to find Jack eyeing her bare limb with interest. She shoved her pant leg back down and wiped her fingers surreptitiously on the damp bandanna holding the ice.

"What's the matter?" he asked.

"Nothing," she said instantly, which was a total lie. That blood had come from someone else. The only place she'd been on her knees had been in the photo room. And it wasn't Twig's blood, because she hadn't been anywhere near him when Jack had knocked him down and made his face bleed, which meant it had come from the filthy carpet.

Her heart raced along with her thoughts. These men had known about Darrell's dirty little gallery, which meant they had been up here once already. Had Darrell been here that time? If so, he hadn't told them what they wanted to know, not if they'd thought she was the only one who could help them find their money.

Why hadn't he talked? Had they loosed the violent Twig on him, or had all of them beat him? Was the blood because they'd hurt him so badly he couldn't talk? Not that she cared much about Darrell after his protracted campaign of intimidation and her suspicions of his involvement in his own brother's death, but the idea of him lying beaten and bloodied in the woods somewhere nearby still gave her the cold shivers.

Because, despite Jack's promise of protection, she could be next. These men may not be wearing patches on their backs, but they were still rough, tough bikers.

She curled her hands on the sides of her thighs, trying not to draw any more attention to her wet knee. Luckily the blood didn't show on the black knit, so maybe Jack hadn't noticed anything.

She hoped not. Because if they knew she knew what they'd done—well, that would not be good.

One of Jack's heavy brows rose. "I've known some women who could lie their way out of damn near anything. Gotta tell you, honey, I'm thinkin' you ain't one of 'em."

Ponytail chuckled. Lindi scowled at Jack, and clamped the ice pack to her face again, hiding from his amused smirk.

Jack reached over and swiped his thumb over her knee, his big hand settling there in a near caress. But then he lifted his hand, and the three of them stared at the red smear on his thumb.

"Keys," he said mildly. "Thought you said they didn't leave a mess."

Lindi peered at the other man. Keys? What kind of name was that? And who were the 'they' who shouldn't have left a mess? Was the rest of their biker gang about to roar up through the trees?

"Didn't think they did," Ponytail said. "See I was wrong."

"You think?" Jack shot him a dour look over his shoulder.

Lindi couldn't stand the suspense any more. She just wanted to know.

"Where's Darrell?" she asked, her voice shaky. "What happened to him? Did you beat him up?"

Jack eyed her for a long moment, an intent study that made her fidget.

"How much would you miss ol' Darrell, if he was to go missing?" he asked her finally.

She snorted. "I would probably fix a free breakfast for whoever caused him to go missing."

But did he mean Darrell had escaped then, and disappeared? That made sense, if he knew these two were after him. She'd tried to run herself. Had Darrell had been more successful?

Keys' blue eyes gleamed with interest. "I like breakfast."

"She gives the best breakfast I ever ate," Jack said. "Serves it up with honey, warm and sweet."

A caressing note in his rough voice sent heat rushing through Lindi. She peeped at him around her ice pack and found his smile had widened, his white teeth gleaming, eyes twinkling. She stuffed down the stupid urge to smile back.

Because, okay, Jack was major sexy-times, but he was still a kidnapper, he'd scared the living daylights out of her, and even if he hadn't hit her himself, it was because he ganged up with sleaze-bags like Twig that she'd been hurt.

Her head throbbed, she was still dizzy and she wanted nothing more than to go home, lock her apartment up tight, crawl into her bed, and have a good cry over the dangers of the world, and the untrustworthiness of men—big, bad-ass bikers in particular.

"What money are you looking for?" she asked.

Jack sobered. He looked to his friend, who nodded once. As if given the okay to share, Jack spoke.

"Keys and me lent some money to Gaspard, on a business deal. He made it back, plus a lot of interest. But he's been playin' coy since then, not only with us but with some other local … investors. Tried to cheat us. We're here to collect."

"Only Gaspard ain't here to tell us where the money is," Keys added. "And sure as hell it's not in a bank, which means he hid it somewhere. We think it's here."

Well, that explained why they'd brought her up here. As Darrell's supposed girlfriend, they'd assumed he would've shared the location of the money with her.

"So what happens now?" she asked. "Since I can't help you." Would they let her walk away now that they knew she was of no use to them? Also, he hadn't actually answered her question about what they'd done to Darrell.

And who were the local investors—a local MC? There were two she knew about, the Devil's Flyers over in Airway Heights on the other side of Spokane, and the Cougars, who were unfortunately very local. The Flyers in particular had a bad reputation, but at least they were forty miles away.

"Well," Jack said slowly, his gaze roving to the cabin, and narrowing on it. "I'm thinkin' that Gaspard did not give two shits about that cabin. But he did take real good care of this shop."

Keys straightened from the wall and tossed his empty beer can into a nearby oil drum. It landed with a hollow clatter. "So if he was gonna hide somethin', he'd probably do it here, not in the cabin."

Jack rose in a lithe movement. "Yup."

Keys reached for the heavy padlock on the door. "Well, reckon I better get busy, then."

He pulled a jangling bunch of metal from his pocket and began to sort through it. The motion lifted his leather vest, giving Lindi a quick glimpse of what lay beneath. She sucked in a sharp breath.

He had a gun tucked in the back of his waistband. A very businesslike pistol.

Jack laid his other hand on her, so that he held both her knees in a gentle, warm grip. "Honey."

Lindi flinched, eyeing him with renewed fear. Stolen money, and now guns, this was way out of her comfort zone. Dave had owned a pistol he carried in his saddlebags, and a shotgun that he'd kept in the bedroom closet, but he'd never fired either one except at a target set up in the woods, at least that she knew of.

Lots of people in North Idaho owned guns, but most didn't carry them hidden in the back of their belt. Well, probably Dave's MC buddies did ... but she'd never spent enough time around them to worry about how they might use them—like on people they didn't want to tell their secrets.

Jack shook his head wryly. "Look, I know you got every reason to be scared. But you got nothin' to fear from either me or Keys. So I'm askin' you to stay calm for a while longer, while we get this sorted. Then we'll get you back to your place, safe and sound. Can you do that for me?"

The slow sweep of his thumbs on her inner knees, soothing even through the thin knit of her pants, was having a strange effect on her, along with his voice and the warmth in his light eyes. When he turned on the charm, the man was as bliss-inducing as a shot of warm cinnamon Jaeger.

Of course, when his eyes turned cold and his jaw steely, he could also be scary as hell.

She licked her lips. "You're not gonna make me, um, disappear like Darrell?"

His gaze on her mouth, amusement tipping up the corners of his lips, Jack shook his head slowly. "Oh no, little honey pot. The very last thing I want is for you to disappear."

This was the look he'd given her at the café, like she was the best thing he'd seen all day and he wanted a bite, or a lick. He leaned forward, his hands pressing her thighs, urging them apart to make a place for him. Lindi watched, hypnotized, as he moved closer, so near she could smell him, warm man, leather and musk. The scent that permeated the jacket now over her shoulders.

This close, his hair glinted with strands of gold and silver in the sunlight, and she could see the speckles of brown in his pupils, the fine hairs in his shadow of beard.

His warm, moist breath soughed across her wet lips, and Lindi held her breath, frozen in place, only not with cold, oooh-hh, no. She was filled with pure, melting heat as he tilted his head to one side and parted his lips, his gaze flicking to her lips.

Metal clanked sharply. "We're in," Keys announced. The door creaked open.

For one instant, Jack paused, his lips a breath away from hers. Then he pulled away, with a last regretful look. "Later, honey."

He gave her knees a last squeeze and let her go. Pushing to his feet, he held one hand out to her, his gaze on the door through which Keys had disappeared.

Wait, wait, wait! What the hell had almost happened here? Horror sluicing through her like ice water, Lindi shot to her feet and sidled away from the man she'd almost allowed to kiss her. After he'd kidnapped her, terrorized her, put her at the mercy of his sadistic sidekick Twig, and as good as admitted he'd beaten her boyfriend's brother until he bled.

Okay, Darrell's beating she just couldn't bring herself to care about right now. On a scale of kidnapping, fear of rape, and being punched in the face by a biker maniac? Not so much. She'd like to put some hurt on Darrell herself for pulling her into this.

Of course she guessed the reason she was here was partly her own fault, because she'd known Dave hung out with bikers who skirted the law, and at times rode their Harleys right across it to the wrong side. But if Dave did so when he was out with them, he'd made sure she didn't know about it. She hadn't wanted to know. She'd just wanted him to come home to her every evening, safe and sober. And bless his big heart, he'd reined in his partying while they were together, because he knew it bothered her when he drank more than two beers.

And she really hadn't wanted to know what his low-life brother was into. Such as whatever activity the stolen money had been the profits from.

For all she knew, Jack and Keys were drug-runners. They were kidnappers, that was for sure. And after that, he expected her to kiss him? Jack Whoever-the-hell-he-was could just wait for it. And hold his breath while he did so.

In a gesture of long habit, Lindi brushed her hands down over her apron. Her fingers bumped the small, hard shape of her phone. She stopped in her tracks.

"I'll just wait for you out here," she said to Jack. "You go ahead and look for your money."

Jack's head snapped around, and his gaze dropped to her hand, closed over the rectangle of her phone in her pocket. He gave her a look. "Huh-uh, sorry, sweetness. You come with us."

Lindi glared, and Jack's eyes crinkled with amusement. Reaching out, he slid his hand to the small of her back and pushed gently but firmly. "You can use your phone after a bit, honey."

Scowling, Lindi stalked into the shop. The sooner these bikers found their damn money, the sooner she could go home. And forget having a good cry. A screaming tantrum was feeling more necessary with each step she took.

Chapter Six

Close behind Lindi, Jack was only a few steps into the shadowed interior of Gaspard's shop when Keys found the bank of switches, and light flooded the space.

Jack looked around with interest, and not a little surprise. Every inch of the place was as tidy and organized as the little café at the foot of the mountain. The walls were bright white, the floor gray-painted concrete, all gleaming with care.

It was as different from the squalor of the cabin as night from day.

The shop was essentially a two-story garage, with a high, open ceiling and stairs leading up to a storage catwalk around the exterior, and to an enclosed room in one upper, back corner. Rolling toolboxes and various other parts and equipment lined the walls.

Through an open door a painting bay was visible. The sanded body of a vintage pickup sat on sawhorses in the center. Spray painting equipment was loaded on a big rolling rack

The main floor held two automotive bays, with steel frames to hold the vehicle and a rectangular hole in the cement below, with a ladder to climb down. One of the bays was empty, but the other held a black-and-silver Chevy Blazer.

Keys paused beside it. "A '74," he said reverently. "Look at those ghost flames. And the suspension ... damn, this is a fine piece of machinery."

Jack nodded. "Sweet ride." If a man had to drive a vehicle other than his bike, might as well do it in a butch rig like this one.

"And look at this beauty." Keys moved on to survey a vintage red and gold motorcycle gleaming from a stanchion. "Hell, this is a '59 Indian. Can't find these for love or money."

It was a pretty bike, although kinda girly for Jack's taste. His own Harley was big and black, with lots of chrome. He looked up the open stairs.

"That Gaspard's office up there?" he asked Lindi.

"I don't know," she said wanly. "I've never been in here before."

Keys turned away from the motorcycle with clear reluctance. "Let's go find out."

The three of them climbed the stairs, Jack's hand on Lindi's back. Her perfume, or maybe it was just her shampoo, tickled his nostrils along with the lingering scent of pancakes. He grinned wryly to himself—kinda made a man want to eat her up. Later, when she felt better. She was still pale, and her eye and cheekbone were starting to swell. Damn Twig to hell—she was gonna have a shiner.

It took Keys less than a minute to unlock the office door. He hadn't gotten his name by accident.

The room held a metal desk, a rolling office chair, two tall file cabinets and an old safe.

"Well, fuck me," Keys said with disgust that Jack shared. The safe door hung open. The interior was empty.

"Someone get here before us?" Jack wondered aloud. "Or did he know we were comin', and clear it out?"

Beside him, Lindi pointed behind the desk. "What's all that?"

Jack followed her gesture. A battered leather satchel sat there, open. But unlike the safe, it was stuffed full of folders and what looked like bank envelopes.

"Hey, now. Let's have a look." Jack moved to pick up the satchel. He set it on the desk, pulled out a manila envelope and read the label. "Title for the Blazer. And this one's for the

Indian. Here's a registration for a '66 Dodge. Another project, I s'pose."

"It was me, I'd keep that shit in the safe," Keys said, moving to join Jack. He pulled out a handful of bank envelopes and opened one. "Receipts for payments."

Jack gave Lindi an approving nod. "Good eyes. I'm guessing Darrell cleared the safe and was packin' up to leave."

"Yeah, now let's see if there's any cash in here," Keys said.

"Go ahead." Jack pushed the desk chair to Lindi, who was swaying on her feet. "Sit down, honey." She looked like she really needed to lay down, but no place here for that.

She plopped into the chair, her lower lip sticking out in a way that said she not only felt like shit, she placed the blame for that squarely on his shoulders. Well, he'd take real good care of her, soon as they found what they needed and could get shut of this place.

Ten minutes later, the contents of the satchel were scattered across the desktop, and Keys leaned on the corner of the desk, scowling at nothing. Jack stood, legs apart, arms crossed, eyes narrowed as he thought. Out loud, 'cause that always helped him organize shit, for some reason.

"Okay," he muttered. "Let's say he's up here. He's figured out we're comin', and he knows we're not happy, doesn't wanna face us. He's gonna clear out, but he thinks he has time to empty the safe, take this shit with him. Some of it to cover his tracks, 'cause a lot of those bank deposits sure as hell didn't come from this garage. But then he hears someone outside. He has to do somethin'—get rid of them quick, so he can come back and finish up here."

He prowled over to the door and stood, looking down at the shop below. Hands on his hips, he pursed his lips in contemplation. "But just in case, he keeps the money on him. If he has to make run for it, that'll take him a long way."

"If he had that amount on him, it sure as hell wasn't in cash," Keys pointed out. "Anyway, if he did, it's long gone, you know that. They wouldn't have missed it."

"Could have had it on him," Jack argued, "Or intended to, if it was in big bills. Benjamins, say."

Keys kicked the side of the old desk in a gesture of supreme disgust. "If he was wearing a money belt, sure as hell the Flyers got it."

Jack shot Lindi a look and saw her good eye widen, the other hidden by her dripping icepack. He gave Keys a warning look not to mention the club by name again. "You sure? Or does it mean Gaspard had it stashed for his travels?"

"Why don't you call Stick and ask?" Keys asked dryly.

Jack snorted. "Yeah, that'd work."

Ivan 'Joystick' Vanko, the president of the local Devil's Flyers chapter would ream their asses up, down and sideways for dipping into club business without sitting down first for a talk in the Flyer's clubhouse. And if Stick learned there was more money, he might expect a cut for the club.

"If Stick has it, he'll sit on it for a while, see if there's any blowback first. But I don't think he has it. Just a hunch, but Gaspard was secretive as all hell. I think he hid it."

His partner shook his head wryly. "Okay, Sunshine, I'll look on the bright side with you. Maybe he did stash it. But it sure as hell wasn't up here."

"Nope." Jack beckoned to Lindi. "Honey, I know you weren't Gaspard's biggest fan, but you knew him. We need your eyes."

She grimaced but rose to go to him out on the landing. He put a hand on her shoulder, enjoying the feel of her warm, supple flesh under his palm, and the way the top of her head fit under his chin. He indicated the garage below with his other hand. "Man tends to stash valuables in other shit he values. Looking around, where do you think he'd hide his money?"

"The Blazer," she said instantly.

"Really?" Keys said, sliding past them. "Thought maybe the Indian. Saddlebags, or a false panel."

Lindi followed him down the stairs, shrugging off Jack's hand, which bothered him more than it should have. What was it about this woman that made him want to keep hands on her? He needed to keep his head on the job, not pussy.

"No," she told Keys. "He wasn't much of a biker. He drove the Blazer all the time. He would have driven it if he was headed off somewhere."

"Stay here," Jack told her, stopping her at the bottom of the stairs, where she couldn't get in the way or get hurt. Because sweet ride or not, he and Keys were gonna tear that Blazer apart if necessary.

* * *

Lindi stuck her tongue out at Jack's broad back, but she lacked the energy to argue with him. She sank to the sixth stair up and propped her elbows on her knees, chin on her palm to watch, the now dripping ice bag once again pressed carefully to her aching head.

Thank God her mother was in Portland with Cissie and her family for the week. When Gail Carson was home in Coeur d'Alene, she often came by the BeeHive for a cup of coffee with her friend Meryl. If she found the café locked up with Lindi's bike still there, she'd be scared out of her mind. Of course she'd then call the cops, which would've been good.

Lindi wondered if her mother had ever found herself in a situation like this. Lindi knew her father had never held a steady job for more than six months at a time, due to his inability to stay out of the bars. She had vague memories of Chuck Carson bringing home friends who like him, smelled of beer and cigarettes, and filled up the small living room of their home with their laughter and loud voices. That was on the nights he wasn't out with them at the local bars.

Whenever his party moved to the Carson home, Gail had shooed her daughters to their bedroom or out in the back yard to play, and most often come with them. Lindi remembered falling asleep in her narrow bed with her mother curled up with her or Cissie, feeling that as long as Mama was there, they were safe.

But had it only been the drinking, or more that led Gail to disapprove of her husband's friends? Not that the drinking hadn't been enough. It had killed him, and the family whose car his weaving pickup truck had struck head-on one night. Lindi and Cissie had grown up knowing that not only had their father been an alcoholic, he'd more or less murdered an innocent family with his carelessness.

Maybe he'd done more.

She looked up, jerked out of her thoughts as Jack and Keys opened the front doors on opposite sides of the Blazer, and leaned in to search through the front seat, conversing in low voices. At one point, Keys climbed in and through to the back seat, while Jack squatted beside the vehicle and shone a flashlight underneath.

Lindi was watching the long, sexy muscles in Jack's back under his snug tee-shirt, and the way his squat highlighted his ass and thighs, when he stiffened. She sat up straight, trying to peer past him at whatever he'd found.

"Keys," he called, a new note of urgency in his deep, rough voice. "Grab a torque wrench, yeah?"

Unable to resist, Lindi hurried down the last few stairs and went to peer over his broad shoulder. Jack trained his light on a black rectangular metal box against the undercarriage above the right front tire. "See that?" he asked her, a smile in his voice. "An add-on. And judging by the shiny marks on the metal, recent."

"Move aside, pretty girl," Keys said behind her. He slid past her, bearing a tool with a long cord attached. "And plug your ears."

Lindi did both, although she noted Jack stayed right at Keys' side as the wrench whined to life. Keys worked with swift efficiency, loosening four nuts one by one.

The metal box fell into Jack's hands. He popped open the lid, and a length of black leather uncoiled, slithering to the cement floor.

"Fuck, yeah!" Keys crowed. He ducked out of the way to dispose of the tool, his blue eyes blazing with excitement. "Money belt!"

Jack grabbed the belt from the floor and rose to his feet, his face glowing in a smile. He held their prize up with one hand, reached out his other arm to haul Lindi to him, and grinned down at her. "You, my honey girl, are good luck."

Then he bent his head and kissed her.

Chapter Seven

Jack's body was hard and hot against Lindi's, his arms strong
but gentle as he slid his hands over her back, one up, one
down. His mouth was a revelation. Warm and hungry, his lips
settled over hers, then parted as he inhaled, breathing her in.

"Knew it," he muttered against her mouth. "Sweet as honey."

Lindi hung in his grasp, shock holding her quiescent as his
lips softened on hers. He tasted exciting and foreign—male,
powerful and virile. Desire flowed through her, warm and liquid.

Something hit the floor with a thwack by her foot. Both of
them ignored it as his hand cupped the uninjured side of her
head, his thumb stroking the corner of her mouth, urging it
open. His lips supped at hers, coaxing them farther apart, and
his tongue teased into her mouth, inviting her to play as his
hold tightened, supporting her head.

Lindi clung to him, her fingers digging into the supple cotton
of his shirt, and the firm pad of muscle beneath. She used this
leverage to rise onto her tiptoes and get closer to him, chasing
his elusive flavor.

Jack growled his approval of this move, and cocked his head
to deepen the kiss, his tongue sweeping into her mouth, tan-
gling with hers.

Lindi hadn't been kissed with this much finesse and heat in a
long time, maybe ever. It was a little slice of heaven. She
wanted it never to stop. Stopping meant she had to start thinking again. Because why did it have to be him who made her
feel this way?

Continuing meant Jack held her tightly in his powerful arms,
her breasts pillowed against his broad chest, and a long, hard,

stiff shape pressing against her mons. One she wanted to feel farther down, against her pussy. She wanted to open her thighs and climb him like a vine.

She moaned as he rubbed his erection against her again, and he ate at her mouth, apparently ravenous for her. His big hands molded her ass, the curve of her back.

"Damn, hate to break this up," Keys said behind Lindi. "But we should probably move."

Jack lifted his head, just enough to give her a glittering look. His cheekbones were flushed, his nostrils flared, jaw hard.

"Go grab that satchel, would you, bro?" he asked without looking away from her. "Don't want someone else finding those papers before we have a chance to go through them."

"Right. Y'all carry on. Lucky bastard."

Key's footsteps thudded away, up the stairs.

Lindi looked at Jack's mouth, tugging at his shirt to bring him back down to her. He slid his hand to cup the back of her neck. "If I kiss you again, I'm gonna fuck you right here, against this rig. That what you want?"

She blinked. Wait, what? He thought they should have sex here? With his friend in the building, and the awful Twig unconscious out in their SUV? Or have sex with him anywhere at all, for that matter.

"No." She pushed at him, her gaze falling to his chest, her face burning. "No, of course not. I ... I don't want that."

She didn't know what she wanted. She knew what she shouldn't want, and that was any part of him. She'd never craved Dave like this—so much her legs were weak as cooked pasta, and her mind was fogged with sheer lust. And she'd loved Dave—as much as she'd let herself, anyway.

Jack was just a sexy smile, a deep voice and a hard body. Just a momentary craving, like catching a whiff of chocolate at the bakery, and then craving frosted brownies all day. That was all. She'd get over it. Starting now would be good, because part of her wanted to throw herself at him, knock him off his feet and get more of those kisses.

Even though her face was throbbing with pain, and her head was woozy as if that Coke had been spiked with rum.

Jack gave her a squeeze, and let her go with what felt like real reluctance. "Later, honey."

She shivered at the loss of his warm arms, then jumped as something clanged beyond him. The outer door of the shop banging against the wall.

"Well, ain't this cozy?" Twig asked, his voice nasal, as if his nose was plugged. "Go on, don't let me stop you, Moran. Go ahead and do the cunt. Be the last pussy you ever get."

Lindi flinched, and Jack's arms tightened. He gave a slight shake of his head, and slowly turned to face the open door, keeping himself between her and the door.

She peeped around his arm and gasped. In the bright fluorescent garage lights, Twig was a horrific sight, blood glistening on the side of his head and streaking his disfigured face.

His eyes were swollen nearly shut, but the blaze of hatred in them was still visible. Worst of all, he held a pistol in his hand. Aimed straight at Jack.

"Oh, my God," Lindi breathed, clutching at the back of Jack's belt.

Jack reached back and gave her a push away from him, toward the Blazer. When he spoke, his voice was calm, almost bored. "'Bout time you woke up, Twig. Thought we were gonna have to split the cash without you."

"You found the money?" Twig moved farther inside the door, turning his head as he peered around. "Where is it?" Only with his swollen sinuses, it sounded more like 'Da muddy? Wer idd it?'

Lindi looked down and winced. The money belt lay in plain sight at Jack's feet.

But Jack lifted the black metal box in his hand and tossed it into the air, catching it, a shiny decoy. "Got it right here. Fucker had it bolted to the undercarriage of his favorite rig."

Twig brandished the gun. "Give it to me."

Jack tossed the box up and caught it again. "You want it? Come and get it, boy."

"No. You toss it to me. Wait—have her bring it."

Jack's hand tightened on Lindi's.

She took a shaky breath, searching for courage. She was the only 'her' present. And if she didn't do what Twig said, he'd shoot Jack. And Jack might be a dangerous biker, but she was pretty darn sure Twig was an actual sociopath—viewing people, especially women as disposable. She'd choose Jack over him any day.

"Okay," she blurted, stepping from behind Jack so Twig could see her. "I'll b-bring it to you." But please God, give her a chance to knee him in the nuts.

He leered, a horrible caricature of a smile on his bruised face. "Yeah, you know who's the boss, don'tcha, babe? Bring it here. Maybe I'll give you a taste of what you're missin'."

"Don't. Move." Jack growled under his breath, his big arm barring her from stepping forward.

"I have to," Lindi hissed. "He'll shoot you—or both of us."

Twig laughed, his annoying high-pitched whinny. "Jesus, you stupid cunt. I'm gonna shoot him anyway. Nobody knocks me around—not and lives to tell about it."

"That what happened to that cop back home, Twig?" Keys deep voice rolled down from the landing, echoing throughout the big space.

Lindi nearly leapt out of her skin, having forgotten he was even in the building. Thank God for his distraction, though—it kept her from having to follow through on Twig's commands, at least for now.

Keys stood in the open door of the office, hard gaze on his nephew. "You the one who shot him in the back? As a little payback for arresting you?"

Twig laughed again. "Yeah, Unc, that's right. I shot the pig. You goin' all moral on me now? Gonna slap my hand?"

"No, Twig," Keys said. "Gonna do what I should've done a long time ago." He shifted sideways, bringing a shotgun up at his side, aimed at Twig. He cocked it with a sharp, authoritative crack. "Gonna send you on your way. You're done—with me and with the club. You got no more chances, so don't try to get back in."

Twig sneered, or tried to. He looked more like a little boy making defiant faces after a playground fight … except for the gun in his hand. He brandished it, his voice rising. "You forget I got the drop on your best bro here? I'll shoot him, I swear it."

"You can try," Keys said. "But you might miss. I won't—not with this baby. Buckshot won't kill you at this range, but it'll hurt like hell-fire. May blind you, if a pellet or two hits you in the face."

Twig made a snarling sound, and held his pistol high. He fired once, twice, three times, Blam! Blam! Blam! Incredibly loud in the metal building, followed by pings as the bullets hit the metal walls.

A shriek burst from Lindi's throat, and then Jack was shoving her back against the Blazer, his body covering hers. Lindi grabbed him around the waist, ready to support him if he fell. "Jack."

He patted her clutching hand. "Not me, honey," he murmured. "Keep still."

Even with one ear smashed against Jack's broad back, Lindi heard Keys voice.

"Get out now, Twig," Keys said, his voice cold as ice. "I see your face again, or hear you been seen around this area, I'll make it club business. And you know what that means. Now git."

"Fuck you!" Twig shouted. "Who the hell needs you anyways, old man? I got plenty of people waitin' to help me out. Fuck both o' you losers."

He stomped out, smacking the door against the wall with a crash as he passed. His footsteps crunched away on the gravel outside. Leaving them alive.

She was alive. Lindi hung onto Jack, shaking. She'd thought for sure she was going to die, right here, and these two men with her … slaughtered in Darrell's classic auto shop.

"Stay here," Jack said, pulling away from Lindi. He jogged over to the doorway and looked out. "Hell, he's takin' the SUV."

Outside, an engine roared to life, and then gravel spit from under tires, fading as the SUV sped down the road.

Keys ran down the stairs, the shotgun aimed upward. He passed Lindi and stopped beside Jack in the doorway, his shoulders bowing as if under a heavy weight. "Goddamnit."

Jack laid a hand on his shoulder. "You had to cut him loose, brother. He was set to shoot me. And you know what he would've done to Lindi."

"I know. Hell, he'd have tried to do both of us for the money." Keys sighed heavily. "He was a cute little fucker once ... used to follow me around when I visited my sister. But this was bound to happen sooner or later—he was just plain rotten, clear through."

"Better get on the phone with Stick, let the club know."

"Yeah. I'll take care of it. Don't want Twig sweet-talkin' any of the brothers into helpin' him before they know the real story."

Lindi stood where Jack had left her. She felt strange, their voices echoing in her ears like slow motion track of a video. She swayed, took a step to balance, and then tripped over something. The money belt, coiled at her feet like a snake.

She watched with dull surprise as it rose up to meet her.

"Get her," Keys called. "She's goin' down."

The floor struck her knees, but the rest of her met a more forgiving surface as Jack caught her in his arms. For the second time that day, her face smacked into his chest.

But this time she hardly felt it.

"I got you, honey," he said from far away, and then even his voice faded.

Chapter Eight

Tuesday

Lindi woke slowly, various annoying facts making themselves known. First, the sun was shining straight into her eyes. She must've forgotten to pull her bedroom shade all the way down last night.

Second, she'd evidently gone to bed half-dressed, as the underwire of her bra was digging into the side of her breast under her arm.

Third, she was so thirsty her mouth felt dry as cotton. Was this a hangover?

Then she turned her head on the pillow and gave a whimper of distress at the pain that shot through her head as she moved. She put her hand to her temple, wincing as her fingertips met a painfully tender lump. Wait, that wasn't from a hangover, that was a bruise—a bad one.

The bed sagged with movement—not hers. Lindi froze, her breath catching in her throat. There was someone in bed with her. She'd sure never been drunk enough to forget bringing a man home with her.

"Hey," said a deep, gravelly voice said behind her. "You finally wakin' up, there, Sleepin' Beauty?"

She tossed back the covers and shot out of her bed. She backed away, stumbling over the edge of the throw rug. Righting herself with a hand on her nightstand, she stared at the man who lay in her old queen bed, taking up, it must be said, more than half of it. The paperback romance she'd been reading the night before fell from the nightstand with a soft thud.

Lindi glanced down at the worn carpet and saw the hero, a vampire warrior, glowering up at her from the cover, as if he didn't appreciate the disrespect. Well, he could get in line, because she had a real man in her bed to deal with.

Jack leaned up on one elbow, the old quilt falling to his waist, and eyed her quizzically.

"W-what are you doing here?" she sputtered. "In my bed?"

He grinned. And unfairly, even with his hair a mess and his tanned face unshaven, his eyes heavy with sleep, he looked just as sexy, maybe even more so, than the first moment she'd seen him. "Makin' sure you're okay. Didn't want you wakin' up hurting, alone and scared."

Oh. That was ... actually kind of sweet.

Lindi jerked her gaze from his bare chest, which somehow looked even broader without a covering of tee shirt. It was dusted with hair a shade darker than that on his head, and when he curled to a sitting position, the heavy muscles in his abs flexed, emphasizing the power in his big body. His nipples were small, brown coins against his tanned chest.

He lifted one hand to run his fingers through his hair, and she watched the bulge of his biceps with fascination. The play of muscle looked even better with no tee shirt covering his smooth skin.

His smile widened in that way that said he found her cute and funny as heck at the same time, his eyes half-closing.

"C'mere, honey" he invited, his voice dropping to a rough purr as he lifted the covers on her side of the bed.

Shaking her head, Lindi took a step back. His gaze flicked down over her and heated even more. Which was when she realized her own lower half was bare—or nearly so. She looked down at herself in horror, at her white tee crinkled up around her waist, at her bare hips and thighs, bisected only by the thin barrier of white bikini panties. Peekaboo lace, which revealed the downy curls on her mons. The area he'd been eyeing with such interest.

"You," she sputtered, grabbing the hem of her tee and yanking it down to cover her crotch. Her rounded hips were a lost cause—there just wasn't that much of her tee. "You took my pants off!"

He chuckled, a deep rasp of amusement. "They had blood on 'em, sweetness. Anyway, you still got your panties on."

"Right. Well, I'm—I'm fine now," she snapped. "So you can just ... go." Leave, vamoose, vanish in a puff of smoke, she really didn't care.

He gave her a look, and then sighed. "Knew it wasn't gonna be that easy with you. Look, honey, you may not recall, but you passed out cold on me yesterday. You've been asleep for ..." he reached behind him, grabbed his phone off the bedside table and looked at it "…over sixteen hours."

"I passed out? You mean fainted? I've never fainted in my life."

He shrugged. "First time for everything. You had one helluva fucked-up day. Don't expect you've ever been threatened at gun point, either. Then too, I reckon you were plain worn out and needed the sleep."

She cringed, the morning chill on her bare skin now registering along with the inner chill of memory, raw and all-too real.

"You kidnapped me," she whispered. "And Twig hit me." She touched her aching temple and wrapped her other arm around her middle as she shivered. "He shot at us."

"Nah, he was just shooting at the ceiling. Stupid as Twig is, he's got enough sense not to aim at one of us. Keys would've filled his ass with buckshot, and I would've finished beatin' the shit out of him."

He scowled, tossed the covers back, revealing long, brawny legs and dark, low-cut briefs, and slid across the bed to her, coming to his feet in one smooth motion.

Before Lindi could move, he caught her in a gentle grip, one hand on the small of her back, the other cupping the side of her throat. He peered down into her eyes, his expression adamant.

"The worst part is he hit you," he said. "No woman should have to deal with that. But that was just a sample of the shit he was capable of. Remember the cop Keys mentioned? They couldn't prove it, but everyone knows Twig shot him in the back. If I'd been able, I would've handed the evidence to the cops myself, so would Keys. Also, there was this gal back in California—well, you don't need to hear that shit. My point is, he's long gone and no loss."

"I hope you're right." She remembered the savage glee in Twig's eyes when he'd hit her—he'd enjoyed it. He'd enjoy doing more. Her skin crawled at the thought of him putting his hands on her, jerking her legs apart and forcing himself on her, no doubt as brutally as he could manage. And when he was done, he wouldn't want to leave her able to tell on him

"I am right," Jack said. "Keys may be easy-goin', but he can also be a scary mother. Twig knows better than to show his face where either of us can see him. We take care of our own, good or bad."

She scowled. "Well, if he does show up again, I'll take Keys up on his offer to hold him so I can slap his face a few times—see how he likes that."

Jack gave her a squeeze and grinned. "That's my girl."

"But Darrell," she remembered. "He's still out there—and he'll be back."

Something shuttered in Jack's gaze. "No, honey. He won't. Now, you go on in and get in a hot shower." He turned her toward the bathroom door, open in the corner of the small bedroom. "Get yourself cleaned up, take some pain pills. Then we'll get some coffee and breakfast, and we'll sort this out."

Lindi nodded, because the thought of being warm and clean and headache-free was the only thing keeping her from diving back under her bedcovers, whimpering like a puppy.

Obeying the gentle push of his big hand, she walked into the bathroom. The door swung closed behind her, sticking halfway shut as usual, because none of the doors in the apartment hung straight any more. She ignored it, leaning into the tubshower to turn the taps on, and then stripping off her tee and undies and dropping them into the wicker laundry basket in the corner. She gulped a glass of water and two pain tablets as she waited for the water to heat.

In the shower, the hot water sluiced over her head and body like a benediction. She huddled under it until her shivering abated. Finally, when she was warm, she poured a dollop of soothing honey-chamomile shampoo into her palm, and washed and conditioned her hair, being ultra-careful of her bruises. She soaped her body and rinsed, managing to do all of this without thinking of anything in particular.

As soon as she turned off the water, her bath towel appeared around the edge of the shower curtain. Lindi gasped, then grabbed it and clutched it against her as she pulled the plastic curtain open just far enough to frown at Jack. "Get out of here."

He shrugged wryly and reached down to flush the toilet. "Didn't think your neighbors would appreciate me takin' a piss on the front lawn."

Lindi jerked the shower curtain shut and began to dry herself off at record speed, her heart pounding. He was the most irritating man she'd ever met. "Well, don't get any ideas about climbing in here until I'm out."

"Nah. Brought you some undies, though. Since you forgot 'em."

The bathroom door closed, and she peered out. He was gone. She dried her hair and climbed out of the tub, but stopped short as she saw the bra and panties draped over the edge of the sink. Her face burned with embarrassment.

He'd not only dug in her underwear drawer, he'd somehow managed to find the black lace peekaboo bra and thong that Dave had given her two Christmases ago. She'd only worn them a few times at Dave's request, but she hadn't had the heart to throw them out after he died.

Well, she'd have to wear them now, because she wasn't going out of here in only a towel. Thank goodness she'd shaved her legs and armpits the morning before, so all she had to do was moisturize before donning the undies. She wrinkled her nose as the thong immediately rode up between her ass cheeks.

When she stuck her head out of the bathroom, her bedroom was mercifully empty. She could hear Jack out in the main room, opening cupboards in the little corner kitchen. Lindi scurried over to force the bedroom door shut before dropping her towel and selecting a denim skirt and knit top from her tiny closet.

The short, stretchy skirt was only because her jeans were all in the laundry, she told herself. And if the top was a new fitted sweater from the sale rack at Kohl's, soft gold batik dyed with a pattern of faux topaz around the low neckline? That was her business and no one else's.

She shoved her feet into her flip-flops, hesitated, and then kicked them off and slipped on her platforms with the enclosed toe instead. They made her legs look longer, and she could use a few extra inches of height when she looked Jack in the eye and told him he had rescued her, but now it was time to go.

Back in the bathroom, Lindi used her bath towel to wipe the shower steam from the mirror. Then she stared at herself in horror.

"Oh, my God," she muttered, lifting a hand to her right eye. She looked like she'd been in a one of those tacky, late-night TV wrestling matches ... and lost. Her eyelid was swollen, with dark bruises above and below. The bruising extended onto her temple as well. The rest of her face looked fragile, in contrast.

No wonder it had hurt so badly. And no wonder Jack had spent the night. He'd probably feared she'd keel over on him, and he'd have her corpse to explain to the cops.

So much for her imagining he'd crawled into her bed to follow up on that kiss. She was such an idiot. He could have any woman he wanted, why would he want one who looked like a BBW wrestler who'd lost her round in the jello tub? Unless he was into pity sex.

She blinked furiously, fighting the hot tears that threatened. No. Wait a darn minute. Just because the revolting Twig had called her fat, didn't mean she had to internalize his hate-filled words. She was past that kind of crap. Dave had loved her curves, and so would another man, when the right one came along.

"Screw you, Twig," she whispered. "Wherever you are."

She hoped he was shivering under a bridge somewhere. Because she wasn't the first girl he'd roughed up, and she wouldn't have been the last. Also, he'd killed a cop, for which he deserved to be serving life in prison.

Lindi shuddered as she remembered the gunshots echoing through Darrell's auto shop.

She wished she could turn back time, so none of yesterday had happened, and she was still the same more-or-less care-free person she'd been when she woke up in the morning, with nothing more on her mind than worrying about her sister, running her café, and trying to figure out a way to stay out of Darrell's way and get ahead of her bank payments.

Okay, so maybe not exactly carefree, but ordinary anyway. Her own stressful brand of ordinary.

Her life had now slipped the bounds of normal—that was for sure. More like, Jack had ripped her from those boundaries. Boy howdy, did she have a story to tell Sara and Kit at their weekly dinner out. But her girlfriends would have to wait. Right now, she had war paint to apply and a biker man to send on his way.

As she opened the medicine cabinet, her hands shook with anger. She may have been a victim yesterday, but she was done being one with any man—including Jack.

Today was going to happen on *her* terms. And maybe she could get in the habit of that, so when Darrell showed up again—which he would, she was sure—she could face him down too.

Chapter Nine

When Lindi walked out into the main room of her apartment, Jack leaned against the counter, legs crossed, one bare foot canted. He wore his snug, faded jeans, but nothing else. He held a cup of coffee poised at his lips.

He froze, staring through the steam curling up from her Seattle skyline mug. His gaze took in her face, then traveled slowly down her body to her toes and back up.

His lids heavy, he smiled at her. "Damn, honey. Thought you were pretty in your waitress getup. But you clean up real nice. Even disguised those bruises for the most part. And I like your hair all sleek and wavy like that."

Lindi tossed her head and sauntered across the room toward him. He watched her come with a predatory satisfaction in his face, and an answering thrill of feminine triumph sang through her. She was woman, hear her roar. He could admire her all he liked, she was still kicking his ass out.

"Thank you." She reached past him for another mug, this one with the words 'Lake Girl' on the side in pink, and picked up the pot to pour her own coffee. Next she moved to the old refrigerator, took out the vanilla creamer and poured a dollop into the dark brew.

Turning, she took a long drink and regarded Jack over her cup. His gaze was on her bare legs.

"As you can see, I'm fine now," she said. "So you can go."

His gaze flew to meet hers, and the atmosphere in the small room changed, charged with a tingling current.

He lowered his cup. "'I can go now'," he repeated. He shook his head chidingly. "Honey, you think you can lay in my arms and kiss me like you did yesterday, trusting me to make it sweet for you in the midst of a shit storm the likes of that one, and today I'm gonna walk away from that?"

He reached to set his mug on the counter without looking away from her.

"Nuh-uh. C'mere, Lindi." His deep, rough voice held a note of beguilement that was worthy of one of the vampire lords from her favorite paranormal romances beckoning his next mate.

If vampires bred with bikers, that is. They didn't, did they? With her luck, she had one in her kitchen right now.

A fine trembling seized her, and Lindi had to clench her hands on her mug to hold it steady enough to take another drink, but she did it, and curled her toes in her sandals to keep her feet planted where they were.

What the heck was going on? There was no way she should be this attracted to a man who'd dragged her straight into danger and mayhem, even if he had given her a sweet and heartfelt apology for the mayhem part of it, his regret evident in his beautiful eyes.

Temptation tugged harder, reaching deep into neglected parts of her body and causing them to clench with need, the way they had when he kissed her yesterday. Only her innate caution, hard-won over a lifetime of watching her mother work to get over tying herself to the wrong man, held her back.

She shook her head at him, seizing on the first protest she thought of.

"I don't think so, Jack Whoever-you-are. I don't even know your last name."

He straightened from the counter. "Moran. James Michael Moran, although you call me anything but Jack, I likely won't answer."

As he prowled toward her, Lindi took another gulp drink of coffee, then winced and swallowed hastily as the hot brew burnt her tongue.

"And where are you from, Jack Moran?" Not from Coeur d'Alene, that was for sure. There was no way she could've missed two hot guys like him and Keys cruising their Harleys through this small town on a regular basis.

"Spokane originally," he answered, closing in on her, bigger, broader and more male with each step. "Although I've spent the last ten years in California. You wanna know more about me, ask me later, I'll tell you. For now, somethin' else you'll learn about me, Lindi honey—when I ask you to come to me, that's what I need you to do."

Her mug of coffee was a false shield. Her inner bad girl sighed with excitement as he took the cup from her and set it aside, then slid his hand down her back, fitting his palm to the curve of her ass as he pulled her against him.

Oh, dear Lord. Her hands met his chest, bare and warm and intriguingly smooth under the soft curls of dark blond hair. She lifted them away, then touched him again, pushing at him, doing her best to quell her bad girl.

"You can expect all you like," she told him, her voice quavering. "I don't take orders from you or any man."

"That's too bad," he said, his lips quirking up as he bent his head to her. "'Cause you want to. I can see it in those big eyes of yours."

Never in a hundred years would she admit something so shamefully retro, not even to herself. Not even when he was leaning over her, surrounding her with acres of delicious, hot, hard, bare man, the smile in his eyes deepening just for her. She shook her head, her hair swirling about her shoulders, even as his hand slipped underneath the waves to cup her nape, warm and possessive.

"Yeah, you do," he rasped against her lips. "You melt so sweet for me, honey. Your sweet mouth and your soft curves all over me. And when you give me all of you, it's gonna be even sweeter. I'm gonna make you come so hard and often you'll forget what it was like not to have my cock deep inside you, my hands and my mouth on you."

Then, while she was stunned and melting from this amazing speech—she hadn't even known men could talk like that outside an erotic romance—he followed his words with full oral contact. The protest forming on Lindi's lips turned into a moan as he plundered her mouth in a long, wet, carnal kiss.

Pleasure sang through her veins as she kissed him back. Oh, what he could do with those lips and that tongue. The taste of his kiss—coffee and pure Jack—the feel of him under her hands was divine. And this time, there was no one to interrupt them.

So, okay, maybe just a little more smooching before she pointed him at the door. She deserved something sweet out of this, didn't she? Everything in her responded to his deep, rough voice, the heat in his gaze, and the naughty twinkle that said his plans included getting naked and raunchy.

Jack was just passing through, she knew that. But it had been over a year since Dave died, and she was tired of being alone. Tired of turning to romance novels and her vibrator for sexual fulfillment, instead of to a real man, one who made it his business to take care of her needs along with his own.

She missed the way Dave had looked at her too, like she was Christmas and his birthday wrapped into one, but she'd never have that again. Her heart squeezed painfully with all too familiar grief, then thumped with excitement. Dave was gone for good, but she had a real man in her arms right now.

Maybe 'fun' with Jack was what she needed. And if that included sex, well, bring it. He'd give her a great orgasm, or maybe even two, and then he'd be gone. She wouldn't have to worry about whether it would develop into anything more, anything that could hurt her when it ended, because it would be over nearly as soon as it began.

Thus, when he boosted her up onto the counter and stepped between her open thighs, Lindi slid her arms up over his shoulders and around his neck, holding on. Oh, she loved the way he could pick her up like she was a tiny, slender thing while kissing her—that was sheer male strength ... and talent.

One big, calloused hand stroked up her bare thigh, and between them, straight to her center. Lindi flinched, letting out a tiny squeak, and then melted as he cupped her in his big hand. He made a deep hmm of pleasure in his chest as he traced the fabric over her mons, already damp. He found her clitoris, and Lindi moaned into his mouth as pleasure feathered under his touch

Kissing her harder, Jack delved two broad fingertips under the edge of the thong, and stroked her wet, swollen labia. At the shock of the hot, graphic caress, Lindi's thighs clenched on his narrow hips, and she dug her short nails into the back of his neck as he found her opening and thrust one, then two fingers inside her.

Bliss coalesced around his big, calloused digits as he stroked in, out, then in again. She moaned, her voice rising in a plea for more. In answer, he hooked those two fingers, finding the magical mass of nerves inside her vaginal wall and pressing as he circled her clitoris with his thumb.

Lindi whimpered, her attention narrowing to his hand, his mouth and his body against hers, all exactly what she wanted, needed.

"You gonna come to me when I call you, Lindi?" he asked, nipping at her wet lip with his teeth as he caressed her with swift expertise.

"Jack," she protested, tipping her head back as the tension inside her coiled tighter. Oh, God, if he stopped now she'd die. Maybe she would if he didn't, but what a way to go.

"Are you?" he asked, biting the cord of her neck this time with a tiny sting of his teeth. She couldn't quite remember the question, but at this point she'd agree to give away her café if he'd only keep petting her right there. She arched into his touch, moaning again as he did so.

"Yes," she groaned. "Yes, Jack." Oh, God, yes to anything and everything. If he wanted her to shout it out the windows, she'd do it.

"That's my good girl," he crooned. "Now come for me, honey. Come all over my hand."

She did, clinging to him as the pleasure imploded inside her, her pussy clenching around his fingers with joyous suction. "Jack."

He held her and stroked her until she sucked in a deep breath and collapsed on his shoulder, her face against his skin, her body limp with relief and pleasure.

Then he withdrew his hand, set her thong to rights and lifted her face for another slow, wet kiss.

"Now I gotta go take care of myself in your shower," he said wryly, palming his own groin. "'Cause the first time I have you, it ain't gonna be on a goddamn counter, it's gonna be in a bed, and I'm gonna be cleaned up so you'll use that sweet mouth on my cock before I eat your pussy and then fuck you until you come your brains out. Okay?"

She gazed up at him, her mind whirling with the hot, graphic imagery he'd just planted there. He raised his brows in a silent demand.

"Okay," she mumbled.

Jack kissed the tip of her nose. "That's my sweet woman." He set her on her feet, held her until she was steady, and then stepped back. Lindi's gaze flew to the long, thick shape pressing against the fly of his jeans, and her knees nearly gave out. She was not averse to taking care of him now—any way he chose.

"Later, honey," he promised. Then he turned and sauntered away to the bedroom, pausing to grab a black leather satchel from the sofa as he passed.

Lindi watched him go, feeling as if she'd stepped onto the peaceful lake shore and been swept away by a warm, tropical tsunami. Anyway, that answered one question. Jack found her sexually attractive, all right.

Almost immediately, a cold chill of guilt slithered in under her warm glow of sexual satisfaction. What kind of person did it make her, if she'd allowed a stranger to touch her the way Jack just had? One who only the day before had kidnapped her and put her in danger?

She grabbed her cup and slugged down another big drink. At least she didn't burn her mouth this time, as her coffee had cooled off while Jack was heating her up.

Maybe she was the slut Darrell had accused her of being.

Or maybe Jack was just that good at getting through her defenses. He might have decided to keep her safe physically, but he could be just as dangerous to her emotionally. She'd do well to remember this, and stick with her earlier resolution to send him on his way before she let him in any deeper.

Because once he was in ... she might not get away without being hurt in ways much worse than the punch Twig had given her. Those bruises would fade, and along with them the ache.

A blow to the heart could last for a long, long time. And as much as she loved her mother, she didn't want to follow in her footsteps, falling for the wrong man, even making a family with him, before realizing he wasn't the kind of man who stayed, emotionally as well as physically.

She'd been with Dave for a year, lived with him for half that year, made love with him, cooked for him, done his laundry … but he'd been the one to say 'I love you'. The one to help her follow her dream, supporting her while she did so. And then, before she could gather the courage to meet him halfway, he'd died.

And now she'd never know if she would've womaned up and said those three words back to him. She'd been afraid if she did, he'd ask her to marry him. And that, she knew she lacked the courage for.

She drained her coffee and moved to pour another cup. Good thing Jack wasn't going to be around for long.

Chapter Ten

Jack walked back into the kitchen as Lindi was thawing lefto-ver cinnamon rolls in the microwave and stirring scrambled eggs in a skillet. Because no matter what, people had to eat, and a good breakfast set them up for the day.

Half a dozen eggs, part of a container of creamer, a small chunk of cheddar and a half-wilted head of lettuce had been the sum total of the contents of her frig, aside from bottled condiments. She'd been planning on grocery shopping yester-day afternoon.

Looking over at Jack, she blushed as she met his eyes. In his faded jeans, another snug tee, this one black with a Harley logo, his wet hair combed back from his face, he looked clean and relaxed, a flush riding his cheekbones, his eyes lazy.

She blushed hotter as she pictured what he'd done to get that way. Handling himself under the warm water in her shower. Leaning one long arm on the tiled wall, the other soapy, work-ing his cock. Did he groan, or just shudder silently when he came?

She already knew he was a talker—he'd urged her to come on his hand. She could imagine him pouring hot, blue words in her ear while he was deep inside her.

She yelped as steam from the eggs scalded her fingers. Well, no wonder, she was standing with her hand poised over the skillet, indulging in dirty thoughts when she was supposed to be focused on her craft. She knew better—cooking was a dan-gerous profession, with cuts, scalds and burns waiting for the careless.

And thinking sexy thoughts about Jack was just as dangerous in a different way. He was not the man for her—not for more than one night, and she had to remember that.

"You need some help?" he asked, pausing at her shoulder. Lindi sidestepped, trying to ignore the warm, enticing scent of her soap and shampoo on his skin.

"No, I need to get to my café," she said as she dished steaming eggs onto two plates, sprinkled finely shredded cheddar over them and then added a warm, mammoth cinnamon roll to each plate. "I left money in the till, and I have to finish yesterday's clean-up."

To which she was not looking forward. The grill and dishes covered in egg and dried syrup would be disgusting by now.

She also hoped no prowling teens had found her bicycle parked behind the café. It was the only transportation she had at the moment. Her old Caprice needed repairs, and she really didn't want to spend the money now. Put another way, she didn't have the money now.

What she really should be doing today was calling to apply for that part-time waitress job at another café in downtown Coeur d'Alene. Maybe they'd be willing to let her work after-noons and evenings, around her current BeeHive schedule. Dinner tips were better anyway, because people were drinking and in an expansive mood.

Jack took the plate she handed him and carried it to the other side of the small table crammed in between the stove and the door to her tiny patio. "I'll run you out there as soon as we're done here," he said, sitting down. "Any more coffee in that pot?"

She refilled his cup and her own, then grabbed the creamer from the refrigerator, the salt, pepper and hot sauce from the cupboard, and brought them to the table with her.

Her stomach growled loudly as she picked up her fork. Jack saluted her with his loaded fork. "This looks great. You as good with dinner as you are with breakfast?"

Lindi took a bite of scrambled egg covered in a thin layer of melted cheese. Her stomach shuddered with bliss as she chewed and swallowed. "Dunno. Depends if you like Cheese Whiz and lime Jello on Ritz crackers. I'm awesome with those."

"Smartass. Gimme a real dinner menu."

Huh, Jack was a foodie. Well, it stood to reason he didn't maintain his big, muscular frame without eating and enjoying it.

She tore a piece from her cinnamon roll and bit into it. The sweet, spicy dough melted on her tongue. As he chewed and waited expectantly, she shrugged. She liked talking about cooking, and at least it was safe conversational ground.

"Well, unless I'm at the café, I don't have much room to get real creative. But I do great lasagna, roasts, stir fry, and a mean meatloaf. My mac'n'cheese and twice-baked potatoes are also to die for."

"Marry me," he said, shoveling up another bite of eggs. "You just may be the perfect woman."

Lindi rolled her eyes and took another drink of coffee. "You're easy."

"Damn straight," he agreed. "For a pretty blonde with tits and ass, I'm easy. For a woman who looks like you and cooks, I'm a sure thing."

She couldn't help laughing, he was so ridiculous. And okay, maybe the fact he was so good with his hands and his mouth had softened her up too.

His eyes twinkling, he wolfed down another huge bite.

This seemed the perfect time to ask him those questions he'd promised to answer.

"So, you're from Spokane," she mused. "Any brothers or sisters there?"

"Got a sister, Bridget, but she lives in D.C. Her husband's career Army."

"What about your parents? Are they still around?"

"Dad's gone. My ma's in Cali."

Lindi nodded encouragingly, but he was eyeing her plate. "You gonna finish that cinnamon roll?"

"Please, help yourself." She pushed her plate toward him. Despite missing lunch and supper the day before, there was no way Lindi could finish one of the huge, gooey rolls.

"You make these too?" he asked, scraping the remains of her roll onto his plate.

"No, I get them from a little bakery over on Sherman. They sell me two or three dozen a week. I freeze, then reheat them when customers order them at the café."

"Sherman, that's the main drag through downtown, right? Loaded with tourist shops and shit." Finished eating, he leaned back to drink his coffee, which he took black.

Lindi nodded as she rose. She slid their dishes into a sink full of hot, soapy water. "It's quieter on this east end. A few older businesses and some new ones coming in. The Sherman Bakery's been there about five years, I think."

He looked thoughtful. "Town's grown from what I remember, but it's still a sweet place to live. Cool downtown with pubs and restaurants. Room to get out in the woods or on the water, do what you want, not bump into other people every minute. Good place to settle."

"I love it here," she agreed. She couldn't imagine living anywhere else. The area was crawling with tourists and outdoor enthusiasts in the summer, but there always seemed to be plenty of room for everyone.

"You grow up here?"

"I did. Rathdrum, a wide spot in the road just north along I-95. I moved over to Spokane for a while, went to junior college, but ... I don't know, I decided higher ed really wasn't for me. I moved over here, and then I met Dave."

Something darkened in his gaze, but his voice was gentle as he asked, "He treat you good?"

"Yeah. He was ... a great guy," she said, her voice cracking a little. "He helped me buy into the BeeHive. My grandma left me a little money, and Dave put up the rest for the down payment. He worked in an auto-repair shop up in midtown. But then he ... died."

"And Darrell made his move." Jack was scowling now. "He ever touch you?"

Lindi shuddered. "No, but I think he was, um, working up to it. Escalating, my friend Sara calls it. She works in the DA's office. She wanted me get a restraining order on him, but he hadn't done anything, so while the police were real nice, but they said they couldn't help."

There was a unique and painful embarrassment in discussing another man's obsession, especially while the memory of the picture wall hung in the air like a graphic mirage.

"Fuckin' stalker laws," Jack shook his head in disgust. "Someone's gotta get hurt or worse before the cops can step in. In my world, a woman don't have to worry about that shit, 'cause her man takes care of it, and his brothers back him up."

Lindi shifted uncomfortably, but she couldn't very well disagree with him. She'd been becoming progressively more afraid of Darrell as the summer rolled into fall. She was so done with men like him and Twig, who thought having a dick gave them the right to be one, and use their strength to intimidate women.

And Jack was right—while Dave had been alive Darrell hadn't dared do anything but make occasional comments to her. But now Dave was gone, and Jack wouldn't be staying. What if Darrell decided to come back? Would he?

She opened her mouth to ask Jack this, but he preempted her.

"What about your folks?" he asked. "You have a daddy or a brother around?"

She shrugged. "My dad died when I was six—driving drunk. I have a sister in Portland. My mom's out there staying with her for the summer, helping with my nieces."

"You never told them about Darrell," Jack guessed, his eyes narrowing. "What the fuck, Lindi? That's just stupid. You have nieces, you got a brother-in-law, don't you?"

"Don't you call me stupid," she said indignantly. "Neither my mom, my sister, or her husband could do anything about Darrell. Chad is an accountant, for Pete's sake. And he has enough on his plate now. I didn't want any of them worrying about me, when Cissie needs them more."

His gaze softened. "What's wrong with her, honey?"

"She's ... sick," she said, looking away. Her chest tightened as it did every time she thought about her big sister's ordeal, and tears threatened. She really did not want to talk about that right now, or she would cry.

Thankfully, instead of demanding more information, Jack rose and walked to her. He squeezed her waist with his hand, and she felt his lips on the top of her head. "That's rough. Sorry you gotta worry about her."

"Besides," she said, resisting the treacherous comfort of his embrace, "if you think I should've reported Darrell, maybe I should call the police about you."

Jack's heavy brows shot together and he opened his mouth, but a raucous guitar riff sounded from his pocket. "We'll get back to that later."

His hand heavy on her back, his gaze holding hers, he pulled his phone out and put it to his ear. "Yeah."

He listened for a moment, then his brows flew up. "What? You sure, man? Well, I'll be fuckin' damned. That's unexpected but sweet, ain't it?" His eyes twinkled with secret amusement. "Yeah, we're still at her place, but she wants to get to her café. Meet you out there—say half an hour."

* * *

"Keys is meeting us at the Honey Pot," Jack told Lindi, sliding his phone back into his pocket. He grinned to himself. She was gonna be a very happy woman soon as she heard the news Keys had for her. And Jack planned to reap the dividends of that. He was gonna take her out to celebrate, and then he was gonna get in there, where she was hot and wet and sweet.

She glared at him, her hands in the dishwater. "It's the Bee-Hive, and you know it."

She was feisty—he liked that. Right now she was shooting sparks from those big blue eyes of hers. His cock twitched as he remembered the dazed look in them earlier after he'd made her come right on this kitchen counter.

He'd jerked off in her shower with a handful of her shower gel, imagining exactly what he was gonna do to her when he got her in a bed. Suck those gorgeous tits, eat her pussy and then fuck her until neither of them could walk—then do it all over again in as many positions as he could talk her into.

"Anyway, why is he meeting us there?"

He patted her round, firm ass. "Because, the three of us gotta talk. And by the time we tell you some news you're gonna like a lot, you'll see callin' the cops is a dumbass idea."

Lindi opened her mouth, and he shook his head. "Not now, honey. Gotta make another call, then we'll go." He turned to go into her bedroom, the only place in her shoebox of an apartment he could make a phone call he didn't want her to overhear.

"We'll go when I'm ready," she called, scrubbing as he walked away. "Unless you're going to help with these dishes."

"I wash dishes," he called back. "And I barbecue a mean ri-beye steak. If you're sweet, I'll fire up a grill and show you sometime."

He'd started washing dishes in the clubhouse kitchen when he was a kid to pay the club back for all the help they gave his mom, sister and him. Learned to cook too, and he loved to barbecue. He'd like to see the look on Lindi's face when she bit into her first bite of one of his grilled steaks.

"If you're around," she muttered.

Already pushing a familiar phone number on his phone, Jack paid no attention to her.

A familiar hoarse voice grunted in his ear. "Yeah?"

Ivan "Joystick" Vanko had immigrated to the Pacific North-west as a baby in his Ukrainian parents' arms, but he still had traces of an accent, from growing up in their home. He was also one scary, badass MC president … except maybe to someone like Jack, who'd seen his two little blond boys riding him like a Harley in his backyard.

"'lo, Stick?" Jack said. "Jack Moran. I'm over in Idaho—Coeur d'Alene."

He pushed the bedroom door closed behind him. It stuck, and he had to reach back and give it a hard shove. Christ, this old building was sagging everywhere.

"Moran," Stick said. "Expected you yesterday at church. Passed the collection plate just for you and Keys."

Why the meeting of MC club members at their private table was called 'church' Jack didn't know. The name was ironic as hell, considering that many of the decisions made at these private meetings had to do with mayhem, mischief or outright murder. The Airway Heights Devil's Flyers committed their share of the first two. And if he was right, they'd done the latter, and recently. It had been a righteous death, though, so he had no quarrel with it.

"Yeah, we'll be sure and tithe when we get over there," he said wryly, "but it won't be for a couple of days. Got a lot of shit to take care of here."

"We took care of most things before you arrived," Stick said. "Even took out the trash."

"That's good, but whoever you had on cleanup didn't do their job. They left … traces of the party." Which Lindi had of course gotten on her knee.

"Really." Stick didn't sound too worried. "Well, the party boy went for a quiet evening cruise on the lake. Very quiet, very nice. No hangover, no blowback."

"Did he now?"

An after-dark cruise in a small power boat with no running lights, Jack would bet. Probably to one of the deepest parts of Coeur d'Alene Lake, the surface of which ironically was visible from downtown. Jack knew about the deep spot because Keys had gotten curious and Googled it on his phone, and because that's where he and Jack would've dumped him, they decided.

Jack's eyes narrowed in satisfaction. "Can't think of a better way for him to end the day."

Hundreds of feet deep, chained to a chunk of cement or heavy steel at the bottom of the big lake until the lake trout saw to it there was nothing left but bones. Would anyone miss the cheating asshole? Doubtful.

"We're having a barbecue on Saturday," Stick said. "You'll be here."

"If I'm in town, yeah. Wouldn't miss it. If I'm not, catch you the next time. And I'll bring my tithe."

"Good. Then I won't have to find you to collect."

Chapter Eleven

Jack would not tell Lindi what Keys wanted to discuss with her. Finally, Lindi gave up asking and scowled out the window of the black SUV which had magically taken the place of the one Twig had driven away.

To Lindi's shock, Jack got busy the moment he walked into the café, helping her clean up the remains of yesterday's dishes, and then sweeping and mopping the floors while she finished scraping the grill and the myriad of other small tasks that were involved in shutting down a kitchen for the night.

He worked with an ease that said he'd done this kind of work before and didn't mind doing it now. And she really liked watching him. Big, sexy man in snug, faded jeans cleaning her café? Bring it, sistah. She surreptitiously whipped out her phone to take a couple of photos of him pushing the mop, smiling to herself at the results. Fun, even if he did have all his clothes on.

Keys arrived as she was dropping the last cleaning cloth in the laundry bag. He wore much the same thing he had the day before, a long-sleeved Henley, this one faded blue, a leather vest, jeans and boots, silver pendants round his neck. His silver hair suited him, highlighting his blue eyes and tanned skin.

Jack's friend rocked the biker look. Almost as much as Jack. Now if she could just get a photo of Keys washing her counters … she'd have double the eye-candy to show Kit and Sara.

"Babe," he said, looking her over appreciatively. "Lookin' good."

"Thank you," she said, her face warm. She might be into Jack, but that didn't mean she was impervious to this man's charm.

Keys peered hopefully toward the kitchen. "Got anything to eat?"

"Get her to heat up a cinnamon roll for you," Jack called from the far side of the café. "Awesome."

Lindi heated the last cinnamon roll in her café freezer, and microwaved some bacon, both of which Keys ate with gusto.

"Although," he told her with a grin, licking his fingers, "this does not let you off the hook. You still owe me a real breakfast."

"Um, how long do I have to make it for you?" she asked, her gaze flickering between him and Jack, who had just returned from stowing the mop in the back.

Jack turned, a frown furrowing his brow. "You mean as in, how long are we gonna be around?"

"Exactly. A few more days, a week? You have nothing to hold you here, now that you have your money."

The two men exchanged a look, communicating without words, the way people do who know each other really well.

Lindi ignored them. "Tomorrow," she said. "I'll fix you a great breakfast, and then you can hit the road."

Well ahead of the sheriff, because she should report what had happened, at least to make sure Twig's assault was noted. Keys may have scared him away from the MC, but he could still decide to hang around Coeur d'Alene.

"Not tomorrow," Jack said. He set his hand on her back, urging her toward one of the booths by the front window. "All right, your café is clean. Time for you to hear some good news."

Lindi sat, and Jack slid in beside her, laying his arm along the back of the booth behind her shoulders. Warm afternoon sunshine poured over them.

Keys lifted a familiar leather satchel—Darrell's—onto the table beside him, pulled a sheaf of official-looking papers out of it, and looked her in the eye.

"You ready for some good news?"

She nodded, still bewildered.

Keys grinned at her, and proceeded to rock her world.

"Okay, babe. I went through all of Darrell's papers last night, and I found some legal documents. Including these." He tapped a document unfolded on the table before him, and then pushed it over in front of her, followed by another. "I ain't in favor of legal shit, but these don't exactly stink. Two wills. This one says Darrell and Dave's folks left their homestead— including the cabin, shop, and if I read the plat map right, also the land running clear down to the lake by the café here— nearly eighty acres all told—all to your Dave."

"They did?" Lindi stared at him. "But … I assumed Darrell got the land. He lived up there."

Keys shook his head. "Reckon they weren't stupid. They either knew what kinda person Darrell was, or they just wanted to look out for Dave.'

'Anyhoo, your boy was no dummy, either. He hooked up with you, he got busy and wrote himself a will too—this one here. Left *ev*-ery-thang—all the property, all his worldly possessions, of which it don't sound like he had much—to you. But the land, now—it's worth a whack. And, since your man died, Darrell's been basically squattin' on your land."

"Dave left it all to me?" Lindi took a shaky breath, still struggling to absorb this. "But—but … is that even legal?"

"Yeah, it's legal, honey," Jack said. "Anyone can write their own will, leave property to whoever they choose. And it's a damn good thing your man did. If he'd died without a will, everything would've gone to fuckin' Darrell, and then to any shirt-tail relatives that surface."

Lindi put her hands carefully on the paper and smoothed it out. Her hands were shaking. Well, no wonder. It wasn't every day she found out she was an heiress.

She found the date at the bottom of the document, beside the notary seal. June 14 of the summer before. Oh, God, Dave had written the will when they moved in together. He'd clearly believed that they would end up married, together for good.

Finding out he'd planned so carefully to take care of her sent sorrow and guilt running through her like a river. He'd given her a gift she could barely comprehend, and she'd give it all back in a heartbeat if she could only have him, sitting here with them. She'd tell him … she'd tell him to be careful, because the world needed him in it. With his goofy smile and his big heart. And she'd tell him she was so, so sorry she'd dragged her feet about marrying him.

"I can't believe he did this," she whispered, her eyes blurring as they filled with tears. She sniffed, hard, and swiped under her eyes with her fingertips. "He never said anything to me about it. Why didn't he say anything?"

"Probably thought there was no reason, honey," Jack said gently. "Guys in their early thirties don't think they're gonna die."

This was true, and neither did the people who loved them. She'd struggled to believe it when the deputies had shown up at her apartment and told her that Dave was gone. Hadn't really been able to take it in until she saw the image of him lying in the morgue, a sheet pulled neatly to his chest, the near side of his face cold and still, the far side one massive bloody bruise.

Darrell had arrived with them, full of spurious sympathy. He'd even told the cops they could go, that he would stay with her. Luckily she'd roused from her fog of shock and grief long enough to let them know she did not want him around. She'd called her mother, who had come right away.

"That—that *sonofabitch*," she realized, her tears drying as anger burned. "All that time, Darrell wasn't stalking me for me, he just wanted the land." And she'd let him creep her out because she felt ... guilty, ashamed. As if it his lusting after her was partly her fault, as if she'd caused him to behave that way.

"Oh, I think it's safe to say he wanted you too," Jack said dryly, giving her nape a gentle squeeze. "He wanted the place, and you along with it, bein' sweet to him like you were to his brother. Bein' a fuck-head, he had no idea how to win you the right way. Thus his stalker shit."

"Oh, my God. This must be what they fought about," she realized. "The night Dave died. It makes sense now. I heard them, outside Dave's apartment, yelling at each other. Dave said something about Darrell could stay up there and rot, he didn't care, as long as he left us alone. Then Darrell said something back, and Dave came unglued, tried to drag him out of the Blazer. Darrell drove away, and Dave followed him on his motorcycle. I ran downstairs, but he didn't even hear me, just blasted out of here."

Jack gave her another comforting squeeze. "And then he slid off the road?"

She looked out the window to the south, where a glimpse of Coeur d'Alene Lake could be seen through the evergreen and birch trees, blue under the bright sun. "Just west of here, on the curve around the bay. That stretch always gets icy in the winter. It had been snowing that day, and it was packed down."

"Wonder what Darrell said to make Dave follow him?" Keys mused.

"I think he threatened me somehow," Lindi said. "I don't know what else would've made Dave so angry." Angry enough to follow his brother at top speed on the slick streets of the first snow of the previous winter ... straight to his death.

"And you been carrying a load of guilt about that, haven't you?" Jack guessed with unerring accuracy. "Y'know, honey, he may've had help goin' off the road. Darrell Gaspard was that kind of low-life."

She nodded. That was also true, or highly probable anyway. "I've wondered. I'll never know, though." Because even if Darrell reappeared, he'd never admit any involvement.

"Nope. Some things you just gotta live with," Keys said, his gaze on his hands, which were knotted on the table.

Embarrassed by her self-absorption, Lindi reached out to touch his sleeve. "Thank you for saving Jack and me. I'm sorry you had to send your nephew away. Family is important."

Keys shook his head in wry acknowledgement. "Hell, babe, it was bound to happen, sooner or later. My sister's long gone, so I tried to look out for him. But the kid has a screw loose somewhere. If I hadn't sent him off, he would've spread his brand of shit all over this little town, and Spokane. And there's some local brothers who would not put up with that." He turned his hand over and squeezed hers gently. "But thanks."

"You mean the Cougars?" She looked between the two of them uneasily. "Are you ... affiliated with them?" The Cougars were a local MC right here in Coeur d'Alene. Every one of them big, blond and muscular, with gazes which always made her think of real cougars with lunch on their minds. Jack could fit right into their group.

"Nah," Jack said, trailing his hand down her back. "We just know 'em."

"Oh," Lindi she wasn't sure what to make of this information. "Aren't they pretty dangerous?"

Keys' lips twitched.

His eyes twinkling, Jack pulled her closer to him and pressed a kiss to her temple.

"Honey, not sayin' you wanna mess with the Cougars, but trust me, you got nothin' to worry about from them. Nothin' at all. Xavier Chase is their pres—he's a good guy. Owns Chase Cycles up on 4th Street. The rest of 'em are mostly his family, cousins and the like."

"Most of the shit you hear about them is just rumors," Keys added.

"What about the stuff I've heard about the Devil's Flyers over in Airway Heights?" she asked, letting herself lean, just for a moment, into Jack's heat and strength. It felt like a safe haven from all the shocks that just kept coming. Even knowing his embrace was only temporary didn't make it any less comforting.

Jack and Keys exchanged another look.

Keys raised one brow at his partner. "You gonna tell her?"

"Tell me what?" Lindi asked, trying to shift away from Jack. He did not let her go.

"Some of the shit about the Highs you can believe," Jack said, his hand wrapping in her hair and tugging her head back far enough to give her a look that said he was dead serious. "But not all. For now, if they come in here, you treat them with respect but you don't give them your sweet smile, and you don't get where one of 'em can misbehave."

"You mean they might mistake me for someone else?" Lindi asked him, widening her eyes. "And try to, say, make me go somewhere with them where they can force me to talk?"

Keys snorted, but Jack's heavy brows drew together, saying he was not amused. "Yeah, only in their case, they wouldn't be forcin' you to talk."

"He's right, babe," Keys told her, sobering. "There's some guys in that club that do not respect women. An' Joystick can't control their every move."

"Which means he should cut them loose," Jack added. "Let 'em go find a chapter in another state that'll put up with their shit."

Keys lifted his chin in acknowledgement of this.

"Okay," Lindi said, "I'll keep an eye out."

"But if they're a problem for you, I'll deal with it," Jack went on, his voice weighted with portent that sent uneasiness skittering down Lindi's spine.

"What? How?"

"'Cause Keys and me are Devil's Flyers," he told her. "Independents, which means we visit when we're in town, and ride when we're needed, but we're not members of the local chapter."

Lindi stared at him, stunned. A heavy weight seemed to be pressing down on her chest. "Oh, my God," she mumbled. "I knew you were a real biker the minute I saw you." And now he told her he and Keys belonged to the same club Dave had hung around.

"Yeah. Which means I can keep you safe from the knot-heads in the Flyers," he shot back, his grip on her hair tightening. "I let Joystick know you're under my protection—and Keys' too—so none of 'em will say boo to you. 'Cause nobody messes with a brother's woman."

She sucked in a breath, and grasped his thick wrist. "I am not your woman."

He let go of her hair, but with that irritating grin that said he found her indignation amusing.

"Also, you really need to get someone else in here to work with you," he said. "So you're not alone. This place ain't exactly in sight of other businesses."

She opened her mouth to say she couldn't afford to hire help, and then closed it. Her heart thumped as she realized that if she could sell some of the Gaspard property, she could hire help and more. Maybe even pay off her bank loan.

The plat map showed the land ran clear down to the water. That was important. People around here paid big money to build houses overlooking Coeur d'Alene Lake and even more if they could own their own dock and lakefront.

She could use Dave's legacy to get the café out of debt and expand her business plan, to live her life free of the constant worry of losing it all. And damn Darrell to hell if he tried to take it away. She'd call the police on him, this time for real.

She smoothed her hand over the will again, and then folded it to tuck into her purse, her hands shaking. She needed to find a good lawyer and then a Realtor.

"Also, the Flyers do come in, charge 'em extra for coffee refills," Keys grinned. "Stick can afford it."

"Reckon he can, if he got what he wanted out of Darrell," Jack said.

He jogged Lindi gently with his elbow. "Seems to me, you can relax a bit, now that you're an heiress, yeah? Go shoppin', get your nails done—all that shit women love."

Lindi shook her head. She wasn't into spending money before she even had it. And she might need to pay a retainer to whichever lawyer she hired to make sure Darrell couldn't try to break Dave's will.

If Darrell had been anyone else—say, a decent human being, she'd feel guilty about taking his family's land. But, instead he was a creep who'd had a hand in his own brother's death, stalked her, and had a dangerous MC after him. She wanted him gone.

Something else about their mention of Darrell was bothering her too.

"You keep talking about Darrell in the past tense," she realized, looking from Jack to Keys. "But listen, I know him ... at least enough to know that he won't give up. He'll be back to try and take everything back from me—I know he will."

"Honey," Jack repeated, his hand heavy on her nape. "Relax. Gaspard is no longer a worry for you. He ain't comin' back."

Across the table, Keys lifted his chin in agreement. "He's right, babe. Ol' Darrell won't be bothering you again."

"But how do you know that?" she asked. "I mean, he's never given up yet, and now he's going to be really pissed."

Keys choked on his mouthful of coffee, and coughed into his fist, avoiding her gaze.

Jack sighed. "Fuck, woman. You don't trust easily, do you?"

"No," she agreed, staring at the small puddle of cold coffee in the bottom of her cup, "I don't." She'd been trained not to by her own father.

"Well, you can trust my word," he said, his gaze boring into hers. "In fact, you don't, it's gonna piss me off."

Lindi gazed up at him, a chill penetrating the warmth of the sun and his hand on her neck. He was very serious ... but, trust the word of a rambling biker, without proof?

Keys shifted, tapping his hand on the table. "About the land, babe. Get yourself a good lawyer, but far as I can see, it's yours legally, free and clear. You can always parcel it. Make a shitload of money that way."

Lindi contemplated this new financial wonder.

"I guess I could do that," she said. "I sure don't have any use for the shop, and as for the cabin, ugh." She shuddered. "I wish it would just burn down."

"Damn good idea," Jack drawled. She stared at him, suddenly worried he was contemplating starting the fire himself.

"Also," Keys said, leaning forward to get her attention, his gaze serious. "I hope you've already forgotten the ugly shit Twig spouted at you, Lindi. You're a hot babe. Jack wasn't glarin' holes in me right now, I'd make a move myself."

Lindi smiled at him, ignoring her burning cheeks. "Um, thanks."

He winked at her, and she nearly winked back. The man was hot, no doubt. If Jack wasn't around, she might let him make his move.

"Quit flirtin' with my woman," Jack said, but his voice was easy.

His hand tightened on her waist, and he looked down at her, a heated look as if Keys weren't sitting right there. "Now, you're finished here and I got nothin' goin' on. So how about you and me get out of here, and go have some fun?"

She raised her brows at him. "I'll consider it."

Jack leaned in to give her another kiss. He tasted delicious flavored with coffee. "Good girl. You do that."

Keys' chair scraped back. "Well, reckon I'll see you tomorrow," he said. "Gimme a buzz when y'all surface, yeah?"

Lindi's blush spread down her throat and chest, and Jack took this in with a grin. "It won't be early," he said without looking away from her. "Sometime in the afternoon."

Her eyes widened and he chuckled. "I get you in a bed, ain't letting you out till I've had my fill of honey."

"Fuck, now I got a hard-on," Keys grumbled good-naturedly. "Later."

The door jangled as he strode out to the big Harley on which he'd arrived.

Lindi took a breath and looked over at Jack. "We should talk," she said.

"Sure, honey. Right after I get a real kiss."

As he pulled her close and cocked his head to kiss her again, she sank against him. Outside, Keys' bike roared to life, and then rumbled away. Inside, it was quiet, the only sound the rustle of their clothing as Jack stroked down her back to squeeze her ass while he used his warm mouth and his tongue to work his black magic on her.

Finally, when she was in a daze rivaled only by the one he'd put her in earlier, Jack lifted his head and smiled at her. "How about we get out of here?"

This time she nodded, and he gave her an approving squeeze before letting her go. "You make sure everything's locked up," he said. "I'll turn off the lights."

He really could be thoughtful. When he turned on his take-charge, caring side, he made it seem having a man around could be a very good thing in more ways than one. In some ways, he was a real catch.

It just wasn't going to be her who caught him. Besides, she might have money coming her way, but there were nightmares

that even a fortune couldn't quell, and as soon as she got
home, she had to deal with a huge-ass one.

Chapter Twelve

Lindi's euphoria dissipated as she followed Jack out to the black Escalade.

Jack opened her door for her and held it. "Hey. You okay?"

"I'm fine," she said. "I just need my bicycle."

"Climb in. I'll get it and put it in the back."

She climbed into the big vehicle and watched Jack saunter around the back of the café. He came back wheeling her bicycle and put it carefully in the back of the SUV.

They drove west on the curving lake road toward town. The afternoon breeze was up, driving whitecaps across the main body of the lake, with puffy spring clouds scudding overhead. The usual walkers and bicyclists thronged the paved path along the shoreline, and elderly folks sat on the park benches placed to catch the best views of the lake.

To Lindi's relief, Jack let her be as he retraced the familiar route past the resort golf course, and then west onto the tree-lined avenue that was Sherman, past an old cemetery, and a couple of motels, a bar and café, and other small businesses.

He turned left again, toward the lake. Her apartment stood on a shady street near the new city hall, library, and a park bordering the lake.

When Cissie, Blake and her nieces had visited late in the summer, the girls had had a ball racing around the play structure and the acres of new green grass. Thinking of Cissie and her family made Lindi's stomach knot. Before she did anything else, she had a phone call to make.

When Jack pulled to a stop on the street before the old house that had been parceled into apartments, Lindi opened her door.

"Hey, slow down," he said. "I'll get your bike, and you can show me where you stow it. Then maybe you'll share whatever has you so deep in your own head—'cause I'm thinkin' it's not the land."

"No, it's not." Lindi hopped down onto the curb. They had to wait again for a mother with a stroller and a little boy on a tricycle before crossing the tiny front lawn. Lindi led him along the crumbling walk to the side door, and showed him where to wheel the bike into an old sunporch which had been converted into tenant storage slots.

Then she hurried through the lower hallway and into her apartment.

Jack seemed to fill the small, familiar space with his male presence. Standing in the midst of her ragtag assortment of pastel cushions, faded quilt throws and flower prints, he stood out like a Harley in a home decor shop. Tall, broad and unshaven in his black leather and denim, he was such a *man*, so overflowing with testosterone and purpose that the woman in Lindi wanted to give way before him, follow willingly wherever he led.

He frowned at her. "All right, you wanna tell me what's goin' on under those blonde curls?"

"I need to make a call," she said. "Check in on my sister."

Just then, the opening bars of the rock classic, 'Mama told me not to come' burbled from her palm. Lindi put her phone to her ear and perched on the edge of her sofa, forgetting Jack.

"Hi, Mama. How was it?" she asked, her heart in her throat.

Her mother's breath hitched, and Lindi's heart plummeted.

But when Gail Carson spoke, her voice was ebullient. "Oh, Lindi, baby, it's a miracle! The whole area around the lump is clear—nothing in her breast at all. The cancer is *gone!*"

Lindi closed her eyes, relief filling her until she felt as if she might float right up off the floor. Cissie had had a checkup the day before, to determine whether the first round of treatments had worked on her breast cancer. This morning she'd met with her oncologist to learn the results.

"Oh, Mama," she managed. "That's so great. Oh, my God. I can't believe it."

Her mother laughed. "I know, I know, baby. We're all feeling the same way. Can't believe it's quite real. Chad bawled like a big ol' baby, and so did I."

Lindi plumped down on the edge of the sofa, tears streaming down her face. But at the same time she wanted to ask questions, get every detail, and then hear it all over again.

She totally understood her mother's inability to believe the good news—she felt the same way. Cissie and her doctors had been battling a vicious disease that often outwitted all modern medicine, so to hear that the treatments had worked, was difficult to take in.

"Oh, Mama," she said. "It's really gone? They checked everywhere?"

"They did. They truly did. It's gone."

"Oh, I wish I were there. Can I talk to her, please?"

"Of course you can. I'll bring the phone to her."

The other end of her old sofa sagged as Jack sat, nearly tipping Lindi into his lap. His arm wrapped around her, and she let herself slide sideways into his warm embrace. He gave her a squeeze and tipped his head to grin at her.

Then her sister's soft, tired voice sounded in her ear. "Lindi?"

"Hi, Cissie," Lindi said, smiling and crying at the same time. "So, you decided you've spent enough time flirting with that hot radiologist, huh?"

"I guess so," her sister said. "Oh, Lindi-Lou, can you believe it? I don't have cancer anymore!"

Tears flooded Lindi's eyes and spilled over for the second time that day. She leaned her head against Jack's chest. "I know, sweetie," she said. "I know. Wish I could be there to give you a great big old hug." Jack's arm tightened in a surrogate embrace that made Lindi smile through her tears.

"Me too," Cissie said. "But you gotta keep those bees buzzing over there, making honey for your pancakes."

"That's right," Lindi sniffled. "My hive is busy, at least in the mornings. Wish I could fly out there and stay for a while. Save you from Mama's cooking."

"That would be nice—to see you, I mean. Mama is a good cook, you know that."

Lindi smiled at her sister's loyalty. Their mother was good at opening packages of ready-to-mix pastas and adding burger or chicken and frozen veggies. She also opened cans like a pro, but beyond that she had little interest or aptitude for cooking. She'd always said the last thing a tired woman wanted to do was cook when she got home from being on her feet all day.

Lindi had taught herself to cook in self-defense, and then discovered she loved it. Her mother and sister had appreciated her talent.

"I'll come out as soon as I can," Lindi promised. Maybe now that she was a property owner, she could afford to fly to Portland once in a while. For certain she wouldn't trust her car to make the five hour drive.

They talked for a few more minutes and then Lindi's mother took the phone back and told her Cissie was tired out.

"Oh, I almost forgot," Gail Carson said, her voice lifting. "Chad's best man stopped by last evening. You remember Kyle? He asked about you. I could let him know when you're flying out—maybe the two of you can get together."

"Uh ... we'll see, Mama." Lindi had met Chad's best friend when she flew to Portland to be in Cissie's wedding a few years before, and again when she and her mom visited them last Christmas. He was a good guy, but he did exactly nothing for Lindi's libido. He was hamburger-noodle bake to Jack's prime cut beef.

"Such a nice boy," Gail went on, "He's buying his own home, you know, in a new subdivision near here. He says it's a long-term investment."

Jack's chest quivered on a silent chuckle, and Lindi's face flamed. Nothing like having her mom extoll the virtues of another man while Jack could hear every word.

"That's great, Mama. Listen, I'll call tomorrow evening, when the girls are home, okay? Bye for now."

Clicking her phone off with mingled relief and joy, Lindi tipped her head back and peeped up at Jack. "Sorry about that. My mother is kind of single-minded ... even now."

Her breath caught on a sob as she recalled the important part of the conversation. "I can't believe my Cissie is finally over that freaking cancer! I mean, I know the next few years are still risky, but for now … it's gone."

He pulled her closer, and pressed a kiss to the top of her head. "Hey, it's okay, honey. Let it out. I get this has gotta be a huge relief for you."

Well. How was she supposed to resist a man who, instead of recoiling in horror at the first sign of tears, invited her to cry all over him?

"I'm so happy, but still so—so angry, you know? I hate that Cissie had to go through that crap," she said, swiping her wet face with her hand. "She's been so weak and sick. And I couldn't do anything to help her. I felt so helpless."

A feeling with which she was all too familiar lately, with Dave's death, her mountain of debt and Darrell's stalking on top of Cissie's illness. Not to mention Jack grabbing her, and Twig roughing her up.

"Breast cancer, that's fucked up," he agreed. "But I'm bettin' she knows you would've taken it on yourself if you could. And now she's good. You're goin' to see her soon, right?"

Lindi nodded. She was, if she had to ride a Greyhound bus.

"All right then," he went on. "You're gonna go to her when you can. Meanwhile, she's got your mama, her man and her girls to celebrate with. How's about you and me get out of here and celebrate a little?"

Uh-oh. Just as she'd realized that first moment he smiled at her through her café window, this man was impossible to re-sist.

"Okay," she agreed. "I'd like that. Unless it involves doing body shots at an MC party or something—I am not down with that kind of celebrating."

Jack's brows flew up, and then he tipped back his head and roared with laughter.

"No," he said, his voice still quivering as he pulled her up off the sofa. "I think we can avoid that kinda shit. I ain't down with lettin' other men, even my brothers, get a look at your sweet tits. Get your purse and shit, and we'll go."

Lindi was smiling as she got her purse and jacket.

Jack wasn't a forever kind of man, not for her, but to celebrate with? Oh, yeah. That she could do.

It turned out that Jack's idea of getting Lindi's mind off things was to take her to a Harley shop on the interstate west of Coeur d'Alene.

She watched in sheer bemusement as he went straight to the women's racks and with every evidence of knowing what he was doing and enjoying it, chose a little black leather vest, a long-sleeved pink and black burnout tee, a cream tank with tiny motorcycles embroidered on it, and a black jersey tank with a zipper—all things she might have chosen herself, if she were feeling sexy and adventurous—and rich.

"You like these jeans?" he asked her, indicating the racks of bootcut blue jeans. Most of them had embroidery and bling on the rear pockets, some on the leg as well.

"Well, yeah, but ... I wasn't planning on shopping," Lindi said, with a guilty look toward the clerk, a slim redhead in Harley black.

Also, she wasn't sure the store would have anything that fit her. Her size always seemed to disappear first from clothing racks, leaving the tiny I-live-on-yogurt-and-salad sizes. She knew this assessment was not fair, because some women were naturally slender, but this didn't stop her from wishing stores would get a clue that they needed to buy more of the larger sizes.

"Well, you're shoppin' now," Jack said. "And I'm buyin'. Tell you what, I'll pick out the shit I like. What are you, a size eight?"

"I wish," she muttered. "A ten or a twelve, depending on the brand."

He winked at her. "Now I should've known that. That ass of yours is definitely a ten."

Her heart melted a little, until he held up a pair of jeans with holes frayed at the crease of the groin. "Love the peekaboo slits."

Lindi wrinkled her nose. "I don't think so." She did not want that portion of her anatomy playing peekaboo, thanks very much.

She moved over to the sale rack and flicked through the hangers.

Hallelujah, this shop was prepared for biker chicks of a larger size. She chose a pair of hipster bootcuts with cute sequins on the back pockets. "I'll try these."

Jack shrugged, then beckoned the clerk, who moved forward with alacrity to show them to a changing room.

He sprawled in one of the leather chairs and crossed his arms, and Lindi went into the dressing room. A few moments later, she blew her hair out of her eyes and glared in disgust at the mirror.

The sequined jeans were too tight in all the wrong places, cutting into her waist and leaving her upper hips bulging over the waistband. The crotch seam dug into her mons, leaving what Sara called a camel's nose effect … or was it a camel's toe? Whichever, like both ends of a camel, it was not attractive.

Lindi wriggled out of the jeans and tossed them on the bench, wanting nothing more than to don her own clothes and leave the store. She'd rather make do with her old ratty jeans than go through this torture.

She heard Jack and the clerk talking, although she couldn't hear their words. She was just slipping her skirt back on when an armful of clothing appeared over the top of the door.

"Here are some more things in your size," the clerk said.

Lindi opened her mouth to say she couldn't afford to pay regular prices, then shrugged. It wouldn't hurt to at least try the things on. There was a pair of bootcuts with pretty blue stitching, and a pair of skinny-legged jeans with black stitching and black lace trim, plus the tops Jack had chosen.

The second pair of jeans and cream tank fit like a dream, the jeans smoothing her curves and the top emphasizing her waist and the swell of her breasts. And when she slipped the black leather vest on and zipped it up under her breasts, it did killer things for her cleavage. Her waist never looked this small in street clothing.

She grinned at her reflection. Maybe she was meant to be a biker chick—yeah, in her next life. In this one, she was a short-order cook and café owner.

"Hey, gimme a look," Jack called.

Lindi hesitated. It was one thing to daydream in the mirror—quite another to present herself for a man who had no doubt been with lots of gorgeous women, most of them more slender than her.

"Lindi, do I need to come in there?"

"No." Lord, he was bossy. She opened the dressing room door and stepped out.

Jack's gaze ate her up from head to toe and back again, lingering on her breasts. He twirled his fingers, and Lindi rolled her eyes but pivoted on one foot, turning in a circle for him.

"You're definitely gettin' that outfit," he said, his gaze searing her ass through the snug jeans. He looked over at the clerk, who stood nearby. "You got any little leather skirts to go with that vest?"

Chapter Thirteen

Lindi dove back into the dressing room. A leather mini-skirt on her ass and thighs? "Not wearing one even if they do," she called.

Jack and the clerk laughed together, and she mimicked them silently in the mirror. Ha ha, wasn't she funny? Not.

She donned the black-zippered tank and black lace-trimmed jeans, a little revenge on her mind. He wanted to see her dressed like a biker ho? Fine. Drawing the zipper down to reveal most of her cleavage, she fluffed her hair out to there and opened the dressing room door to stand, hand on her outthrust hip, the other hand on the door.

Jack stopped in mid-remark, his mouth open a little ways, his heavy brows slowly rising. Lindi reached up to twine a lock of hair around her finger, her eyes wide. "D'you like it?" she asked with faux innocence.

Without a word, his narrowed gaze taking her in, he unfolded his length from the chair, pulled his wallet from his hip pocket and handed a credit card to the clerk. "We'll take 'em all," he said.

The redhead beamed. "Gotcha. I'll take care of it."

"Hey, wait a minute," Lindi called after her. "He's not buying me anything."

"C'mere, Lindi," Jack said.

When she looked back into his hot, caressing gaze, Lindi forgot clerks and credit cards. Her breasts and belly tight, her legs loose as warm honey, she walked to him.

Jack waited until she stood with only a breath separating them to slide his arms around her, his hands fondling the slope of her ass and squeezing. "You look hot as hell in this. You're wearin' it when I take you out for dinner and drinks," he told her.

"Kind of cool in the evenings for sleeveless," Lindi murmured, her gaze on his mouth, more a token resistance than anything.

Dinner and drinks with the sexiest man she'd ever met? Oh, heck yeah. Just one evening more, that was all. Then she'd force herself back to reality. She just hoped it wasn't a reality that had been forever changed by this man, to the point she wouldn't want to settle for less.

"Nothin' cool about this outfit with you in it," he muttered. "But we'll get you a leather jacket."

This startled Lindi out of the daze of lust caused by his nearness. She could get drunk on his scent alone—she wanted to bury her nose where the strong column of his neck flowed into his broad chest and sniff him like—like warm bread just out of the oven.

"No, we won't." She'd seen the price tag on the leather vest, and she was not spending even more on a jacket. She had a little black cardi that would work. "And you can just get your credit card back from the clerk. I'm don't need all this."

She'd buy Cissie a cute top she'd seen on the sale rack, though.

His eyes narrowed, his jaw tightening as he leaned closer. Impressive and a tiny bit scary, although not as much as that morning when she'd first learned his initial purpose for meeting her.

"Jacket, boots, and no arguments," he countered. "Can't put you on the back of my bike with bare arms and tits, and no protection for your feet except those little fuck-me sandals."

"Why, are you planning to dump me over in the road?" she teased, even as excitement crackled through her like fireworks over the lake in July. He was going to take her on the back of his bike! Oh, my Gawd. She'd ridden with Dave on his bike, but a Harley ... yum!

Jack's hand tightened on her ass, and his eyes narrowed in admonition. "Don't insult a man's riding skill, woman. Unless you're crankin' for a spankin'."

Lindi shoved at his chest. "Don't you threaten to take your hand to me, Jack Moran—or this is over before it starts. And you are not buying me clothes."

"Says you. We're well past start, woman. You can't afford to buy here, I get that. But, I can. Now go get the rest of your shit, and we'll get goin'."

"Oh ... fine. You want to throw your money around, go for it." Giving him a glare, she stalked back into the dressing room. She changed into the other outfit and gathered her own clothing, leaving the other things behind.

Then she went and grabbed the long-sleeved tee in baby blue with a lacy black Harley logo on the front, in size small, because Cissie had gotten the slender gene in their family. When they were younger, Lindi had to work not to hate her just a little for this, but now Cissie was too thin, and Lindi wanted to wrap her in the softest, cuddliest things she could find. Her PTA-attending, mini-van-driving sister would get a kick out of the Harley tee, she hoped.

However, it soon became clear that just like that morning, Jack was once again set on getting his way. He strode back into the dressing room, come out with all the other clothing over his arm, tossed it on the counter before the highly amused clerk, who was watching them like the protagonists in a reality show. Jack then towed Lindi, his arm around her, over to the racks of leathers.

She didn't know whether to laugh or scream with frustration.

Even if he and Keys had recovered money that Darrell owed them, the way Jack was spending gave her a bad feeling, a tight knot in her chest.

She'd seen first-hand what happened when a man let money slip through his hands like water, putting practicalities like food and a roof over his family dead last. Personally, she'd rather live the rest of her life without ever again experiencing the fear and want of nothing left to pay rent or buy groceries. Even though Lindi had been a little girl, she remembered the look of desperation on her mother's face.

"Jack," Lindi said, trying to wriggle free from his powerful arm. "No more. You can't keep buying me stuff."

Their minor tussle ended when he crowded her gently against one of the racks, lifted her chin with his thumb and forefinger. She stilled at the sober look on his rugged face, and the rueful tenderness in his hazel gaze.

"Honey," he said. "I started off by making a huge, fuckin' mistake and scaring the livin' shit out of you. I'd consider it a big favor if you'd let me do somethin' nice to say how sorry I am. Doesn't mean you gotta do anything in return. We walk outta here, you want me to take you home and say goodbye, I'll do that. But first I wanna do this. And stop worryin' about breakin' my bank. The thing with Gaspard ain't the only deal I got goin'."

She vacillated for a moment between her own determination and the sincere regret in his gaze. He truly seemed to need to do this. And he was an adult, had been for more than a few years—if he wanted to spend money, let him.

"Well ... okay. If you're sure."

His lips curved up in a satisfied smirk, and he dropped one eyelid in a wink. "Good. And just to say, you do decide to boot me out tonight, that don't mean I won't be back tomorrow to give it another go."

"Of course you would." She definitely should've seen that one coming. But she was smiling as she turned to the racks of leathers.

She chose a jacket that was loose and covered her ass.

Jack gave her a look. "Nope. Try this one. Safer and warmer to have leathers that fit snug." He pulled a short, body-skimming jacket from the rack, and Lindi pulled it on and fastened it up.

Jack leered, and patted her on the ass. "Sexier, too. That one, for sure."

Blushing, Lindi looked in the mirror. The jacket did look fabulous on her. Okay then, biker chicks did not hide their curves, they rocked them.

Jack then wandered off while the clerk fitted her with a pair of kick-ass black leather boots that screamed 'naughty biker-cowgirl', and chose himself three tee shirts, a pair of jeans and a helmet.

Only it turned out the helmet was for her, as he brought it to the checkout counter and pushed it onto her head with careful precision, checked the fit and then nodded.

A short time later, Lindi climbed back into the Escalade as Jack stowed two fat, glossy orange shopping bags with black Harley logos in the back.

"Thank you for the biker apparel," she said as he stepped into the driver's seat. She stroked her palms over her thighs, now encased in velvety worn denim. Her new jeans totally rocked. "I'm ready to ride, that's for sure."

"Glad to hear it, 'cause have I got somethin' for you to ride."

"I'm sure you do." She sneaked a sidelong look at his groin, heat flushing her skin.

He winked at her. "And you're welcome. There a mall around here?""

Lindi's jaw dropped. "What? You want to do more shopping?" In her experience, nothing made a red-blooded biker man run screaming in the other direction like the words 'shopping mall'. She was pretty sure Dave hadn't been near one since he was a pre-teen.

"I thought we were going for a ride on your bike." It was a beautiful late afternoon, with the clouds dissipating to leave behind blue skies.

"I'll take you for a ride down the lake tomorrow mornin'," he said. "I packed light for this trip. I need underwear, and so do you. I like the black lace set, but the rest of your shit, hell no. All that white made me feel like I was riflin' through a high school girl's things, and that's just wrong."

"Jack," she protested. "I absolutely cannot accept anything more."

He backed out and accelerated out of the parking lot onto the frontage road. "Somethin' you need to get, honey. Darrell was not into me and Keyes for a little money, he owed us a fuck-wad of it." He glanced over at her. "Nearly a mil. And we just got it all back, plus interest."

Lindi gaped at him. That money belt had held nearly a million dollars? "What in God's name are—or were—you and Darrell into?"

Jack pulled a pair of aviator sunglasses from the sun visor, slid them onto his face and reached over to lay a warm hand on her thigh.

"Gaspard was into shit you do not need to know right now," he said, his voice brooking no further questions. "Things work out with us, I'll fill you in, tell you everything you wanna know. But that time ain't here yet. You need to learn you can trust me, I need to know the same, yeah?"

"It wasn't … drugs, or, um, prostitution, was it? Or weapons that will be used on law officers? Because those things—no."

"Hell, no. I ain't into that shit." And that, it seemed, was all Jack had to say.

But at least he'd given her that much. Any of those would've been a deal-breaker for Lindi. If an adult chose to take money for sex, that was his or her business, but prostitution too often seemed to consist of underage teens being horribly exploited. And she knew some MCs ran girls, illegal weapons and drugs.

She was hugely relieved Jack and Keys were not into those activities. Wait—what had he said? If things worked out with them? Double, triple, oh my Gawd.

"Does that mean you're planning to stay around for a while?" she asked. "I mean, around the area?" she added quickly. Geez, she didn't want to sound like she was asking him for a commitment, because she was not.

She clutched her purse, her short nails digging into the soft leather. She'd be crazy to even contemplate a relationship with a man with a shady background like his. One who was in some ways, so much like Lindi's own father, whom her mother should have thrown out, but instead stuck with until he died. Gail Carson was not a whiner, but she'd shared with Cissie and Lindi a little about the boom and bust of living with a man who threw money around until it was gone.

Jack might not be a drunk, but she needed to remember to expect nothing more from him than the moment. Even if he stayed, he'd no doubt be be moving on to a flashier woman soon, one who understood and accepted his world. Probably a—a stripper from one of the clubs at State Line, or someone like that.

And why this depressed the heck out of her, Lindi didn't want to think about.

"I'm thinkin' I may just stay here," he said. "I like this area. Not as many people as Cali. I need to scout around, see what opportunities there are."

Right. Opportunities for what? A legitimate business, or more shady deals?

She shifted nervously. "Okay. But ... um, are you likely to be arrested in the near future?"

"Nope," he said instantly and unequivocally. "I ain't on any law enforcement radar, neither is Keys."

She waited for him to scowl at her for asking too many questions, but to her shock he gave her thigh a friendly squeeze before accelerating onto the interstate.

"I respect you for askin', honey. A woman's gotta take care who she hangs with. You wanna call one of your girlfriends and give her my name and driver's license number, that kinda shit, go for it," he added. "You can send a picture of me on your phone and tell her where we go and what we do every step of the way, if you want. From this point on, I got nothin' to hide."

Lindi looked at him, sitting tall and strong and capable in the driver's seat of the SUV, one brawny arm draped over the steering wheel, his eyes hidden behind the sunglasses, his hair waving carelessly about his ears and neck.

She sighed. He was like an extra-large box of chocolates—no doubt bad for her, but pretty much all her naughty fantasies rolled into one big, virile, rough-talking but easy-going male package. And from the sound of it, he'd be around for another week or so, at least. Just long enough for a wild fling, but not long enough to worry about anything permanent.

So why shouldn't she let him make her feel good, just for the time they had? In his company, she could celebrate the good things—Cissie's reprieve from cancer, Dave's incredible gift, and even the fact that while Jack had kidnapped her, it truly had been a case of mistaken identity, and he and his partner had banished the man who had hurt her.

And it wasn't like she was signing on for life ... just for a fleeting good time.

"Okay," she agreed. "I'll send your deets to my girls."

Sara for safety, and Kit because she'd be crushed if Lindi left her out of this information loop. She was always trying to talk Lindi into going out with her to hook up with guys, but no matter how Lindi's healthy libido often craved a man's touch, she knew herself. She was not the kind of person who could hook up randomly on a regular basis, walking away without regrets. She was certain Kit wasn't half as tough and carefree as she portrayed herself either, but that was another story.

Jack grinned as she pulled her phone from her purse to take his photo. "Lucky that's my good side," he said.

"Right." She laughed, pretty sure it would be impossible to find an unflattering angle from which to take a photo of him.

She snapped a photo of him from the side and then held her phone out toward the windshield to take another. "That's a good one," she approved. "Now take your sunglasses off for one."

He did, and Lindi took a photo of him smiling straight into the camera, sunglasses shoved on top of his head. She couldn't help smiling at this captured image of him. Sara was going to swoon, and Lindi herself might never delete it. And he even had his clothes on.

'Hi,' she texted her friends. 'Meet Jack Moran. Met at café, we're on date. Since he's a stranger, letting you know I'm with him.'

She paused for a moment before sending the text, well aware of the irony of how much her terse words left out.

But then she couldn't very well text 'He kidnapped me because of Darrell, who as you know is a major lowlife, but discovered it was a mistake, so saved me from his creepy associate who slugged me and then tried to kill both of us. He's also a member of a scary MC. Despite all this, for some reason I trust him—physically, at least.'

"Driver's license?" she asked, holding out her hand.

He levered himself up in his seat far enough to reach into his hip pocket and pull out his wallet. Flipping it open, he handed it to her. The brown leather was warm from his body, and supple from use.

"Huh," Lindi said. "You even take a good license photo. I always look like I've been arrested for kiting checks or something."

Jack chuckled. She entered the number into her phone. He had a California driver's license.

"Did you like California?"

"Cali's okay," he said, slowing to turn off the highway. "Helluva lot of people, though. You can drive for miles and never get out of the sprawl of businesses and shit. Gets old fast."

Lindi nodded wisely. "Like the Sons," she said, folding his wallet shut and handing it back. "Jax and the guys are always riding through those rough, industrial areas that go on forever, when they meet up with the other MCs."

Jack pulled to a stop at a stoplight on the interchange. Lindi gave him an innocent look as he stared at her quizzically. "Honey ..." he began, but his lips quirked and he shook his head. "Fuck me, you are a small-town girl, aren't you?"

"Joking." She let her grin break free as she reached over to poke his hard thigh. "I know California's not really as lawless as it is on SOA."

"Well, in some places it is," he said, turning right and accelerating along a road that wound toward the Spokane Valley Mall. "There are definitely gangs, MCs and shit. But it's not quite the wild, wild MC west portrayed on that show."

She groaned, pressing the back of her hand to her forehead. "Please, stop! Next you'll tell me there's no Jax Teller. I won't be able to stand it."

They rolled into the huge parking lot surrounding the mall. Jack swung over into an empty space, braked to a stop, turned off the motor, and reached over to unbuckle her seatbelt.

"Hey," she said in surprise, "Jack, what are you—?"

He set his hands on her waist and lifted her bodily across the console, sliding his seat back at the same time to make room for her astride his lap. She perched there, her mouth open. She hadn't appreciated his strength this morning, but she surely did now. She wondered dazedly if he would mind repeating that lift in slow-motion so she could watch his muscles bulge and relax. She wasn't exactly a lightweight, either. He was really strong.

Jack pulled her close with one hand on her nape, the other on her ass. "You think you can say shit like that and I'm not gonna kiss you till you forget every man but me—including some fuckin' pretty boy actor?"

Oh, well then. Lindi sank against his hard torso and tipped her face up, her lips already tingling for his. "Do your best, biker man."

Chapter Fourteen

Jack did his best, kissing her into a daze the likes of which Lindi hadn't experienced since ... wait, since this morning, on her own kitchen counter.

Rocking her feminine parts against the long, stiff shape in his jeans, and her breasts against his hard chest, which in the thin bra and tank was a turn-on all its own because her nipples loved the friction, she sighed against Jack's mouth.

"Are you sure you wanna go shopping?" she asked him. Okay, it was more of a whine, but who cared? This was her day to throw off the traces of ordinary life, and she wanted him. Wanted him inside her, wanted him to help her lose her mind. And to her surprise, she wanted to make him lose his mind while she watched. This would be as much of a turn-on as getting off herself.

He groaned, and his hands tightened on her as he flexed his lean hips under her. "Woman, after this, I won't even be able to walk. Not until you do somethin' about the monster you've created, anyway."

Lindi's sex squeezed tighter, and she nearly whimpered with shock and excitement. Oooh, this just kept getting wilder and hotter. "You ... you want me to, um ..."

He grasped her wrist and guided her hand down between them, folding it over the bulge of his erection. "Hell, yeah, I want you to 'um'. I want you to open my jeans, take my cock out and use this sweet mouth to suck me dry." He pulled her head back and nipped at the tendon in her throat, pressing his hard, swollen cock up into her grasp. "You willin' to do that for me, honey?"

Lindi shuddered with desire, then stiffened as a car with two women rolled to a stop two spaces over. "Um, should we maybe go somewhere else?"

A jacked-up pickup drove slowly along the next aisle and pulled into a spot nearby. There were people everywhere. Thank God most of the kids were in school.

"Honey, this rig has dark tinted windows. No one can see in here, no matter what we do."

"Well, for heaven's sake, lock the doors," she blurted as a young guy leapt down from the pickup and jogged by, headed for the mall.

He reached past her and hit a button on the door console. Four locks clicked closed.

Then he pressed another button, and the seat began to move under them, leaning Jack back into a nearly reclining position. One that gave Lindi room to wriggle back toward the steering wheel, she soon discovered, and room to bend over his lap. Oh, my God. She was really going to do this. She was going to suck him off in a parking lot.

"Are you sure about this?" she asked him, one hand on his chest. He was warm and solid, and touching him quelled the nerves jumping in her middle.

Jack traced a finger over her cheek, his eyes heavy and hot. "You got a desperate man here, honey. Have mercy."

He was at her mercy. Feeling daring and naughty, Lindi unfastened his jeans. His cock sprang out. She stared in awe. He was beautiful, long and thick and hard, the turgid length suffused with blood, the broad head spangled with a drop of arousal.

Hesitantly, she traced her fingertips up the underside. He was like hot silk, and she giggled nervously as he leapt under her touch, smacking against her palm.

He stroked his thumb across her lip, his gaze searching hers. "Baby, you're hesitating. You ever done this before?"

"Well, to the finish? Only once," she admitted, "And I was kind of drunk. I don't really remember much."

Dave had loved it from what she could remember, and she'd gone down on him again, but he'd always pulled out, telling her he'd rather come inside her. That had been fine with her.

But now, she wanted to go all the way. She practically craved the taste and feel of this man in her mouth.

Jack groaned. "Fuck me, you're practically a virgin. Well, don't you worry about a thing. Papa's gonna teach you everything you need to know."

And he did. Urging her down to him, he showed her how to taste him, licking the drop of cum from the crease in the broad head of his cock, and swirl her tongue around the head, moistening it and her lips before opening her mouth to take him in. He filled her mouth, and she shivered with pleasure as she imagined taking his cock inside her sex, having this power and girth thrusting deep and strong. Her pussy clenched with need, and she moaned.

Her hair hung in a curtain around her face, hiding her and what she was doing in a private space, a naughty secret from the people in the parking lot outside. He smelled good down here, too, his musky male scent stronger, but tinged with her shower gel.

"That's right, honey," he praised her, his voice even rougher than usual. "Now, wrap your little hand around the base and hold on. Stroke me while you suck. Fuck, yeah. Just like that."

He surged up into her mouth, then cursed when she gagged. "Sorry, sorry. Christ, you got me hot as a high school kid. Just take as much as you can, honey. I'll be still."

He was, holding her head in a gentle grip as she licked and sucked him. But a thrill of pleasure and triumph coursed through her as his hands tightened in her hair, and he quivered in her grasp like a bucking horse when a cowgirl dropped onto his back, ready to ride.

"Yeah," he groaned. "So good, honey. So hot and sweet."

Reveling in the power she held over this big, strong male, Lindi took him as deep as she could, then again and again.

He stiffened, his hands pulling on her hair, his body quivering under her.

"Like that," he muttered. "Ah, Lindi. Gonna come."

With a deep groan, he began to ejaculate, salty, creamy fluid filling her mouth.

Lindi swallowed, triumph brimming as she took all that he gave her and continued to caress him with her mouth and hands.

"Jesus fuck," Jack muttered, stilling her with his hands on her scalp. "Think I just caught a glimpse of heaven there."

Lindi sat up and wiped her mouth on the back of her hand, then watched him shyly as he lay under her, eyes closed, his tough face flushed and lazy the way it had been after his shower.

He pulled her down to him, and gave her a hug, turning his head to kiss her temple.

"Thank you, honey," he murmured, stroking her back. "That was ... amazing."

Lindi bit her lip, although she couldn't hide her pleased smile. "Really?"

Jack opened his heavy eyes, gave her a look of disbelief, then began to laugh, a deep, rollicking sound that wrapped her in warmth. "Are you fuckin' kidding me? Honey, you could make a cool million a year with that mouth in Vegas."

"However," he added, his eyes narrowing, "you use it on any cock but mine, I won't be happy."

Lindi ducked her chin and traced the pattern on his tee shirt with one finger. Wow. That sounded ... proprietary. And she hadn't really been considering it—just maybe having a flash fantasy of him as a Vegas high roller and her as an expensive call girl in a tiny little dress.

Jack leaned up and kissed her mouth, his smiling. "Goin' shy on me, now?" He kissed her again, and Lindi sank into the caress of his lips and tongue, and the taste of him on both their mouths.

"You like makin' me come," he said, with the air of a man making a discovery that pleased him no end.

"Uh-huh," she admitted breathily, her face hot. She had liked it, a lot. When he began to ejaculate in her mouth, giving her his essence, his ecstasy, she'd nearly orgasmed herself.

She'd enjoyed sex with Dave, but sex with Jack was a whole different level of raunchy, earthy, and delicious.

She loved the way he looked, the feel of his big body holding hers, and the way he smelled. Best of all, she loved the way he looked at her, as if he really saw her, and liked what he saw.

Wait, no, maybe the best part was the way he kissed her, as if she were endlessly delicious.

No, it was the way he talked to her. That was her very favorite thing about him, the way he said exactly what was on his mind, what he wanted and what he liked, all in his deep, rough voice.

Until he cupped her mons through her jeans, and lifted her up high enough to nip at her distended nipple through her lace bra and thin tank.

"Pull your top down, honey," he ordered. "Gotta taste your pretty tits."

Her nipple in his hot, wet, inventive mouth, Lindi decided, with the few brain cells that were still working, that she definitely loved this the best. He sucked and then nibbled with his lips and flicked the hard tip with his velvety tongue, sending her into shudders of need for more, harder. And then he gave her that too.

"You could ... make money doing this too," she told him, sliding her fingers into his hair to hold his head to her. "Jack—oh please. *Harder*."

"Sweet as honey. Gotta make you come too," he mumbled around her nipple, unfastening her jeans. "Then we can go shoppin'."

Since he already had his hand in her panties, Lindi didn't bother to argue. She arched her hips forward so he could work two thick fingers inside her, and moaned her approval as he found her clitoris with his thumb.

"Ride my fingers, honey," he instructed. "Give me your other tit, and ride me till you come. Yeah?"

She nodded fervently, and did as he said, until his mouth and his hand, his voice low and dirty in her ear were all that she knew, all that she wanted.

"Now open your eyes," he ordered. "Look at all those poor schmucks right out there, never knowin' what they're missin', 'cause they ain't us."

Lindi obeyed, dragging open her heavy eyes just as two men in business suits threaded their way between the SUV and the car next to theirs. They were so close she could have reached out and touched them, had the window been open.

"Who's got you?" he demanded, stroking her faster with his thick, calloused fingers and thumb. "Who's makin' you come?"

"You are ... *Jack*." Lindi came helplessly, hard and fast, ecstasy imploding through her in a dark, helpless rush. She tipped her face down against his hair as she moaned, high and breathy. "Oh, Jack."

"That's right," he approved, holding her fast. "Squeeze me hard. Gimme that honey, hot and sweet."

When at last she opened her eyes, he was smiling at her. He gave her a last pet, and pulled his hand from between her thighs.

"I like makin' you come, too," he told her. "Hate that I lied to you though."

Lindi stiffened, some of her glow of happiness fading. "You lied to me? About what?"

He shook his head with mock sadness. "Told you I was gonna eat you before you used your mouth on me again. I haven't tasted you yet. That is a bad thing. I want you to come all over my mouth, so I can taste your honey." He lifted his hand to his face and inhaled deeply, then groaned. "Fuck, you smell good."

Her pussy clenched in an echo of her orgasm, and he grinned as if he knew exactly the effect he'd had on her.

"Oh, you." Lindi sat up and tugged at her bra and tank. Jack watched and hindered her efforts by petting her nipples and getting his big hands in the way. But finally her top was straight.

However, when she pulled up the zipper on her tank, he promptly unzipped it part way. Then he leaned up and pressed a kiss to her cleavage. "Too pretty to hide."

Lindi was smiling as she wriggled her new jeans up over her hips again, and zipped them. Her thong felt as if it was jammed up into her crack, but she almost didn't mind as it abraded happy parts of her farther forward.

"Next time," Jack promised her, "I get to have you in a bed ... every way I can think of."

A frisson of alarm danced down her spine. "Um, not every way."

His brows flew up, and then he chuckled, his eyes twinkling wickedly. "No?" he asked, trailing his fingers down between her ass cheeks.

"No," Lindi said firmly.

He levered the seat up. "Just remember, honey, everything's negotiable."

"Oh, no. Huh-uh. Rear entry is not negotiable, not for this girl."

Done talking, Jack opened the SUV door and stepped out, bearing her with him. With a gasp, she hung on until he set her on her feet on the pavement. He smacked her lightly on the ass and closed the door behind them.

"All right, sweetness, let's go shoppin'."

She leaned over to peer at her reflection in the side mirror on the SUV. Oh, great. Flushed, sleepy-eyed, with her lip gloss long gone and her hair a mess—she looked exactly like she'd just been engaging in heavy petting in a vehicle.

Well, she had. And it had been awesome. With a mental shrug, she finger-combed her hair, renewed her lip gloss, took the hand Jack held out to her, and walked with him to the mall.

Chapter Fifteen

Lindi's phone chirped as they were walking through the mall's big glass entry doors. She pulled it from her purse and gave Jack a self-conscious smile. "It's my friend Sara."

He shrugged. "Go ahead and answer. I ain't in any hurry."

However, Lindi winced as she read her friend's message. 'Nice pic. But dating a stranger? R U sure?'

'He's the one who told me to send U his deets,' Lindi fired back. Then she speculated guiltily on what Sara would have to say if she knew Jack had begun by kidnapping her, or some of the other things that had happened. That would not be good.

Belatedly, she realized that her first instinct had been to defend Jack to her friend. Which was a little weird, considering how they'd met. She'd better be careful here—she'd read about some syndrome where victims ended up allying themselves with their kidnappers.

Then she rolled her eyes at her own lurid imagination. Jack was hardly holding her bound in some remote place, waiting for ransom. As soon as he'd discovered their mistake, he'd defended her fiercely, knocking Twig out after he hit her, and then put himself between her and a gun.

He'd also given her a heartfelt apology for his part in her ordeal.

Her phone pinged again. Kit this time. 'OMG, he's hawt! Does he have a friend??'

Keys' lean, knowing face filled Lindi's mind, and she winced. Yup, Jack had a hot friend, but one who'd been around a lot. And no matter how tough the face Kit showed the world, Lindi couldn't help but feel it was only a thin, fragile facade. Kit needed to find a nice, ordinary guy, not a rambling man who'd make her fall for him and then take off on his bike for parts unknown.

'No, sorry,' she texted quickly. 'Just him & me tonite. Talk to u tomorrow.'

She stuffed her phone back into her purse and followed Jack into the nearest store. Then she stopped short as she realized they were in Victoria's Secret, surrounded by mannequin torsos clad in tiny, pretty underthings.

"I know you said you needed underwear," she said, hands on her hips, "But I figured the men's section at Macy's."

"Cute," he shot back. "This is for you."

"Jack," she hissed. "You are not buying me undies."

"Yeah, I am," he said, perusing the nearest rack, which held a selection of candy pink and black bras and panties. "'Cause then I'm gonna take 'em off of you. I like tits and ass wrapped up sweet. These'll go with your Harley shit."

He fingered a push-up bra, and Lindi snorted. "Not that one. I do not wear double-D."

He grinned. "Know that, honey. I figure you for a C-cup."

"Thirty-four C." She didn't want to think about why he was so accurate at guessing bra sizes. "Size 6 panties. And no, I am not buying any more of those." She grabbed the thong dangling from his big forefinger and tossed it back on the display shelf. "I wear bikinis or boy-cuts."

"Cool. Pick some out." His attention had already wandered on to a turquoise set. "And some of these. Mm-hmm, that's what I'm talkin' about."

String bikini bottoms. But at least they weren't thongs. And she'd always secretly longed to shop at Victoria's Secret for undies. And although she felt weird taking all these gifts from

Jack, he was right, he did owe her a nice apology. And—yeah, and she knew very well all her rationalizations smelled like last weeks' café garbage, but still, since he and she weren't going to be long term, if he wanted to throw his money around ... let him.

Jack bought them both fruit smoothies at a popular kiosk, and then walked her through two other stores at the mall, carrying the Victoria's Secret shopping bags with utter unself-consciousness, but to Lindi's relief, his only other purchases were underwear and socks for himself.

When she stopped to admire a store display of spring pastel-hued candles and soaps, she found he had moved on a few feet in front of a jewelry store window sparkling with diamonds.

Lindi giggled quietly as she joined him. "You're the first man I've ever seen look at jewelry voluntarily."

He slurped the last of his smoothie and tossed the empty container in a trash can. "Jewelry is for chicks, but they're not the ones who buy it."

"I suppose."

"You're not into jewelry?" he asked.

Lindi shrugged. "I have other priorities."

Would she like to stroll into the store and choose a pretty ring? Sure, especially the one with a big diamond in the center and golden gems around it in an asymmetrical swirl, but that wasn't going to happen, so no sense even dreaming about it.

The only jewelry she owned was a little gold cross on a chain from her grandma, and a few silver pendants and rings she sometimes threw on together for an evening out. They were good enough for her. Dave hadn't been into buying her jewelry. Just leaving her a chunk of valuable property.

She turned away from the temptation of the glittering gems. Diamonds weren't in her destiny, but that was all right. All she really wanted was to be able to hire some help to keep the BeeHive open longer hours, afford paid advertising, and thus make a profit above and beyond what she owed the bank. To be a businesswoman, dependent on no one but herself. To be safe from the nagging fear of ending up with nothing, both literally and emotionally.

Now, maybe she had a chance at that ... if Darrell didn't show up to harass her before she could put it into action.

Jack insisted on carrying all their purchases in one hand, and continued to hold her hand in his big, warm, calloused one as they strolled farther along the mall. This, Lindi liked a lot. She couldn't remember ever shopping with anyone except her mom and sister.

Sara made good money but wasn't a shopper, and Kit existed from month to month, wearing outfits thrown together from Goodwill or borrowed from Lindi's closet, and at times sleeping on Sara and Lindi's sofas and eating their food. Not that either of them minded. Kit was good people, but she was ... lost, in a way Lindi worried could never be fixed.

That a rough, tough biker man like Jack seemed to be willing to take all the time in the world to wander and shop, with families and groups of giggling teens now out of school for the afternoon eddying around them, not only surprised Lindi, it made her like him even more.

He may have scared the daylights out of her when he grabbed her at the café, but every hour since revealed more of his easy-going side. And this felt like a piece of the real Jack Moran, not a facade he drew over himself to blend in or hide a mean nature.

He guided her to a stop before a sign giving locations of the mall businesses.

"Hey, good deal," he said. "There's a steak house right across the parking lot. How about I go get the SUV and pick you up outside those doors right over there? We'll go have a couple drinks and an early supper."

"Okay," she agreed. It had been a while since breakfast at her apartment, and she was hungry. Also, she hadn't had good steak in months. It was so much cheaper to buy burger for herself, not to mention easier to cook up with pasta or rice on the stovetop in her tiny kitchen. Steak required a grill.

"Call me, so I'll have your number," he said, digging his phone from his pocket. "I'll text you when I'm back with the rig."

Lindi did this. She smirked when his phone blared AC/DC's You Shook Me All Night Long, and then sat down on a nearby bench to watch him walk out of the mall.

She was not the only female eyeing him, either. Had that brunette really just brushed against him on purpose? Skank. When Jack ignored her and held the glass doors for a young mother with three kids, Lindi sighed, hand to her heart. What a guy.

She gave the brunette a smile that may have been just a teensy bit smug. The woman tossed her long hair as she passed. Whatever—she had a bony ass and wore too much makeup.

Grinning to herself, Lindi crossed her legs in her killer jeans and swung her foot as she texted Sara again.

'Dinner at the Ribeye by SpoVal mall w Jack.'

A moment later Sara texted back, 'OK, now I'm just jealous! Have fun.'

Lindi intended to.

'All-nighter!' Kit texted. 'Don't let him go till u get great sex.'

Lindi squirmed a little in her seat as she remembered the great sex she'd already gotten from him.

Then she smiled to herself. 'Okay,' she texted. 'I may just do that.'

* * *

When Jack ushered Lindi into the restaurant, the place was still in a late afternoon lull. It was nice and clean, smelled great, the bar looked well-stocked, and the hostess smiled as if she was genuinely glad to see them.

They were shown to a corner booth with a big, semi-circular seat, and a gold-toned hurricane lamp casting subdued lighting on the table. He stood back to let her in and slid in after her, so far pleased with his choice of venues for their dinner.

"You a highball girl?" he asked, taking Lindi's hand and pulling it to his thigh. "Or d'you like those fancy blended drinks?"

"I'll drink either." Huh, low maintenance, that was sweet. She looked prettier than ever in the soft lighting, her brown eyes smoky and mysterious, her glossy lips tempting with their shadowed curves. Her tousled hair made him want to run his hands into the silky mass and use it to pull her close for another kiss.

"Good evening," said a smiling, middle-aged waitress, appearing by their table. "Would you like to hear our drink specials?"

"Ask her," Jack said, nodding toward Lindi. "I'll have a Crown and Coke."

Lindi ordered a mojito. It arrived in a tall, frosted glass garnished with fresh mint leaves. He watched her sip through the straw and heat stirred low in his groin as he remembered the extremely fine blowjob she'd given him in the SUV.

"Damn, watchin' you put those pretty lips around that straw gives me a hard-on all over again," he told her.

She promptly choked on her drink. Jack chuckled wickedly as she coughed into her napkin, her eyes wide over the white fabric.

"You need to behave," she hissed when she could speak.

"Why?" he asked, still grinning. "You know anyone in this place?"

There was wait staff, a manager, and two other tables of patrons talking animatedly, but they were all several feet away or more.

"No," she admitted, "but still—"

Jack squeezed her hand on his thigh, enjoying the softness of her hand in his own. "Don't worry, I won't get us booted out before we eat, but you might as well know, Lindi, I don't censor my mouth for anybody, unless I see a good reason. And since it's just you and me and these monster plants, if I wanna tell you how sexy you are, I'm gonna do that."

She rolled her eyes at the greenery hanging behind him. "I believe those are ferns."

"Don't give a flying fuck what they are." He tugged on her hand, pulling her closer so he could slide his arm around her. She was a fine armful, all soft curves that a man could get a good hold on. "You take my point?"

She pursed her soft lips, glistening now with lip gloss or some such shit, and raised a brow at him. "Sure, Jack. You do what you want, say what you want, and ignore anyone, including your date, who might not like it. Did I get that right?"

He returned her look for good measure. "You're lucky I remember how good that sassy mouth of yours felt wrapped around my cock." And he planned to get it back there later.

Their waitress chose that instant to appear around the bank of ferns. "Are you folks ready to order?"

Her face flushing pink, Lindi stuck her nose in her fancy drink and avoided the woman's gaze.

Jack nodded at the waitress, who was a real pro. If she'd heard anything, she didn't show it. "I'll have a ribeye steak medium-rare, baked potato with everything, salad with ranch, and another one of these." He raised his half-empty glass. "How about you, honey?"

"That sounds fine," Lindi said.

When the waitress had gone, Jack stroked the back of Lindi's hand with his thumb, and grinned at her. "No arguments about the food, I see."

She wrinkled her nose at him. "Ribeye is an excellent cut, so I see no point in making the waitress stand around while I study the menu. Anything else I don't like, I'll push aside."

"True. Although, dessert we're gettin' from room service at the hotel," he told her. "You can choose that."

Her eyes widened again, and then she licked her lips, processing this. Jack grinned at her, because yeah, he knew what he was having for dessert—her. Maybe with some whipped cream.

And tonight he was gonna get to see all of her, and touch and taste and ... shit, no more thinking about fucking right now. He reached down and adjusted himself in his suddenly too-tight jeans.

"Where are you staying?" she asked.

"Coeur d'Alene resort," he said. "Got a room that looks out over the lake. Real pretty, especially with the lighted docks, park and shit."

Lindi blinked. "Wow, the resort is a five-star hotel. You must have been sure you'd get your money back from Darrell."

Christ, he never knew what she was gonna come out with next. Jack tipped back his head and let loose a laugh. He squeezed her hand. "Honey, I got a lot more goin' for me than that loan. Don't you worry, I can afford to drop a few dollars here and there."

Then he lifted his hand and pushed her hair back, his finger trailing over her bare shoulder, and enjoying the shiver that ran over her silky skin. "I'm real glad I got a room like that to take you back to. King-sized bed, and a mirror wall in the bathroom." Okay, so he was still thinking about fucking—bite him.

To his shock, the corners of her mouth turned down, and her gaze fell, her long lashes veiling her eyes from him. "Yay, mirrors," she muttered.

He cocked his head and gave her a searching look. Then he shook his head, marveling at her lack of self-confidence. She gave as good as she got when she was cornered, but in this, she was clueless.

"You really have no idea how fuckin' hot you are, do you?" he said quietly. "Honey, I can't wait to bend you over that big bed, my hands full of your world-class ass while I fuck you, watch your tits bounce while you take all I wanna give you."

Her eyes widened, her pupils flaring, and then she gave a little squirm, the kind that said she was suddenly feeling her new jeans rubbing on soft, wet parts of her. Oh, yeah, his honey pot liked it when he talked dirty to her.

"Fuck," he muttered. "You keep lookin' at me like that, I'm gonna drag you into the nearest bathroom and have you on the countertop." He slid his hand around the back of her neck, and pulled her in for a kiss. She tasted of mint and fresh woman, hot and sweet.

Finally he forced himself to draw back, nearly groaning at the smoky, dazed look in her eyes, and the soft wet of her mouth.

"I got no objection to foreplay in public," he told her, stroking her throat with his thumb, and dropping his gaze to where her hard nipples poked at the thin lace of her bra and knit top. "And if we were at the T-rack up in Hayden, I wouldn't say no to sex in the women's john, either, 'cause it's a biker kinda place and that shit happens there. But we're here, and we both need to eat, to keep our strength up for what I got planned later. So we better behave ourselves long enough to eat our steaks."

His timing was good, as their waitress appeared again, this time bearing their salads and a basket of warm bread. "Enjoy, folks. Your steaks will be out shortly."

They were, and Jack's was delicious. The tender, flavorful meat practically melted in her mouth. He chewed with enjoyment, and watched as Lindi closed her eyes and chewed her steak with what looked almost like sexual pleasure.

"I like to see a woman who enjoys her food," Jack approved, slicing off another bite of his own steak. "Means she ain't afraid to enjoy other things."

Lindi forked up a bite of loaded baked potato. "Or it could just mean she likes good food."

He gave her a wink, because they both knew she liked sex too. She rolled her eyes at him and went back to her dinner. Jack did the same.

"You mentioned the T-rack," she said after a few moments. "I've never heard of that."

He grinned. "The Tamarack. Great brew pub on the shore of Hayden Lake. Gets a little wild on weekends and summer nights. The Chases hang out there."

"Oh right." She nodded. "I was there once, with Dave. They're right by the public beach. We swam, then went up for a drink. We left when a fight broke out on the porch, though."

He nodded. That sounded like the T-rack.

They went back to eating. Finally, she sat back and sighed. "That was delicious."

He eyed her plate. "That all you can eat?"

Lindi nodded. "I'm full." Then, she gave him a look from under her lashes and ran her tongue over her upper lip. "Besides, I'm saving room for dessert."

That sultry, teasing look sent every bit of blood in Jack's body straight for his cock. His gaze on her mouth, he set down his knife and fork, and lifted one arm for the waitress. "Damn straight," he agreed. "And you better believe you're gettin' somethin' that will fill you up."

She bit her lower lip, like maybe she was having second thoughts, and clutched her drink so hard her fingers whitened.

"Hey," he said, putting a hand on her thigh. "It's okay, babe. Remember, you choose. Right?"

She took a breath that did interesting things to her tits, and then nodded. Thank fuck, 'cause he meant it—he'd quit whenever she told him to, but at the same time, if he didn't get in there where he'd had his lucky fingers, and *soon*, he was gonna go fuckin' crazy, howling at the moon.

Chapter Sixteen

When Jack opened the door to his room on the eleventh floor of the resort hotel, the first thing he did was flick on the lamps in the small vestibule, and guide Lindi through the room to the floor-to-ceiling windows overlooking the lake.

He stepped behind her, his torso warm against her back, his arms around her. Since she was shivering a little with sheer nerves, his warmth was welcome in more ways than one.

"Pretty, ain't it?" he asked, his voice rich with satisfaction.

Lindi nodded. Below them lay the resort marina, full of pleasure boats, some with their winter coverings off already. A wooden boardwalk stretched around the outside perimeter. The scene was limned with the glow of old-fashioned lamps that glittered off the still, dark waters of the lake.

To the right, a floatplane and a big tour boat were moored on either side of a cement jetty jutting out from the lake shore, and beyond that a sloping beach and city park full of grand old trees and a band shell. Beyond twinkled the lights of the little resort town.

The lake stretched to the south and west within the shelter of low, evergreen-clad mountains. The western sky bore the last vestiges of sunset, a faint peach fading up into the vault of night laced with small clouds and a few stars.

"I always wondered what this view was like," Lindi said, for something to say.

Was she crazy to be here with him? Could she give him her body and protect the rest of her, the parts that were essential— her heart, her emotions? What they'd done in the SUV had been hot and daring, but she hadn't let him breach the final frontier, slide deep inside her.

And while other women might be able to have sex and walk away with no repercussions, she wasn't sure she was one of them, especially with this man. Jack Moran was like a force of nature, blowing into her narrow life and ripping her protective shell wide open.

She only had a short time to decide how much more of him she could handle.

"You've never been up here?" Jack sounded surprised.

She shook her head. "There's no reason to spend money to stay in a fancy hotel in your own hometown."

Jack's chuckle rumbled through her. "The view is one reason." He leaned his head down and murmured in her ear. "Want me to show you some others?"

Since he followed his words by trailing his warm lips down the side of her neck to nibble at her skin above the collar of her jacket, Lindi responded by leaning her head back against his shoulder to give him better access. He reached up, found the zipper of her jacket and pulled it down, baring more of her throat.

This time he found that sensitive spot just where her neck and shoulder met, and sucked. Lindi's insides turned to liquid, and she sighed. He groaned, his arms tightening. "That mean yes?"

"Yes," she managed. "Yes, Jack."

The heck with her worries about the emotional cost of sex with him. She'd known, really, from the moment she agreed to spend the day with him how it would end. And she wanted this, desperately. As her mother always said, there were two people to whom a woman should never lie—her doctor and herself.

"Thank fuck," he muttered. "C'mon, honey." He walked her to the huge bed that took pride of place in the room. The sheets were turned back, the pillows plumped invitingly.

With Lindi's back still to him, Jack unzipped her jacket the rest of the way and pulled it from her shoulders. He tossed it aside and stroked his hands down her bare arms, then set one on her waist and cupped her jaw with the other, tipping her head back against his shoulder for a kiss.

Surrounded by his heat and strength, she parted her lips and kissed him back, accepting his tongue into her mouth and sucking on it. He groaned deeply, flexing his hips to drive his erection against her bottom.

"You want this inside you?" he muttered against her cheek as he found her hem and tugged it upward. "Want all of me?"

Lindi nodded, and he let her go. "Good. Now, take off that top for me, yeah?"

He moved around her to sit on the edge of the bed, leaving her standing before him, her tank tangled over her breasts. As she hesitated, he reached back with one hand and grasped his own shirt and pulled it off over his head, tossing it aside. "There, now you catch up."

She would rather have had a moment to take in all that was Jack, but when he raised his brows at her, she realized the sooner she got naked, the sooner he would touch her, and vice versa. She tugged the top up, freeing her breasts, and then pulled it over her head, shaking her hair back as she lowered her arms.

Jack's gaze slipped over her breasts in the thin, lacy black bra. "Damn, woman. Prettiest set of tits I've seen in a long, long time." He lifted his hands and cupped her breasts, weighing them in his palms, and flicking his thumbs over her thrusting nipples.

The action abraded the lace against the sensitive tips, and Lindi reached for him, seeking support as pleasure streaked from under his touch.

"Unzip your jeans, honey," he urged, his voice tender, his touch edging on harsh.

Her hands shaking, she fumbled with the snap and zipper on her new jeans. "I can't—" she panted. "Stop—just for a sec."

He rolled her nipples between his thumb and forefinger, watching her face. "Ain't stoppin', Lindi. Hurry it up, I want these in my mouth, but first I wanna see you in nothin' but skimpy, sexy black lace."

Every tug on her nipples went straight to her pussy and to her brain, until all she could think of was getting Jack's mouth back, and her body plastered against his with no space between them, just all that hot, bare, hair-dusted skin against hers.

Somehow even with this potent distraction, she managed to shimmy the snug jeans far enough to push them down. When she wriggled her hips, impatient to be free of the soft denim, Jack froze, his hands still on her breasts, but his gaze now much lower, on the black thong that bisected her full hips, and cradled her mons in a peekaboo tease.

Slowly, he let go of her and sank back on to his elbows. The pose widened his legs and set his groin in prominent display. Eyeing the long, hard shape behind his snug jeans, Lindi saw with relief that he certainly didn't seem to be thinking she was too plump to wear a thong.

"Jesus fuck," he growled. "You been hidin' this from me? God damn, woman."

She couldn't help the smile that broke across her face. Feeling beautiful and sexy, she stepped all the way out her jeans and moved between his knees.

"C'mere and straddle me," he ordered, reaching out a hand to her. "C'mon, honey. Up."

She obeyed—anything to get close to him. She set her knee outside his on the bed, took his hand and climbed up astride him on the bed, her other hand on his bare chest. Her hair fell forward around her shoulders.

His warm, calloused hand cupped her bare ass, and stroked and squeezed, as he took her in. "So fuckin' pretty," he approved, his voice a sexy rasp. "Hot and sweet."

He levered himself away on his elbows, up the bed, grabbed two pillows and stuffed them behind his head, then lay back, his hands on her ass, pulling her down onto his groin. "Now, take your bra off. Real slow."

Lindi was busy, petting his chest, luxuriating in the hard bulge of his broad pecs, exploring the tiny coins of his nipples, and admiring the bunch and swell of his biceps. She wriggled a little, experimentally, on his erection, and sucked in a shaken breath at how good it felt on her swollen sex.

Jack's right hand lifted, leaving cool air behind. Then he gave her a sharp smack on her bare ass cheek.

"Ow!" Lindi scowled at him as she rubbed the sting.

He gave her a look. "That's what I give naughty girls who don't mind. Now be good and do what I told you."

"Huh," she huffed. "You better be worth your bull, Jack Moran."

He shook his head chidingly. "Seriously, honey?"

The lazy heat in his eyes said he was a man completely certain of his appeal and prowess. And she wanted to scratch out the eyes of every woman on whom he'd perfected his skills. But more than that, she wanted all of him for herself. Just his body, she reminded herself. This was just sex. But she had the feeling it was gonna be mind-blowing sex.

Reaching up, she pulled one bra strap from her shoulder, then the other, holding it in place as she shrugged out of the straps. Slowly, his gaze following every move, she unfastened the catch between her breasts, and let the bra slip free, but kept her hands over the full mounds.

Jack growled in his throat, his eyes heavy, his groin tightening under her. "Yeah, like that. Tease me."

His hands slid up her back, and he pulled her closer. "Now let me see 'em. Ah, fuck yeah. Look at you, so round and white, and those pretty pink nipples. Nice and long, just right for suckin' like a lollipop."

His heartfelt groan of appreciation was everything she could have hoped for. Her breath hitching with excitement, her body trembling with need, Lindi leaned down to him, and kissed him, her breasts pillowing on his bare chest. His arms closed around her, and he held her close, stroking her back and her ass as he kissed her in return, hot and wet and deep.

His chest was so hard and hot under her bare breasts, the soft curls of hairs abrading her sensitive skin and teasing her nipples.

His hand swept up her back and cupped the back of her head, tousling her hair. "Soft," he murmured against her mouth. "Soft and sweet, all of you."

"Hard," she mumbled back, rubbing herself on him. "All of you."

He groaned, and stroked his hand down her ass to delve between her thighs, his fingertips probing. "For you, honey. Jesus fuck, you're wet for me."

Since he slid two fingers into her pussy as he spoke, Lindi cried out against his mouth, and arched her back, asking for more.

Then she cried out again as he moved, rolling over in the bed and carrying her with him so she was under him. But when she reached for him, he was already headed south, his denim-clad legs forcing hers apart, his torso settling between her thighs. "Tits first," he said. "Then I eat your pussy. Then I'm in you."

His mouth on her breast was a revelation. His soft lips closed over her nipple, then he sucked it in, so hard his cheeks bowed in, his hand and gaze on her other breast. His mouth was hot and wet and the things he could do with his tongue were amazing. And every lash of his tongue, every suction of his lips shot sensation straight down through her.

He ate her up like she was manna and he was starving, until Lindi was writhing and whimpering under him, her fingers in his hair, her thighs locked around his ribs.

"Jack," she pleaded. "Oh. Oh, harder. Oh, my God."

Still suckling her, he stroked his hand down over her bare ribcage, over her hip, and lifted her leg high and to the side. Nuzzling her wet nipple, he pressed a kiss into the valley between her breasts, and then moved downward again.

"Hang on, this is gonna be quick," he warned. "You gotta come on my mouth, honey, but fast. Can you do that?"

Looking up at her, he thrust those two fingers into her again, and plumbed her soaked depths. He tweaked the thong aside with his thumb. "Lindi?"

She looked down at him, sprawled between her bare thighs, his fingers in her pussy and his gaze taking in every nuance of her expression. Clutching at the sheets, she gasped as he found her G-spot and stroked it teasingly. Holy wow, he knew his way around a woman's body.

"I can do that," she managed. *Amen.*

"Good," he said. "Then I won't have to spank you again."

"Huh-uh," she agreed, shaking her head. "Wait—spank me for what?"

"For nearly makin' me shoot my load in my jeans," he said, caressing her G-spot again. "Now hush up and concentrate, woman."

Then he put out his long, wicked tongue and tickled her swollen clitoris with the warm, wet tip. Lindi let out a shriek, letting go the sheets to clasp his head in her hands. "Jack. Oh, my God, *Jack.*"

He laughed, a deep, raunchy sound in his chest, then proceeded to drive her crazy with his velvet tongue and his hard, probing fingers. Then, when everything inside her clenched around his touch and she began to come, he sucked on her clitoris as he had her nipples, and Lindi let go with a high wail and surrendered completely to his touch, pleasure imploding inside her.

Jack caressed her through her orgasm, then turned his head to wipe his mouth on his bare shoulder, and rose like a conqueror over her on his knees, and shoved down his jeans to free his rampant cock. It prodded the air between them, quivering with eagerness, long and thick and beautiful.

Lindi reached up for him. "Let me do that," she offered, her voice still sultry with repletion. She closed her fingers around him and stroked the silken, broad head. He jerked in her grasp. "Jack, please. Wanna taste you again."

Jack shook his head emphatically. "Oh, no. I've waited two fuckin' days, now I want in there." He pulled a condom from his pocket, ripped it open with his teeth, rolled the thin covering over his cock, leaned on one hand to kick free of his jeans. Lindi had only one quick look at his, long, brawny, bare legs before he knelt between her thighs.

He kissed her, and shoved his forearm under her thigh, lifting her leg up and to the side again. "You gonna put me in you, honey?" he asked. "Do that for me this first time?"

Suddenly shy again, Lindi looked into his hooded gaze and nodded. "Yes, Jack."

She reached between them, circled her fingers around his turgid length, and guided him to her opening. He twitched in her grasp, then shuddered as he watched himself push into her channel. "Fuck, that's beyond hot. Little blonde pussy, takin' all of me."

He thrust again and slid deep, and Lindi's moan of shock and pleasure mingled with his poignant groan. He came down into her arms, his elbows at her sides, his arms under her shoulders, and kissed her again, smelling and tasting of her. Lindi wrapped her limbs around him and held on as he began to move in long, hard strokes.

He was almost too big, stretching her to the edge of discomfort, but at the same time he felt so good, so perfect that excitement squeezed her even tighter around him.

"Jesus fuck, you feel good," he told her hoarsely, his forehead tipped to hers. "Christ, I'm comin' already—can't wait."

He thrust twice, three more times, and then went rigid in her arms, his skin damp with sweat, and his breath harsh in her ear.

Lindi held him, stroking his back slowly, and knew a thrill of joy at having pleased him. After a moment, he raised his head and grinned down at her, his face flushed, eyes heavy. He lifted one hand and stroked her cheek with his thumb

"Knew it'd be this good, first minute I saw you, so shy and pretty in that café window," he said. "Your tight little pussy is sweet as those little honey bears you were settin' out on your counter."

Even after all they'd done, Lindi blushed. He chuckled, the sound vibrating through her. "Feel your pussy squeeze me. You like pleasin' me," he said. "Next time, I'll make sure you come too. I can usually wait for my lady, but damn, you got me hot.

"Tell you what," he offered, "let's take care of you, then we'll order dessert."

He withdrew from her and moved off the bed. "Be right back."

Lindi watched him saunter into the bathroom, because no woman with eyes in her head would miss the sight of his big, nude body. His broad shoulders and back tapered into lean hips, and his ass was even more gorgeous nude, tight and round, flexing with each step. His thighs were brawny, his calves long and tapered.

Realizing she was lolling nude on the sheets, she jackknifed to grab the covers and pull up the sheet over herself.

Jack came back out of the bathroom, still nude, and walked toward her with a sly smile on his face. "Shy, huh?" he teased. "How about we order that dessert? Don't care what you get, long as it comes with a bowl of whipped cream."

Lindi took the menu from him. "You mean, you want whipped cream on top?"

"No, I mean I want a bowl of whipped cream on the side," he said, grabbing the phone beside the bed and sliding under the covers beside her. He dropped the covers over himself, and raised his brows at her. "I like it on all my dessert."

"Oh," she breathed, her pussy clenching again as she finally got his meaning. "Okay."

She perused the menu quickly, then took the phone from Jack. "Room service," said a polite male voice. "How may I help you?"

"Um, we'd like an order of chocolate mousse pie and, um, a side bowl of whipped cream," Lindi said.

"Yes, ma'am. That will be about twenty minutes."

"Thank you." She put the phone down with relief. Jack set it back on the bedside table. "I can't believe I just ordered a side of whipped cream," she snickered, hands to her hot cheeks. The hotel staff would know exactly what they planned to do with it.

He snorted. "You think that's the first time they've gotten that order, think again."

He pulled her close under the sheets, and turned onto his side facing her, pulling her near leg up over his thigh. "Now, how about you make good use of that twenty minutes, and come on my fingers again?"

She wriggled self-consciously as he cupped her mons in his big hand. "Jack. You don't have to—"

He shook his head. "I know I don't have to, woman, this is about doin' what I want. Now hush, till you're ready to make those sweet little sounds you make when you get excited."

Lindi opened her mouth to tell him she did not make sounds, but he stroked her own wetness up over her clitoris with one broad fingertip, and she moaned. He smiled at her, and bent his head to kiss her bare shoulder.

"That's right, honey. Now push the sheet down so I can watch. Love lookin' at you."

Her hands shaking, Lindi pushed the sheets down for him, and he petted her with a gentle, expert touch, his gaze flicking from her face to his hand on her pussy.

"Come for me, Lindi," he ordered. "Let me feel it."

She came for him, pleasure pulsing from under his touch until she had to cry out to the quiet room, and to him.

"That's my girl," he approved. "Now come here."

He pulled her on top of him, and kissed her leisurely, until a sharp rap sounded on the door. Then he stepped into his jeans and went to answer the door.

Sitting in the pillows like a pasha, Jack let her feed him bites of delicious chocolate mousse pie in a dark chocolate crumb crust.

Then he set the plate aside and showed her where and how he liked his whipped cream, and where he wanted her to eat it off of him. When they were both sticky and aroused all over again, he fucked her again, this time until she screamed with the perfection of his cock inside her.

Lindi could have fallen asleep right then and there, but Jack hauled her, protesting, from the bed and into a warm shower. The bathroom did indeed have mirrors, but they soon fogged over, so Lindi ignored them.

She was getting good at ignoring things she didn't want to think about.

Chapter Seventeen

Wednesday

"So what do you think?" Jack asked. "How does the resort breakfast stack up against yours?"

Lindi took another bite and considered as she chewed. In a scene of sheer decadence, they were eating breakfast in bed.

They sat against plumped-up pillows, Jack with the covers to his waist while Lindi held them tucked under her arms. Outside, morning sun sparkled off the blue waters of the lake, and boats were nosing their way out of the marina. On the shore, people walked, jogged and strolled along the esplanade and through the park.

A legged tray between Jack and Lindi held coffee, dishes of plump, fresh berries and plates of thick, sugar-dusted French toast and crisp sausage links. She was dipping each bite into a small dish of huckleberry syrup, while his plate swam with maple syrup—although, he told her with a wink, it wasn't as good as her warm honey. The coffee service was just as fancy, with cream, whipped cream, sugar and even spun sugar sticks.

"It's good," she decided. "The sourdough bread adds tang, and there's plenty of egg. Although it could use a little more nutmeg."

Jack grinned at her over his coffee cup. "That's my girl. Figured you'd think of a way to improve the chow."

She shrugged. "It's a professional thing. Always critiquing."

"You should be on one of those reality TV shows," he suggested, forking up another big bite. "Where the chefs scramble around, screaming at each other, waving sharp knives and winning prizes."

She nodded enthusiastically. "Top Chef. Chef Gordon Ramsey is my hero. I'd love to meet him."

Jack raised his brows. "Thought Jax Teller was your man. Now you're tellin' me I got even more competition?"

"Hel-lo, fantasy versus reality," she said. "Chef Ramsey is real, and he gives advice on how restaurant owners can step up and save their businesses."

Jack grunted. "Watched one of those once. Some lazy fat-ass sittin' at the bar all day instead of workin', then wondering why his place was failing. Bunch of bullshit. You wanna be a success in business, you gotta hire good people and work harder than any of them."

"This is true," Lindi agreed. "As soon as I can afford it, I'm going to hire some help, keep the café open longer hours."

He smiled at her, his gaze warm. "You like runnin' your café."

"I do. The moment I saw it sitting empty, kind of … I don't know, forlorn … the former sign gone from the marquee, the parking lot empty, I just got this feeling inside me. I knew it was meant to be mine." Her chance to fulfill her dreams of making a living at cooking and serving up wonderful food. She would make it work, no matter the odds against her.

She eyed him, waiting for him to chuckle or something, but he merely nodded.

"Gotta follow your dreams. Tell you what though, make your first hire a man. Anyone comes in thinkin' they're gonna pull shit because you're out there alone on the lake road, they see a man behind the grill, they'll think twice."

Lindi took a drink of coffee and raised a brow at him over her cup. "Would you have thought twice?"

"Yup. Would've come to your apartment instead. Make no mistake, I'd have gotten to you, but it wouldn't have been at the café."

She rolled her eyes. "So having a man at the café would have done me no good."

"Yeah, it would, because no one else is gonna grab you for the reasons we did. And here's another thing I should've done different—fuckin' Twig should not have been anywhere in the deal, and you should not have gotten hurt. But it's done now, so we learn and we move on."

He wiped his mouth with his napkin and tossed it on the tray. "You full, honey?"

Lindi nodded, and Jack lifted the tray away and set it on the service cart. Lindi watched him slide naked from the bed, moving with the easy, unself-conscious grace of a male animal in his prime.

His words echoed in her head, and uneasiness snaked its way into the warm coziness of their luxurious nest. 'It's done now, so we learn and we move on.' But was it over, or was trouble waiting in the shadows to bite her when she least expected it?

Jack disposed of the tray, and then sauntered back to the bed, his lids heavy in a way that signaled he had sex on his mind. Not to mention the way his cock was rising, long and thick.

"Now, you got two choices," he said, pulling back the corner of the duvet. "We can get up, shower and head out on my bike for a ride. Or ... I can fuck you again and we'll let the rest of the day take care of itself."

Lindi's body reacted instantly, her already sensitized pussy clenching, her nipples tightening, her breath quivering in her chest as he leaned over her, caging her with his long arms. She squirmed with anticipation, her hand clenching on the quilt. She wanted a ride on his bike, but she wanted him even more.

Taking in her response with his predator's gaze, Jack's jaw tightened, his nostrils flaring, and he nodded slowly. "Door number two it is. Good choice, honey."

He leaned closer, so that his lips brushed the shell of her ear. "Now turn over and get your gorgeous ass in the air for me."

Lindi sucked in a sharp breath, even as excitement at his graphic command roared through her in a wave of responsive heat. She searched his gaze uncertainly. "Jack ..."

He raised his heavy brows in a challenge. "What do I like, honey?"

She licked her lips, the urge to yield already fluttering low in her middle. "You like me to come to you when you say."

His gaze warmed. "That's right, honey. You gonna gimme that?"

She took a breath, and nodded. Then she rolled over in the tumbled sheets, and drew her knees under her, and got her ass in the air for him.

Jack smacked her lightly on the inside of one thigh, a small, sweet sting. "Spread for me, gorgeous. That's right, show me everything you got for me."

Her face and breasts in the soft mattress, Lindi spread her knees wider, until she knew all of her was on full display for her biker man.

And then she waited, stark embarrassment warring with delicious uncertainty. What was he thinking? She could feel his gaze on her—did he like what he saw, or was he thinking 'fat girl on display'? It was all she could do to remain still, waiting for him to act, to speak.

Jack shifted in the bed behind her, and his warm, calloused hands settled high on her hips, then stroked slowly over her ass cheeks, squeezing and fondling her. His hard, hair-dusted thighs brushed her inner calves.

"Mm-hmm," he approved. "Been waitin' to see you just like this since that first look. Saw you smilin' at me through the window, and swear to God, a picture of this popped into my head. Knew I'd have it, sooner than later."

A sound of shock escaped Lindi's throat. She dug her fingers into the sheets, a blush suffusing her face and flooding down-ward. He'd thought about this? Anticipated it, looked forward to it? And now, he liked the way she looked. He thought she was hot.

Jack chuckled, low and dirty, and leaned down to press soft kisses to the small of her back, and then the curve of her ass. "You're so wet, you're drippin' for me."

He stroked his hand down the crease of her ass, tickling the tight rosette of her anus, and then thrust two big, knobby fin-gers into her pussy and back out again. The wet, succulent sound was loud in the quiet room, as was Lindi's whimper of pleasure. Her pussy clenched around his fingers, and she mewed with disappointment when they withdrew.

"You wanna please me?" Jack asked, thrusting his fingers in-side her again. "You wanna make your man happy, Lindi?"

She nodded quickly, pushing back against his touch. "Yes, Jack."

He made a deep sound of pleasure. "That's good. Gonna fuck you just like this. Wanna see every inch of me swallowed up by your little blonde pussy. I'm gonna give it to you the way I want, and watch you takin' it that way. You want that?"

"Yes, Jack. Oh, my God. Please."

Lindi squirmed, panting with eagerness as she heard the rustle of a condom wrapper. Then he was prodding into her wet folds, and all she could do was brace herself and take the thick, hard, hot cock thrusting into her depths. It was perfect, it was maddening.

Jack gripped her hips, and began to thrust, long slow strokes that drove clear to her center, and raked every nerve ending in her tight, wet sheath.

"Jesus fuck, that's good," he growled. "Need you with me, honey. Pet your clit for me."

She slid one hand between her legs and fingered her swollen clitoris, moaning as her own touch magnified the sensation of his cock inside her.

Jack grunted, his grip tightening on her ass. "Christ, felt that. You're gettin' close, aren't you?"

"Yes," she breathed. "Oh, Jack."

He shifted, deepening his stance, and thrust harder, jolting her with each long, solid stroke. "Fuck, yeah. Feel you milkin' my cum right out of me. C'mon, woman, give it to me."

With a high, breathy moan, Lindi gave it to him, arching back to meet him, her pussy clenching in paroxysms of utter joy around his thick, hot shaft.

Jack gave a muted roar of completion and stiffened over her, his thrusts short and jerky until at last he bent over her, buried deep inside her, his hot, damp body cupping hers.

At this evidence of his pleasure, Lindi came all over again. "Jack," she moaned happily.

"Yeah, honey," he muttered, stroking her bare hip with a lazy stroke of his thumb.

He pulled out of her and toppled onto the bed beside her as she curled on her side. A heavy arm over her waist, Jack pulled her close, and nuzzled his face into her tumbled hair.

"You like pleasin' me," he whispered again.

Lindi ducked her face into the sweaty, musky curve of Jack's powerful shoulder and throat, hiding her bashful smile. She more than liked it, she loved it. When this powerful, virile man lost control because of her, she felt like she'd done something delicious and naughty and triumphant. Knowing she'd made him come had sent her flying again too.

She snuggled close and draped her arm over his torso, tracing the whorl of silky hair that circled his belly button. Jack lay still, only his thumb moving in a slow caress on the high curve of her hip as he dozed. Lindi's body was relaxed and liquid.

However, as if it had been denied too long, her mind was working, her conscience nudging—no, by now it was more like outright shoving her along paths that she knew she could no longer deny.

"Jack?" Her voice was soft and hesitant, even to her.

"Hm-mm?" He sounded half-asleep.

Lindi lifted her head, looking into his face, a funny feeling swelling in her chest at the sheer, rough masculine perfection of him. He was all man, and logically she knew he wasn't the handsomest guy she'd ever seen, but he was definitely the sexiest.

He cracked one eye and raised a heavy brow at her. "What, honey?"

She swallowed, her throat suddenly dry. Oh, she would so much rather not have to have this conversation. But she needed to know, so she opened her mouth and blurted it out.

"Jack, what really happened to Darrell?"

Under her, Jack tensed, his body coiling like a spring. Alarmed, she curled her legs under her and pushed up onto her hands.

"We really gotta talk about this now?" he asked.

Lindi nearly shook her head, anything to back away from what she sensed was going to be a very uncomfortable discussion.

But she forced herself to nod, her fingers twisting in the sheets. "I need to know that Darrell isn't going to show up and—and take everything away."

Jack sat up in the tangled sheets, scrubbing his hands over his face. He did not look happy.

Feeling even more vulnerable in her nudity, Lindi slid backward off the bed and looked around for her underwear. Her panties were nowhere to be seen, so she grabbed her jeans and pulled them on, then tugged on her bra, and pulled her tank over her head. Suddenly chilled, she picked up her leather jacket, and put it on too.

Combing her hair nervously with her fingers, she turned back to find Jack watching her movements, that hawk-like intensity back in his gaze. Her heart skipped a beat. His face was hard, as if he knew exactly what she was doing, armoring herself against things she didn't want to hear.

He slid off the bed and reached for his own jeans. He eyed her as he pulled them on, and tucked himself carefully inside before fastening them. Then he straightened.

"All right, I can see you got a load of shit in that blonde head of yours. Might as well get it out."

Lindi twined a lock of hair nervously in her fingers as she eyed him in return.

"I ..." she began, and then nearly lost her courage as he waited, his face impassive, eyes impaling her. "Jack, I ... I know you and Keys must've killed Darrell—whether it was accidental, or—or self-defense or whatever. And he—I hated him, but ... it's still wrong. So much of what has happened these last few days was wrong. I just can't ... I don't know how to deal with it."

The atmosphere in the room shifted, and Lindi nearly looked over her shoulder at the window, sure she'd see that a thunderstorm was gathering. But the dark tension emanated entirely from Jack. He was staring at her as if he could not believe his ears.

"What the fuck?" he repeated in a soft, terrible voice. "You know I killed Darrell?"

Oh, how did he manage to invest her words with so much disbelief, even derision?

He continued to study her until she nodded again, her nerves jumping.

"You mind tellin' me," he asked, his voice growing louder with each word, "just how the hell you came up with that?

Lindi shook her head, her face hot, uncertainty niggling at her now. "Well, you—there was the blood—and you said to Keys, 'I thought you—or they—cleaned that up,' and he said—"

She flinched as Jack moved, turning away from her, striding to the heavy wood console that held the TV and slapping his big hands down on it so hard the floor underneath rattled. Then he turned on her again, his countenance holding a storm, his eyes the lightning.

"Yeah, I said that," he mocked savagely. "But here's the deal, Lindi. I gave you what I thought you needed—told you Darrell wasn't comin' back. Why can't you just leave it at that, huh?"

She swallowed, miserable but determined. "Because I ... can't. I need to know."

Jack shook his head. "All right, you wanna know it all, here it is. Keys and I found Darrell dead in your little photo gallery.

Double tapped—" he jabbed a finger at his forehead and his chest and snapped his fingers each time, making her flinch with each snap "—with a big caliber revolver. The signature of a certain MC. I won't say which one, 'cause nobody involved needs you prancing in to the local cop shop and stirring up a shit storm the likes of which this little burg has never seen."

She ignored this insult. "You mean, the Dev—I mean, bikers killed Darrell? But they were Dave's friends."

Jack snorted. "They may've been, don't mean they were Darrell's. Hell, he killed his own brother, according to you."

"But what did he do to them? Did he owe them money too?"

Jack shrugged. "Nobody's business but theirs—sure as hell isn't yours."

"But ... what happened to his body?" She shuddered. At least he hadn't still been lying in that room when she arrived.

He shook his head impatiently. "Why the fuck do you care? Can't you leave anything alone, woman?"

Her heart sank to her toes as she realized that he was more than angry—he was furious. "Well, you said—I mean, you asked if I'd be sorry if he was gone," Lindi fumbled, foreboding flooding her in a chilling tide, "and so I thought—"

He cut her off with a sharp slash of his hand between them. "Jesus, shut it. You're just diggin' a deeper hole for yourself."

"Then explain it to me!" she shouted back, her control gone, throwing her hands out. "Tell me what happened, Jack. Please! I'm begging you—give me something to trust, something to believe." Something that let her know Darrell's body wasn't going to gruesomely turn up on her doorstep, or up on the property, so she was yanked in by the police and questioned. So she could be rid of him once and for all.

"Fuck that," Jack ground out, his gaze fiery. "I tried to give you what you needed, so you could go along with your life, and not have to hear the dirty details. Why couldn't you trust me enough to let me do that for you? And if you don't trust me, what the hell are you doin' here?" He swept an arm out to indicate the rumpled bed behind him.

Lindi stared at him. What was she doing here? That was easy. She'd been swept up in the force of his powerful personality, his charm, all that was Jack. He was like a big Harley roaring through her quiet little life, rocking it on the foundations and carrying her along, until all she could do was hang on for the ride.

"Well, you ... I—I wanted ... I like being with you," she fumbled.

She winced as he gave her a look that said he thought that was as lame as she did.

He smiled. It was not a nice smile—sort of like the one a big shark would give the little fishy before he bit her in half. "Not to mention, you let me buy you all that shit, spend money on you when you don't trust me to do right by you, what's that make you? Huh?"

Was he calling her a—? Lindi stared at him, trying to form words around the pain slamming into her chest.

Jack nodded, his mouth twisting savagely. "Yeah, that burns, don't it, baby? Women who take money and shit from men they don't respect—got a name for that."

"No!" she moaned. She backed away from him, shaking her head. Had he just called her a *whore*? "I respect you, I just ... I just can't be with a man who ..." A man who wouldn't promise her she'd never be stung again.

She did respect Jack ... or at least, she hadn't thought about that. She'd thought about how she trusted him with her body and her safety, despite their dangerous beginning. She'd thought about how he made her feel—so much more *alive* than any other man she'd ever met. She'd thought about how maybe, in spite of everything, he was *the one*.

But none of that mattered now.

Because if he didn't understand why she needed proof that life wasn't going to turn and sting her so hard she couldn't get up again, she wanted nothing more to do with him, or his gifts. He had no right to look at her this way—with contempt that burned deep, leaving a gash straight through her heart.

Lindi grasped the lapels of her new leather jacket and ripped it off. She held it out to him with a shaking hand. "Here, take it back. I don't want it."

Jack folded his arms across his chest and sneered. "Oh, don't stop there, sweetheart. Take off the rest. Maybe if I like the way you do it, we can have us one last good time."

She gasped. "Oh. You—you *bastard*. If you think I'd let you touch me now, you're crazy!"

He leaned toward her, his gaze fiery. "Honey, five minutes and I could have you panting for it."

Scalding shame suffused Lindi, because a tiny part of her was very much afraid he was right. But fury followed it, and she put one hand on her hip and returned his glare with one of her own.

"Sorry, Jack. There's not enough leather in that Harley shop to make *that* worth my time again."

She threw the jacket at his feet, turned on her bare heel and stalked toward the door. Her purse and sandals lay on the closet floor alongside Jack's motorcycle boots. Lindi grabbed them and yanked open the door.

She would've loved to slam it behind her, but the stupid thing was on a pressurized hinges, so it closed with a hushed, yet final sound.

Ridiculously, even as she hurried toward the elevators, she hoped to hear him calling to her, telling her to wait, that they'd talk this out. But only her angry sobbing breaths accompanied her along the quiet hallway.

Chapter Eighteen

After shoving her feet into her sandals, Lindi pelted toward the elevators.

The nearest was open, an older man inside with one hand on the buttons, a startled look on his face as he saw Lindi. She rushed in and stood, back to the mirrored wall, arms tight around her middle, eyes squeezed shut as she fought back more tears.

The doors closed, and the elevator slid downward. "You all right, young lady?" the man asked. He was bowed with arthritis, but weathered and tough in golf apparel and a straw fedora.

Lindy scrubbed wetness from her face with the heel of her hand. "No," she said. "But I will be. And he can just k-kiss my ass."

The man chuckled. "That's the spirit. Give him hell. We men mostly deserve it."

Lindi sniffled. That was for sure.

But this time, she was achingly aware that she might just deserve a big, fat share of blame herself. Then she remembered Jack's slashing words, and nearly moaned with pain. Why couldn't he have just told her everything would be fine?

The elevator stopped and the doors opened to reveal the main floor hallway, and a group of luggage-laden people. They stared curiously at Lindi, and she ducked her head, shaking her hair forward around her hot face.

A hand touched her elbow. "Excuse us," said her fellow passenger in a voice that rang with authority. The waiting people moved aside, and the man waved Lindi through. Holding onto her composure by a thread, she walked out of the elevator ahead of him.

At the corner of the lobby, she looked back. "Thanks," she said, her voice growing stronger as she spoke. "If you're ever out at the BeeHive Café on the north shore, the coffee's on me. I also make the best breakfast on the lake."

He raised a finger to the brim of his hat. "Thanks, hon. I just might take you up on that. And you remember this—you're worthy of respect. So whoever he is, don't you let him come on back unless he treats you right."

Lindi smiled crookedly even as her eyes welled with tears again. "Okay. It's a deal."

The trouble was, she wasn't so sure she deserved his kind words.

Then she thrust her sunglasses onto her face and hurried out of the resort into cloudy afternoon. It was damp and chilly, and it was then she remembered she now had to make her way home with no jacket.

It was a cold walk, with a breeze blowing through the park, straight off the chill waters of the lake. To Lindi, with her tousled hair and tear-stained face, it felt like the walk of shame. She stalked along the sidewalk above the park, where jacketed children ran and played in the sun, whooping with laughter, while their parents chatted idly on the sidelines. She felt as far removed from their happiness as the lone raven flapping slowly along overhead, doleful cry echoing as he headed for the tall evergreens on the point.

Back at her apartment, she went straight to her bedroom, where she dug the Harley shopping bags from her closet. Then she began to pack. She didn't stop until the bags contained every single item Jack had bought for her.

She took a hot shower, scrubbing Jack's scent off her skin. But of course the smell of her shampoo and shower gel reminded her of how the products had smelled on his skin. Not all the hot water streaming down her face came from the shower.

Dressed in her own jeans, tee and workout jacket, she piled the bags into her car. It started with a rough sputter, but then quit before she made it out of her parking space. And would not start again, no matter what she did.

Lindi leaned over and thumped her head three times on the steering wheel. Then she burst into tears, and sat and had that long-overdue cry. It took a while, because she not only cried over her fight with Jack, but Cissie and Twig and Dave and her stupid car were all jumbled in there too.

When she finally wiped her swollen, wet eyes and looked out of her car, she yelped in shock. A man stood just outside her car, lounging against the next vehicle, arms crossed.

For one wild moment, she thought it was Jack, but then she realized it was Keys. When he didn't go away, she slid her sunglasses over her swollen eyes and rolled down her window reluctantly. "What do you want?" If he was here to yell at her too, she was rolling the window back up until he gave up and went away.

Jack's friend gave her a look of mingled compassion and ex-asperation.

"Question is," he drawled, "what are you doin', cryin' in your car, babe? Thought you were partyin' with Jack."

Lindi hiccupped on a sob. "H-he called me a whore."

He winced audibly. "Whoa, that's raw. You had a blow-up, huh?"

She nodded.

Keys leaned his hands on the open window as if he were set-tling to chat. "Jack has a temper, no doubt. So, you two done?"

"Darn—I mean, damn straight we are." Even cursing didn't make her feel better.

"Huh. Well, I guess that's fair ... long as you don't mind watchin' him with other bitches when you're out and around town."

Of course she would mind. That would *burn*. But she'd have to stand it, because Jack certainly didn't want her anymore.

"He hates me," she mumbled. "And I'm not his biggest fan at the moment either."

"No, he doesn't hate you," Keys said, sounding disgusted. "Christ, I ain't cut out to be a fuckin' marriage counselor."

He pulled her car door open with a loud creak of unoiled hinges. "C'mon, babe, climb out. Let's get you back inside. Doesn't look like this rolling wreck's goin' anywhere, anyway."

Lindi climbed out, and he jerked his chin toward the back seat. "You been shoppin'?"

"No. Those are things J-Jack bought me. Which I am never wearing again."

"Uh-huh. He's not the only one with pride, is he? Well, best not leave those bags here, or you'll find your windows smashed in for it. This is a nice little town, but you still got a criminal element, an' Harley shit is worth good money."

She couldn't argue with any of this, especially when he hauled the bags out and waited. Sniffling, she locked the car and led him into her apartment.

Her neighbors, two college coeds, were just leaving. They looked her and Keys over as they sauntered past. Lindi heard them giggling behind her. Stupid girls—what did they know about anything?

In her tiny living room, she sank onto the sofa. "Why are you here?" she asked, belatedly curious.

Keys dropped the bags in the corner and sat on the only other chair, elbows on his knees as he regarded her. "'Cause I called Jack about somethin' else, and he, ah, mentioned your spat."

She could imagine.

"Gonna give it to you straight," he said, "'cause I think you can take it. Jack's got a temper, and a mouth on him, but he's a good man. Best I know, in fact. He's like my brother. I'd trust him with my life, and vice versa. Once he's got your back, he'll do anything for you."

He'd never be that for her.

"Now hold on," Keys said, sitting up straight. "Do not start cryin' again. Fuck, I hate when you women do that."

"Sorry." Lindi gave up on hiding behind her sunglasses. She tossed them aside and swiped the back of her hand over her wet face, grimacing at the smear of eye makeup on her hand. She probably looked like a raccoon. "I'm not usually like this. I haven't cried since—" since Dave died. No, since she found out Cissie had cancer. Whereas today she'd been a regular watering can.

"Glad to hear it. You came across as real feisty the other day."

She smiled crookedly at him. "You guys deserved feisty."

He grinned back. "True that. Jack needs a woman with spirit."

She shook her head. "He needs something. Not sure it's me."

Keys held up his hand, palm out. "Now just stop right there, woman. Who knows him best, you or me?" He waved one finger between the two of them, his brows raised.

"You," she admitted.

"Right. Now, if you two get your heads out of your asses, that ratio may change, I don't know. But I do know, Jack is *into* you. I haven't seen him like this with a woman in years. We've both had a lot of women, fucked more than our share and of those, had plenty that wanted to cling. I've seen him brush them off one after the other, but I've never seen him angry over a woman ... until now."

"Really?"

He nodded, and leaned back to crook one foot over the other knee, arm over the back of the chair. "Really. Swear it."

She bit the tip of her thumbnail. "You may as well know," she admitted, "I ... I thought you guys killed Darrell."

He gave her a dry look. "I know, babe. Jack told me. You over that?"

She nodded. "I'm sorry."

He shrugged, not looking in the least upset. "Don't worry about it. You've kinda been swept up by the whirlwind, and I can see how you'd think that. Jack will too, once he calms down. But you could always get a head start on convincing him."

Lindi eyed his innocent look with suspicion. Now who was stirring poo? "And just what would that involve?"

"Keep it simple," he said dryly. "Fix up pretty again, go back there and a-*pol*-o-gize." He drew the word out with comic emphasis, but the look in his eyes said he meant every word.

Lindi thought about this. "Well. I can do that." Although the thought of knocking on Jack's hotel room door and facing him again kind of made her want to crawl under her own sofa and hide.

But then she remembered the man from the elevator, and his firm advice to demand respect from her beau. That had been darn good advice, and she meant to take it. But that didn't mean she didn't have to give some respect in return.

"No wussin' out," Keys said firmly. "Go on, go get ready and I'll give you a ride over there. And then I'm callin' a tow truck to come and get that excuse for a car, and take it to a shop."

"You don't have to do that," she said, startled.

He shrugged. "Consider it a down payment of sorts. I got a business proposition to run by you. But not today. Today you got more important things to do, right? You in?"

Yes, she did. She'd done without her car for a few months, but she wasn't sure she wanted to do without Jack. Could she? Sure. People did, they went on living after they lost those they loved. She'd done without Dave after he died, even though he left a big, gaping hole in her heart and her life.

But if she let Jack in … well, he would be the biggest risk she'd ever taken, emotionally.

From the outside, he looked a lot like the man she barely re-membered as her father—good-looking, charming, easy-going and full of life. But according to Keys, and to her heart, Jack had depth and breadth to his character that her father had never possessed. Jack stood by his friends, and he'd done his best to protect her from harm. She'd trusted him with her body, now she had to trust him with more—to stand by her.

She nodded emphatically. "I'm in."

Keys leaned forward. "And one last thing, babe. If you ain't *all* in, don't do this. 'Cause Jack's my brother. I ain't down with seein' him played and then dropped."

Lindi scowled at him. "I am not the player here," she snapped. "And I have a few things to say to him too."

His best friend's blue eyes twinkled devilishly. "Again, true. Gonna be fun to see if you got what it takes to put a governor on my bro."

Lindi knew, from hanging around Dave, that a governor was a device that prevented a vehicle from going over a certain speed. She wasn't so sure she wanted to tame Jack's velocity—she just wanted to know if she could, and should, hang on for the ride.

Chapter Nineteen

However, if Lindi had thought it difficult to question Jack
about his part in Darrell's disappearance, it was nothing to
what she had to do now. She could apologize, sure. But the
hard part was making herself vulnerable to him. This was going to take every bit of courage she had.

She knocked. Then she had to stand there for a long, suffocat-
ing moment listening to silence from the other side of his
door.

"Jack," she called finally, her voice sharper than she'd intended. "If you're in there, let me in. I need to ..."

Her voice trailed away as the door was yanked open. Her
heart leapt, and she opened her mouth again, but Jack was already turning away. His back to her, he sauntered across the
big room and flung himself into one of the easy chairs by the
window. His face was shadowed, with the afternoon sun limning the side of his head and his heavy shoulders. Crossing one
leg over the other, he waited.

Lindi stepped into the room, letting the door close behind her.
Then, before she could lose her courage, she continued across
the room. She walked past Jack and stopped by the French
doors, turning to face him.

He turned his head to watch her, the light falling over his face,
and her heart sank when she saw his stony expression.

He didn't seem to appreciate the fact she was wearing the
short skirt he liked, or a little black sweater set that revealed
her cleavage and hugged her waist, or that she'd done her
makeup smoky and sexy, and fixed her hair in long, looping
curls. She had to dig her toes into her strappy black sandals to
keep from turning around and scurrying back out the door.

No. She'd come this far, she was not giving up now. She took
a shaky breath and began.

"I came back here to tell you I'm sorry," she said. "I ... should have trusted you, about the situation with Darrell. I see now that you were trying to do the right thing, and protect me."

She looked into his hazel eyes, praying he could see she meant every word. "I'm sorry, Jack. Can you forgive me?"

He let her wait. Then he cocked his head. "Depends."

"On what?" she asked, her heart pounding.

"You gonna do it again?" he asked her, his gaze like an x-ray. "Assume the worst? Or are you gonna trust me?"

"I'm going to trust you," she said instantly. "Although, it would help if you explained yourself once in a while. Especially since I have known you a grand total of, what—three days."

His face relaxed slightly, the corners of his eyes crinkling, and hers narrowed, suspicion crawling in. If he was playing her ... so help her, she would get him for it.

"Also," she snapped, "when we met, you were sweet to me, and all the time, you were really stalking me, planning to kidnap me. Not the greatest way to build a trusting relationship. If I could forgive you for *that*, big shot, you can be a little bit understanding now."

"You were into me from that first look through the café window," he said, looking not even a little ashamed. "You're right, I saw that, and I played on it."

Lindi's face flamed. "I was *not* into you from the first look. I just—"

"Yeah, you were, honey." Now he looked downright smug. "If I'd wanted to, I could've had you right there in your café after everyone else left, with the closed sign on the front door."

All right, that was just enough. She set her fists on her hips, and glared at him. "The same could be said vice versa, biker man."

He grinned slowly. Then he held out one hand to her, palm up. "Honey. It don't work that way. Now, you came to me and apologized nice and sweet, and I appreciate that. Come here and show me the honey I know you got hidin' under that sting of yours."

She tossed her head and regarded him rebelliously, not quite ready to let go of the hurt.

"Lindi," he chided, his look darkening.

Her feet were already moving to him. "Just don't get to thinking that every argument is going to end this way, Jack Moran," she told him. "Because I won't be with a man who can't admit when he's wrong, either."

He pulled her between the vee of his thighs, and looked up at her, a new softness in his beautiful eyes that made her heart thump, this time with joy.

"I can admit it," he said, his strong hands sliding up her back to hold her as if she were a precious vessel, "and I do. And here's my apology. I'm sorry as hell I said that shit to you earlier, honey. I was pissed, and I let fly. Not for one minute have I ever considered you a whore. Saying that was all kinds of wrong."

Her heart swelling, Lindi let him pull her onto his lap, her knees on either side of his hips in the chair.

He leaned his head against her breasts, his breath hot through her thin sweater. "I was an asshole to put that busted look in your eyes, honey. Think you can find it in your heart to forgive me?"

If that didn't melt a woman's heart, she didn't have one. Lindi wrapped her arms around him and kissed the top of his head, breathing in the scent of his hair, woodsy shampoo and Jack, an intoxicating combination. "Oh, Jack. Of course I can."

His shoulders sagged, his arms tightening until Lindi could feel his heart thundering in his chest, and the shudder of relief that went through him. "Thank fuck."

"So," he asked, "you wanna share why you panicked? I get why you might think we offed Darrell, 'cause we both know in the MC world, sometimes people get dead. But why couldn't you take my word he was taken care of?"

Lindi nodded, even though she felt slightly sick with fear. "I'll share."

Jack let her go enough to sit up, although he kept his arms linked loosely around her hips. Lindi traced the design of the Harley wings on his tee with a fingertip.

"It's hard for me to trust a man," she said quietly. "You know it's just me, my sister and my mom."

She looked up and he nodded.

"Well, my dad was a drunk," she said bluntly. "An alcoholic. We had a little house up on Eighth Street, and he worked construction while Mama stayed home with us. But when I was, I don't know, about three years old, he started drinking, and it got worse and worse, until he was spending all his money on drinks for him and his buddies. He'd get fired, but promise Mama he was done drinking. He'd get another job, and then do it all over again. He kept promising her he'd change, get help, all that … but he never did."

Jack nodded, his hands massaging her back. Listening with his gaze intent on her.

"Then, when I was six and Cissie was eight, he—he went out one night, got really drunk, and r-ran his pickup over the center line of I-95. He hit a van head-on, and killed the family in it and himself."

"Aw, honey," Jack muttered. "That's rough."

"Yeah. We lost our dad—such as he was. And since he never bothered to buy life insurance, or insurance on his truck, we lost our house, and had to move into assisted housing. Our apartment would've fit in this hotel room. And Mama started working any jobs she could find." She shook her head, and laid her hands flat on his chest, looking into his eyes. "I'm not telling you all this to make you feel sorry for me, Jack. Mama's fine, so are Cissie and I. We all came through it okay in the end. But—I guess you could say I have issues with trust. Which sounds like such bull-doody when I say it out loud, but it's true." She blew a breath up toward, ruffling her bangs.

"Nah," Jack said. "Sounds to me like three women who got stomped on by a fool who didn't deserve any of 'em, and fought their back to the top where they belong."

He pulled her close, his gaze warm. "Look at you now, Lindi Carson. Queen bee of your own little hive. You got a fuckuva lot to be proud of.

She nodded, soaking in his approval. "You're right. I do."

"Good. I gotta tell you, if your daddy had been in a club, his brothers would've kicked some sense into him, and they'd have looked after your mama and you girls too."

She regarded him with new curiosity, threading her fingers through the thick waves of hair over his ears. "Did you grow up in the club?"

He lifted his chin. "Yeah. I was born in Spokane, but then we moved to Cali. My dad was the sergeant at arms for the Redding chapter of the Devil's Flyers, met ma when he was up here on a run, decided to stay up here for her, even patched into the Airway Heights chapter for a while. My ma knew who and what he was goin' in," he added, his gaze darkening, "but she never took to the life. She questioned every move he made—was it gonna get him arrested, was it enough to keep food on the table. And, every time he went on the road, she was convinced he was with club whores." He shook his head. "They fought like you would not believe. They moved to Cali to try and make a fresh start, but it didn't take. He gave up on her, started spending as much time on the road as he could, then finally just left us behind."

"Oh, no," Lindi breathed, cupping his head in her hands. Jack had a few family issues of his own.

He shook his head, caressing her absently. "Lookin' back, I see Ma did the best she could. She's a born worrier, always fretting about the future. I blamed her for a long time for driving the old man away, but he made his choice—his own life instead of his family."

"I'm sorry," she said. "Sounds like your dad's club should've straightened him out."

Jack's face eased into a wry grin. "Sweetheart, they made sure we had a place to live, and food on the table. More'n that, a club is not gonna interfere between a brother and his old lady. My folks are just happier apart."

"Do you still see them?"

"Yup. Once in a while. They're both back in Redding, Dad lives at the compound, Ma has a nice modular that Bridget and I helped her buy."

"That's sweet," Lindi said. She stared at him, playing with an unruly lock of hair over his temple.

"What?" he asked, giving her a quizzical look.

She blinked. "Oh, nothing." She'd think about Jack's history and her own, and how they had been on a direct line to clash, later.

Jack leaned in, nipped at the swell of her breast through her sweater, and gave her a roguish look up through his lashes.

"In that case, how about you let me show you how much I missed you?"

She giggled, flinching away from his teeth. She smiled down into his face as he surged up out of the chair with her in his arms.

"I was only gone a few hours."

"Yeah, but we were both pissed and we fucked up, so they were long hours"

He was not wrong. "Okay," she agreed. "Show me. But you have to do all the work."

He raised a brow at her as he carried her to the big bed. "You like pleasin' me too much for that, honey. I give you five minutes, tops, before you're beggin' to get your mouth and hands on my cock."

She shook her head as he yanked the covers aside and laid her back in the bed. She kicked off her sandals, arched her back and crooked her legs enticingly, turning them to one side like a pinup girl.

"Not this time. This time it's all you, demonstrating your prowess. See, Keys told me all about all the women you two have gone through, and I want—"

Jack gave a growl of warning, and her words cut off in a gulp of sheer feminine alarm.

He shut her up with his mouth, coming down over her with his thighs straddling hers, and his big hand tangled in her hair. Desire and delight flooding her, Lindi opened her mouth under his and slid her arms up around his broad back, holding on while she kissed him back. She forgot all about those other women.

Less than five minutes later, although she didn't know this because she wasn't watching the clock or thinking about anything but Jack, Lindi was naked and kneeling over him, his beautiful cock in her mouth, and his mouth between her thighs.

He licked into her, making her moan. But then he groaned, and she smiled happily around her mouthful. Her biker man loved what she did to him as much as she loved doing it.

Much later, there was a knock at the door.

Jack, who was enroute to the bathroom, walked to the door. "Yeah?"

"Valet service, sir," said a muffled voice. "Delivery for you."

A moment later, Jack was stalking toward the bed, two very familiar Harley shopping bags in his hands.

Lindi rolled her eyes. Keys, stirring the situation again.

"You know anything about these?" Jack asked her, frowning as he tossed the bags onto the bed. They spilled open, lacy undies falling from one, her leather vest and a pair of jeans from the other.

She wrinkled her nose. "Um, I was sort of planning to return those to you."

He picked up both bags by the bottom and dumped them out in a spill of color and fabric.

"You were gonna return my gifts to me," he repeated, his brows lowering.

She flushed. "Because you said—"

"Know what I said," he cut in. "Also know I apologized, and you accepted it. But what the fuck, guess that means these're mine now, huh?"

She frowned at him. "I guess." Except that she now felt guilty, as if she'd thrown his gifts back in his face. He'd chosen most of the things himself.

Jack looked at her, and back at the heap of clothing.

"Hey, wait. What are you going to do with them?" Lindi asked, frowning. Those were her biker chick things. He'd better not be planning to toss them off the balcony to teach her a lesson, or some such action.

"Just tryin' to decide which outfit I'm gonna let you borrow to wear to supper," he said with an evil grin.

She gasped and scrambled forward. "Oh, no, you don't. Wait. Give me those, Jack Moran!"

Grinning, he held her away with one long arm, while he selected the pink and black string bikini panties, and then scooped her leather jacket from a chair. These, he pushed into her arms and leaned down to kiss her. "There you go, honey. Now, why don't you go get dressed, and I'll straighten up."

"You big jerk. I need more than these." She was so not sitting around this hotel room like a motorcycle magazine centerfold.

He narrowed his eyes at her. "Ah, ah, ah. You talk nasty to me, I'll take those away too. And I won't let you have the clothes you showed up in, either. So you'll be enjoyin' four-star room service bare-ass naked. Which means I will *really* enjoy the cuisine. Come to think of it, that's a fine idea."

He reached for the leather jacket. Belatedly realizing her peril, Lindi scrambled off of the bed in the other direction, the jacket and panties clutched in her arms. "No! You stay away from me."

His chuckle followed her into the bathroom. Jack, huh. Jack-ass was more like it.

She washed up, fluffed her hair, and then donned the bikini panties and the leather jacket, which she zipped up all the way, then unzipped partway again because the high collar was meant for protection on the road, not indoor wear.

She surveyed the way the soft black leather cupped her waist and then ended high on her hips, leaving her lower half bare except for the tiny panties, and huffed a disgusted sigh. Yup, she looked like she should be spread over the seat of a big Harley, giving a come-hither smile at male magazine buyers. Right now, she'd rather flip them off.

Jack was waiting in his jeans and tee-shirt when she came out. He looked her over with a smile. "You warm enough, honey?" he asked. "'Cause I sure don't want you takin' a chill."

"Right." She gave him a saccharine smile. "That's why you let me have my jacket, right?"

"I let you wear my jacket," he corrected her, "'Cause yeah, that's the kind of guy I am. Big hearted. Can you unzip it a little bit more for me, though? So I don't change my mind and take it back."

Giving him a dirty look, Lindi unzipped the jacket another inch.

He cocked his head and ran his thumb over his chin, considering her. "Little bit more," he decided.

She unzipped farther, and he nodded. "Perfect. I do love lookin' at your tits. Now, you want a beer or a glass of wine while we're waitin'?"

Maybe if she drank some wine, she wouldn't brain him with one of the heavy hotel lamps. "I guess so."

"Good," he said. "It's in that little frig down there. And get me a beer while you're there."

She set her hands on her bare hips and eyed the refrigerator, near the floor. He just wanted her to bend over. "I could do that," she agreed. "It all depends on whether you want to drink your beer, or wear it."

He chuckled. "Okay. I'll get your wine if you get my beer."

"Oh, all right." If he was that determined to have a show, she'd give him one—a good one.

From the glazed look in his eyes as she carried his beer to him, he appreciated her efforts. He took the cold bottle and lifted it to his lips, taking a long drink. "Thanks, honey. Need that to cool off, 'cause you are one hot biker mama."

Pursing her lips to hide her smile, Lindi sat down across from him, crossed her bare legs, and took a sip of the wine he'd poured her. Jack's gaze followed every move.

"Nice view from up here," she said, looking out the window.

Jack shook his head without taking his eyes off her. "Nuh-uh. The best view is all right here."

Lindi sat across from him to eat her steak dinner.

But she ate dessert on his lap, and by the time Jack had spooned the last bite of decadent chocolate layered dessert into her mouth, the jacket was unzipped and his hands were all over her.

Then he bent her over the end of the bed and had her that way, still wearing the thong and the jacket.

When she'd come twice and he once, Jack leaned down to lay his head on her back, his hand still cupping her mons inside the thong, his other braced on the bed.

"I'm definitely buyin' the leather miniskirt," he muttered.

She giggled into the duvet. "For you or me?"

"For me. I'm keepin' all this shit," he said. "That way, I say what you wear and when."

He graciously allowed her to wear one of the tanks with the thong to sleep in. Lindi decided she'd put up with it just while they were here at the resort. When she was back home, she'd assert her right to choose her own ensembles, thanks very much.

She snuggled close to his big, warm body and slung her leg over his thighs, sighing happily as he wrapped one arm around her, his hand on her ass, two fingers playing lazily with the string of the thong.

Wearing a thong wasn't so bad if it got her chocolate mousse pie and two Jack-induced orgasms, she decided sleepily.

And opening up to her man was definitely worth it.

Chapter Twenty

Thursday

Lindi woke the next morning to her phone alarm. She smiled, reaching for Jack in the big hotel bed before she even opened her eyes. But her questing hand met only cool sheets and empty pillows.

She sat up and rubbed her eyes. "Jack?" she called, her voice rough with sleep. "Jack?"

Silence greeted her. And no running water from the bathroom, no sounds of a man taking care of his morning business.

She threw back the covers and slid out of bed, hurrying to the little hallway between bathroom and closet. The bathroom counter was empty. She whirled, her heart pounding. The closet held the Harley shopping bags with her new things, but Jack's satchel was gone. So were his boots, his leather jacket, and his wallet and keys from the table.

Five o'clock in the morning and he was already gone? He'd left her, without as much as a word. Like a thief in the night. Or a rambling man who didn't like goodbyes. Just like her father.

Suddenly shivering even in the warm hotel room, Lindi wrapped her arms around her middle, struggling for breath against the huge, icy ball of foreboding that filled her chest.

"Damn you, Jack Moran," she muttered, her voice breaking on the words.

The burble of her phone announced a new text message.

She dashed around the corner of the bed so fast she stubbed her toe on the bottom of the bed, and had to hobble the last few steps, biting back a whimper of pain.

The text was from Jack. 'Mornin', sleepyhead. You were dead asleep, so I didn't wake you. Keys & I on business for couple days. Order breakfast on room tab.'

'Business where?' she texted back, her fingers flying, heart pounding. 'How long will u be gone?'

No reply. Evidently Jack was finished with their conversation. Lindi scowled at his meager words on the tiny screen, as anger and hurt overwhelmed her again.

How much gosh-darned trouble would it have been for him to wake her up and kiss her before he left? Explain why he was leaving, and when he'd be back. Not much, that's how much.

The memory of her mother's face filled her mind, weary and resigned—the look she wore whenever she spoke of Chuck Carson disappearing with his buddies. Mama was past loving Lindi's father, but the residual hurt would always remain.

"If you think this kind of communication is going to work between us, you've got another think coming, Jack Moran," Lindi said aloud.

The utter quiet of the room mocked her.

Well, she wasn't hanging around missing him. She had her own life, and her own business, which she needed to get to.

She didn't need a biker man around anyway.

Her phone beeped again. This text was from an unfamiliar number. 'Caprice is in resort parking garage. Valet has keys. She runs good 4 now, but u still need to replace her. Keys'

Well, that was sweet. Lindi smiled crookedly. 'Thanks!'

Another beep, this time a smiley face icon.

She snickered, though it died as tears flooded her eyes. How hard would it have been for Jack to end his message with something like that ... or maybe even a flower, or a heart?

Not hard at all.

He was in such deep shit.

The Caprice started right up and ran well, although Lindi winced at the cloud of exhaust left behind as she accelerated out of the resort onto Sherman Avenue. Keys was right about looking for a new vehicle.

But, she'd think about that later. She had the BeeHive to run this morning, other business to take care of this afternoon, and she also desperately needed some time with her girls.

At her apartment, Lindi took a quick shower, dressed and hit the road to her café.

There were some early turkey hunters and fishermen, and then things slowed down, so while she ate a late breakfast of her own, Lindi texted Sara and Kit, and set up dinner and drinks at their favorite Italian pizza and pasta place in midtown.

She closed the café at eleven thirty, and headed back to her apartment

There she showered again to get the cooking smells out of her hair and skin, bundled on her robe and got busy on her old laptop. She perused local listings for Realtors and lawyers. Luck seemed to be in her favor, or maybe it was a slow time of year, because she soon had an appointment at two o'clock with a lawyer from a firm she remembered Sara mentioning, Leupold & Leupold.

She fixed her hair and makeup, dressed in her one and only professional outfit, a pair of black slacks and blazer from the clearance rack at Macy's, over a cream top and her black sandals. With her silver jewelry and black hobo bag, she decided she looked like an up-and-coming business owner.

The lawyer, Jace Leupold, met Lindi in the foyer of the firm's offices in a remodeled Craftsman-style home on East Sherman. A handsome, dark-haired man in a pinstriped suit, he smiled and shook her hand, and led her back to a rear office with a large, dark wood desk and two comfortable leather chairs.

And although he looked nerve-rackingly young, the moment Jace began to speak, Lindi was reassured. He was clearly intelligent and knew what he was doing with legal documents.

He perused Dave's will, nodded approvingly when he saw the notary's stamp, and told Lindi he would begin the process of making sure the property title was moved into her name at the county courthouse.

"Give me at least a week," he said. "I hope it won't take that long, but it depends on how busy they are at the county. Sometimes they get backed up, especially with developers lining up projects for spring."

"But you don't think there will be any problems with the will?" she asked anxiously.

He raised his brows in inquiry. "Do you anticipate any?"

Lindi flushed. "No. It's just that I didn't know that my boyfriend—Dave, even had a will until a few days ago. It … turned up suddenly. I just want to make sure it's all legal and above board."

The young lawyer nodded, his face giving nothing away. "Any family members who may contest the will?"

She shook her head, trying not to wince at Darrell's fate. "No. There's no family left."

He nodded again, still silent, and Lindi pursed her lips against the urge to tell him everything. She blinked and looked away from his pale gray eyes. Sheesh, he might be young, but he had a force of will to rival Jack's.

"So, I think that's all," she said. "Unless you need me to sign more papers."

"Not today." He moved around the desk to walk her from the room.

"Thanks for your help," she said.

"Thank you," he countered smoothly. "We appreciate your business, Ms. Carson. You have a very nice piece of property there. When you get ready to sell or subdivide, please let me know if I can assist with any legal questions."

Lindi told him the name of the Realtor she was considering, and he nodded. "Good choice. She has a solid reputation."

"Oh, good," Lindi said. She'd chosen the woman and her office because of her rating on a popular internet site, since she didn't know anyone in the realty business.

By the time Lindi walked into the Italian restaurant at six o'clock that evening, she was at once exhausted and wired. She looked around the low-ceilinged room, peering past pillars painted to resemble Roman columns, and hanging bunches of plastic grapes and wine jugs, searching for her friends. The place was crowded as usual, the air filled with voices, laughter and the clink of dishes and cutlery.

Finally she spotted a familiar auburn head near a window. Kit, gazing out into the parking lot and winding a lock of her hair around her finger. Since a purple headband held her wild curls back off her face, Lindi deduced her friend hadn't had a trim in a while. And judging by the faded black tee, leggings and striped pink-and-black mini-skirt into which she'd stuffed her curves, she hadn't done laundry lately, either.

Lindi pulled out the chair across from her friend and plunked herself down in it, dropping her purse on floor beside her.

"Hello to you too," she said.

Kit finally turned her head and blinked her heavily made-up eyes, as if awakened from a trance. Her black-rimmed, green eyes widened with pleased surprise, her oval face breaking into a smile.

"Lindi, hi," she breathed.

Lindi smiled back, barely refraining from rolled her eyes. Sometimes she felt a decade older than Kit, rather than a few years. "You sound surprised to see me. Forget we were meeting?"

"No," Kit explained. "I was just … thinking, that's all." She raised one brow, only a few shades darker than her hair. "Wow, you look very pro. Whatcha been up to?"

Lindi surveyed the bottle of house red on the table and reached for one of the glasses grouped around it. "I'll tell you both when Sara gets here, okay? I need a drink."

"I'm here," said a voice at Lindi's shoulder.

They looked up to see a statuesque, platinum blonde in a gray sheath dress and gray-and-yellow flowered sweater standing beside the table. She looked tired and stressed, although her rounded face relaxed in a smile as Lindi and Kit chorused a greeting.

Sara pulled out the chair between them and lowered herself into it, grimacing. "God, that feels good. These heels are killing me."

Lindi winced in sympathy. She loved her platforms, which gave her height and leg length without cranking her feet into an uncomfortable position.

"They're so pretty though," Kit said, peering at Sara's discarded stilettos. "Besides, you work at a desk."

"Not when I'm following our idiot new office manager around with my tablet as she inventories every single freakin' paper file in our storage room," Sara snarled.

Then she gave Lindi an apologetic look. "Sorry. Enough about my day. I want to hear what you've been up to with this Jack Moran dude."

Lindi's cheeks heated as both her friends trained looks on her that said she would spill all, or they would know the reason why.

"Okay," she said, before pausing to take a sip of wine. "But pour yourselves a drink, girls. You're gonna need it."

Kit leaned forward, fists under her chin, eyes wide. Sara reached for the bottle and poured. "I knew it," she muttered. "You've gone crazy over a man."

Lindi gave her a quelling frown. "I'll tell you everything." Or nearly everything, she added silently. "But you have to promise not to say anything until I get to the end."

Kit nodded instantly. Sara frowned, but then sighed. "All right, I promise. Now talk."

Lindi talked. She talked through salads and warm rolls, through thick, cheesy lasagna split three ways, because the house servings were freaking huge, and through a last glass of wine.

When she told how Jack had gone from flirting with her to kidnapping her, her friends gasped, Kit in fascination, Sara in outrage.

Darrell's X-rated stalker gallery loosed twin growls of fury.

Twig's attack on her brought looks of horror that were only calmed when she quickly added Jack's knocking him out, and Keys' banishing him.

She left out the part about the guns, because no one had actually gotten shot, and Lindi was not going to bring trouble down on Keys and Jack by gossiping, especially to a friend who worked in the DA's office.

The discovery of the cash, Dave's will and Darrell's final attempt to screw her over by hiding it from her, followed by Jack's showering her with clothing, excellent meals and nights at the resort had them listening raptly.

Finally Lindi sat back. "Okay, that's all of it."

She'd left out the details of her sexual exploits on her kitchen counter and in Jack's rented SUV, because that was her business. Maybe sometime over stronger libations she'd share with these two, but not yet.

"Oh, my Gawd," Kit sighed, hand to her heart. "That is so crazy wild and crazy romantic at the same time."

"It's crazy, all right," Sara said, her blonde brows drawn together. "Romantic? Hmm."

She leaned closer. "Sweetie, are you sure this guy is safe? I mean, a Devil's Flyer? I know Dave was a friend of the club, but these guys are full members."

Lindi returned her look steadily. "My gut says yes. My heart says … might wanna watch out."

Kit nudged her with a foot under the table. "What does your pussy say?"

Lindi's face heated, but she smiled, a trifle smugly it must be said. "It says hang on tight and enjoy the ride!"

Kit let out a whoop and pumped her fist in the air. "Hot biker action, yeah!"

Lindi caught Sara's eye, and then the three of them burst out laughing.

Practical Sara sobered first. "But now he's gone?" she asked. "And you don't know where, or when he's coming back."

Lindi's laughter disappeared like a bubble popping. "Right. And I don't know how I feel about that, or how I want to handle it. I mean …"

"Just like your dad," Sara whispered, reaching to give her arm a warm squeeze, her eyes full of sympathy.

"But you're gonna be rich," Kit chirped, "So you don't need a man, right? Except for a good ride once in a while. On his big hog." She waggled her brows.

Lindi smiled crookedly. "I should behave like a guy, and use him for sex, you mean?"

"Hear, hear." Sara raised her glass. "If you've found one who's good for more than bump, bump, and done, might as well get some of that."

Lindi clinked her glass with her friends and drank. "No, I'm not gonna be rich, but as long as everything checks out with the will, I'm at least out of the hole financially. Which means I can pay off my bank loan."

"Hmm, maybe not the best use of your money," Sara said. "Interest rates are so low right now, you may be better off investing. But we'll discuss that later. I want to know what you're going to do when Jack rolls back into town on his Harley."

"I just wanna know when I can meet his friend," Kit sighed.

Lindi and Sara exchanged a look. "Oh, sweetie," Lindi said. "I don't think Keys is the guy for you. Far as I can tell, he goes through women faster than clean underwear."

Kit sat back in her chair and crossed her arms. "I'm a big girl, and last time I looked, you ain't my mama."

Seeing the hurt behind her friend's defiance, Lindi winced. "I'm sorry. You're right. I guess it's just that I'm in over my head myself, and … I don't wanna drag you in after me."

Kit grinned fully this time, her full lips tipping up over one crooked incisor. "Okay. I'll forgive you … as soon as you introduce me to Keys."

Sara snorted. "You're both nuts."

Kit gave her a look. "Right. Like you won't go cray-cray when that certain hunk of man roars into your life. You're young, gorgeous, and you need to loosen the fuck up, woman."

Sara touched one hand to her French twist and shook her head. "Not gonna happen. Although, I may murder one, if the new office manager doesn't lighten up soon."

A week ago, Lindi realized with a pang, she would've said she was impervious to men too. But looking back over the last few days, she had gone a little crazy—and all because of Jack. If he'd been any other man, she'd have called the police on him and his cohorts, and she certainly wouldn't have fallen under his spell and into his bed.

Heat filled her body, and she pressed her thighs together against a swell of need. Remembering all that was Jack, it might just be worth any heartache she went through when he was gone.

Her phone burbled with a text. Lindi dug frantically in her purse, and pulled it out.

'In Oregon. Headed 4 Cali in mornin,' Jack's text read. 'Tying up loose ends. Back when I'm done. Be good.'

Lindi stared at his words, the heat of anger rising through her in a hot tide. "Be good, my butt," she muttered. "You can just wait for it, biker man."

Not bothering to answer the text, she tossed her phone back into her purse. Then she looked up and met her friends' fascinated gazes.

Sara shook her head. "His ass is fried, huh?"

Kit made an 'eek!' face. "Crispy as a rasher of bacon on Lindi's grill."

Lindi shrugged. "Let's just say I'm not going to be laying out the welcome mat when he finally rolls his 'big hog' back into town."

Sara sighed and turned to wave for their check. "Damn. I'm getting the check. You need to save your pennies for some really good chocolate ice cream."

"With dark chocolate chunks and loads of nuts," Kit added. "You're gonna need it."

They were not wrong.

Chapter Twenty-One

Friday

Jack sent another text Friday afternoon. Lindi thought about ignoring it, but curiosity won. Okay, and she wanted to know he was safe.

'Made it to Cali. Weather's real nice. U hire help at café yet?'

"Ha, ha. Kiss my ass," she muttered. "For your information, Jack, I'm hiring the best looking guy I can find. We'll see how you like that."

Showing great strength of will, she did not answer him.

Not long after, she received a text from Keys. Him, she was glad to hear from.

'How u doin, babe?'

'Fine & so's my car,' she texted back. 'Thx again.'

'Ur welcome. Hey, I know a guy who needs new cook job.' A local phone number followed. Then he sent a photo.

Lindi opened it, and stared at the man pictured, her jaw dropping. Keys' friend looked to be at least part Native American, lean and brown-skinned, with a long, ebony braid trailing over one shoulder. He was grinning into the sun at the camera, his dark eyes crinkled and his teeth a white slash in his hawkish face.

Lindi squinted at his name and then smiled to herself. "Hel-lo, Remington Redhawk," she murmured. "You are fuh-reaking perfect."

Her phone pinged. Keys again. 'Call Jack. He's pissed & taking it out on my ass.'

Poor Keys. She didn't want him to put up with Jack's sulking.

'I'm fine,' she texted Jack. 'Just a little hung over. Out last night. Enjoy your trip.'

There, let him wonder who she'd been drinking with, and hopefully assume the worst.

Next, she called Remington Redhawk and invited him to stop by the café that afternoon. Little did he know he was already hired. Well, as long as he wasn't a complete noob.

She was smiling as she sashayed into her room to shower and dress for the day.

Saturday

Remington, or Remi as he preferred to be called, was waiting outside the café when Lindi putted into her parking lot in the Caprice the next morning. In a faded red hoodie over a white tee, jeans and work boots, he looked to be her age. And yes, he was just as handsome in person.

"I parked my bike around back," he said. "That all right?"

A gleaming black motorcycle stood on the gravel behind the café, at a safe distance from the dumpster.

"Great parking spot," Lindi said. "Come on in and let's get started."

Remi was, as promised, a skilled fry cook. He tied a faded bandanna around his head to hold back any stray strands of long hair that escaped his braid—a look that he totally rocked. He wrapped on one of her black aprons, merely raising a dark brow at the bees, and got to work warming up the fryers and grills, and checking the ovens.

The day was fine, and they were busy from the time they opened the front doors until closing time. Lindi alternated between keeping an eye on Remi, showing him how she did things, and waiting tables. She had the idea once or twice that he was being patient with her, but the BeeHive's reputation now rested on his shoulders as well as hers, so she had to know he was either willing to do things her way, or demonstrate his way was better.

Between orders, he helped bus tables, put a table of rowdy college boys in their place by appearing silent and unsmiling at Lindi's elbow, and generally made himself indispensable.

When another loaded SUV pulled into the parking lot at ten thirty, Lindi called to Remi, "You mind staying a little later?"

"I'm good," he called back.

They stayed open until eleven-thirty, and then Lindi turned the sign on the front door to 'Closed', because they just weren't supplied or ready to serve lunches yet. She wanted to be, but had to choose a menu, get it printed up and a host of other details. Yikes, she was going to need a new soda fountain too.

But excitement lent wings to her feet and an extra sparkle to her smile as she contemplated the BeeHive's busy future. She couldn't wait to tell Jack how well things were going.

Not that he was around to tell. She scowled at the counter she was scrubbing. Apparently he wasn't interested, anyway, since he couldn't be bothered to phone her and have an actual conversation.

At noon, she and Remi sat down to eat a quick lunch of fried egg and bacon sandwiches with a heap of hash browns for him and bowls of mixed berries for both of them.

"So, you like working here?" she asked.

He gave her a considering look, and then shrugged, a glint of what looked like humor in his dark eyes. "Think I will, once my probation's over."

Lindi gave him a level look over her sandwich. "I just need to know you have the skill set you claim, and that you're flexible enough to change if I ask you to."

He forked up another bite of crisp hash browns, and nodded. "That's fair. Yeah, I like it here. Last place I worked in Spokane? Trendy, upscale clientele, but the worst boss ever. Bet the place won't stay open another year."

"They need Chef Gordon Ramsey," she said.

He grinned, looking much younger. "Love that show. Man, I'd pay to see him whip my ex-boss's ass into shape."

"I know, right? And, since you've worked at a variety of places, I'll consider any suggestions you want to make for the BeeHive."

"Cool. Can I help build the new lunch menu?"

Lindi thought this over as she took her last bite of sandwich. "Sure. I'm looking for solid American diner food, but with a fresh twist."

Remi nodded. "We can do that, no problem."

His calm confidence was contagious. Lindi beamed at him. "Yes, we can."

That night, Lindi was lying in bed, having nearly reached the climactic conclusion of her vampire romance, when her phone played the first few bars of a familiar country song. Frowning, she picked it up. Who had loaded Lady Antebellum's American Honey as their ringtone on her phone?

Jack—she should have known. Luckily for him, she was calm and mellow after her great day of business. "Hello?"

"Hey, honey. How you doin'?" he asked, his voice rough. In the background, she could hear loud music, voices and laughter. He and Keys were out for the evening.

"I'm fine," she said. "And you?"

He snorted. "Are we bein' fuckin' polite now? Tell me somethin' sweet, like you're wearin' that little peekaboo nightie I saw in your bureau drawer."

Lindi didn't know whether to end the call or laugh. She settled for rolling her eyes to herself. Only Jack would complain about her phone manners being too nice. "No, I'm wearing a tee shirt."

His voice lowered. "One o' mine?"

"Yes," she admitted, smoothing her free hand down over the soft fabric. His faded black Harley tee, actually, which she'd found tangled in the bed covers. It smelled like him, and the well-washed cotton was soft against her skin.

Jack's voice deepened. "That's good, honey. I like picturin' you in one of my shirts."

Longing pierced her. "When are you coming home?"

"When am I comin' home," he repeated. "Soon as I can. We got some shit to wrap up tomorrow, then we'll see."

"Well, that's … vague," she said.

"No, that ain't vague," he shot back. "That's how it's gotta be, Lindi. I'll be finished with my business here when I'm finished. Fuck, I'm tired, my ass is beat from sittin' my bike for a thousand miles, and it's already hotter'n hell down here. You think I don't have a hard-on, wishin' I was in that bed with you, think again. And you think you're not getting' a spankin' for reamin' my ass when I finally get the chance to talk to you, instead of bein' sweet, *think again*."

He missed her, and still wanted her? A smile breaking over her face, Lindi opened her mouth to tell him she wished he was in this bed too, although not for a spanking.

"Jack," said a husky, feminine voice through his phone. "Hey, baby. Crack said you were here and we came right down. C'mere and show me how you missed me."

Okay, whoever this woman was, her mouth had to be pretty darn close to Jack's face to be heard that clearly. Her eyes narrowing, Lindi waited for Jack to send the floozy on her way.

Instead, he replied, a smile in his voice. "Hey yourself, Coral."

"Jack?" Lindi's voice cracked on his name.

"I gotta go," he said to her. "Call me in the mornin', yeah?"

The call ended with a beep. Slowly, Lindi lowered her phone far enough to stare at the screen in disbelief. Some skank from his past showed up, and he hung up on her, Lindi?

"Oh, no, you did not just do that, Jack Moran," she whispered.

He left in the middle of the night, he communicated only when it suited him, and now this. She ran her fingers through her hair, narrowly refraining from yanking on it in sheer frustration. Was this how his father had treated his mother? If so, she had a new sympathy for the poor woman.

She wadded up Jack's tee shirt and hurled it off her front porch onto the communal lawn, then went back to bed in her usual sleepwear, which was in fact a peekaboo nightie, a Christmas gift from Cissie. It was cream with lace insets and ribbon ties.

Not that Jack Moran was ever going to see it. He'd probably never see his tee again, either. And wasn't that just too bad?

Chapter Twenty-Two

Sunday

Lindi staggered into the shower, then slugged down two cups of strong coffee while she dressed. She had dark shadows under her puffy eyes and a pale, grumpy face.

No wonder—she'd spent half the night lying awake, pretending she was not imagining Jack with the owner of that sultry voice. She was probably everything Lindi wasn't—tall, slender, self-assured. Heck, she probably had her own Harley and a leather miniskirt.

Lindi bundled her wet hair into a messy knot at the back of her head, flicked on the bare minimum of cosmetics, grabbed her purse and headed out to her car. The spring morning was cloudy and still, even the robins subdued in the newly leafed trees.

She'd driven the Caprice away from her parking spot when she suddenly realized she didn't remember unplugging her coffee pot. She had to turn around and go back, which made her late arriving at the BeeHive.

Remi was perched on the metal railing that framed one side of the café's front step. He simply lifted his chin in greeting and rose to follow her around back.

"Sorry you had to wait," Lindi said. "I'll get you a key."

"Bad night?" he asked.

"The worst." As she led the way into her café, Lindi waited for the familiar sights, sounds and smells to reassure her, and buoy up her mood.

But this time it didn't work.

Lindi worried the cloudy morning might bring fewer customers, but instead they were slammed from the moment they opened, first with fishermen, then with the families of cyclists and walkers, including two elderly couples in sturdy walking shoes who informed Lindi as she served their coffee that they remembered when the café had been open before, and they were delighted to return.

"The BeeHive," one of the men said, his faded eyes twinkling. "That mean you serve up honey with everything?"

Lindi ignored her aching head to smile back. "If that's the way you want it, you bet."

She had to force the smile for more reasons than her headache, if she were honest. The thought of what Jack might be doing so far from her, when he would return, and whether she should even want him to return thrummed in the back of her consciousness like a jarring, discordant rhythm.

A family with two toddlers moved into the next booth. The man caught Lindi's eye and snapped his fingers at her. "Highchair here."

Lindi blinked, because really? Had he just snapped his fingers at her like she was his minion? She forced herself to focus on the older people again. "Let me know when you're ready to order."

She greeted another group walking in the front door, and went to pull her one high-chair from a corner. Setting it by the family's table, she smiled with an effort. "Welcome to the BeeHive. Would you like—"

"We'd like water," the woman snapped, "You have sippy cups, don't you?"

"No, sorry," Lindi said. "I can bring the kids' drinks in juice glasses, if you like. Coffee?"

"I don't suppose you do lattes," the man sighed, as if put upon.

"You suppose right." She slapped two menus down on their table. "Let me know if you see anything in here you do like."

Then she turned on her heel and went to wait on another table.

"Well," the woman gasped behind her. "How rude."

One of the fishermen at the counter turned around and slid off his stool, hitching his pants up under his belly. "Oh, for Chrissake, this is a diner, not one 'o them fancy-ass coffee shops," he said, not in a quiet voice. "Best damn breakfast on the lake, too."

There was a moment of silence, and then a man at the other end of the café said, "Preach on, brother."

Several customers chuckled. Lindi managed not to join them, but she beamed at the fisherman as she rang up his order at the till. "Thank you. Have a great day of fishing."

He winked solemnly at her and lumbered out into the morning.

The snooty family followed on his heels.

"Betcha they won't be back," Remi muttered as he passed Lindi with his arms laden with plates of food.

He was no doubt correct. Lindi suffered a moment of worry, which lasted only until she discovered one of the toddlers had upended and squeezed a honey bear, leaving a large, sticky pool of honey on the table. Sheesh, she did not need customers like that.

The remainder of the morning rolled by, leaving Lindi battered in its wake.

"I wouldn't have survived that without your help," she told Remi, slumping at the counter over her fifth—or was it sixth—cup of coffee with cream. She was too exhausted to even worry about the calories.

He slid into the seat beside hers, setting a type-written sheet where they could both see it. "I know, boss. And here's some lunch menu ideas for you to look over, which will make me even more indispensable."

Tired, headachy and heart-sore as she was, Lindi huffed a laugh. "You're probably right. I'll look them over as soon as I can."

This afternoon, she needed a nap.

* * *

Jack had about had it with Lindi, honey sweet or not. She was playin' games with him, and he did *not* like it.

He'd rolled out of Coeur d'Alene Thursday morning beside Keys with a smile despite the chill of early dawn whipping past him on his Harley, remembering the things he'd done with her in that big hotel bed, and how good it had been. The way she gave it to him, so soft and generous, then went wild for him whether he gave her his hands, mouth or cock, it made him wanna throw back his head and howl to the wind.

And, damn, the way she'd come to him at the hotel had been sweet. She'd fixed herself up so sexy for him, and given him her apology and then the reasons why she'd behaved the way she did. She'd bared her soul—he could tell by the look in her big brown eyes, like she was fighting hard to lay it all out when what she wanted to do was hide it deep down where it was safe.

A man couldn't hope for better than that, a woman who thought he was worth that kind of pain, was willing to admit she was wrong, and explain why, so maybe she wouldn't smack him with that shit again. Instead of the same old, same old, like his ma and dad had done, two dogs chasing each other around in a circle, snapping and snarling.

He'd awakened Thursday morning early, with Lindi snuggled up to him, warm and soft and sweet, and his chest had filled with the solid, sweet conviction that this was good, real good. She'd dropped into his life in the most unexpected way possible, but not being stupid, he'd grabbed her and hung on. He wanted what they had to last. And to make it work, he was gonna pull up his ties to Cali, and send down roots here.

So he'd set out to do that, with his best friend by his side.

The ride was great—it was good to be back on the road with Keys at his side. They'd made good time over to Portland and south from there, and the fine spring weather held. Oregon was real pretty, they had some nice views of the coast, and it warmed up the farther south they rode.

But now it was Sunday and he was hot, tired, and saddle-sore from being on the bike for five days. He was also exhausted from negotiating the sale of his third share of a motorcycle parts store in Redding to the other two partners. It was profitable, they were glad to have it all, and since one of them was an asshole and the other his kiss-ass, Jack was glad to have his money *and* be done with them.

While there, he'd checked in with his dad, and listened to the old man badgering him to patch in to his local club. He'd then visited his mom, which was okay, as she was on her best behavior—probably because she could tell right away his dad had not been. He'd made sure she had everything she needed, and promised to call when he was safely home.

Then he and Keys headed back north to the redwoods, where Jack owned half of a bar in Eureka—a venture he'd landed in trying to help out a buddy. It had paid off big time, and now his buddy Gates and his wife were ready to buy Jack out. They were able to do so in a way that pleased everyone, especially Jack, who had never expected to make money on the deal.

Now Jack had his money, he was fuckin' tired of California traffic, and even the partying he and Keys had done with old friends hadn't been as much fun as Jack remembered. He wanted to be back in the cool north, with his new woman at his side, one he was considering making a life with.

Except that now she was playin' head games with him.

It was Sunday evening. He and Keys were relaxing at a beach-side chowder house and bar. They had their feet up on the railing of the verandah overlooking a beach where seals frol-icked in the shallows and gulls rode the evening breezes. Each had a cold beer in their hand, and a basket of clam fritters be-tween them while they waited for their fish and chips.

"You ready to head back to Idaho?" Keys asked. His lean face was sun and wind-burned, his hair hidden under a bandanna, his eyes behind shades. He had a scruff of beard that matched Jack's. No one to shave for on this trip.

"Thought I was," Jack growled, glaring at a seagull that was eyeing their clam fritters from a nearby post. "Now I ain't so sure. Lindi don't stop playing hard to get, she'll find me hard to get. Tried callin' her from that gas station, she didn't even pick up."

"You leave a message?" Keys' voice held no criticism, but Jack felt heat crawl up his neck anyway.

"No. Don't see why I should—she's been chatting with you all friendly on text, but not giving me diddly-squat. Don't need this shit, and didn't expect it from her."

Keys grunted, and took a long drink of his beer. "Well, your thing is pretty new. Don't give up yet, bro." He bent his head and fiddled with his phone, and Jack drank his beer and gazed moodily out at the ocean, silver in the early evening.

"New is one thing," Jack said. "Cold is another. I ain't puttin' up with that. She's got a problem, she can tell me."

Keys sighed, and handed Jack his phone. "Yeah, well here's your problem right here. You see, I *asked*."

Keys had texted *'Babe. U tryin' to fuck up this thing with J or what? Call him.'*

Lindi had replied *'Was he with that woman last nite?'*

Keys *'What woman?'* This Jack read aloud, his brows lowering in a thunderous frown. The whole conversation was beginning to sound like a bad replay of his parents' shit.

Lindi *'The one who was all over him when we talked. Coral.'*

Keys *'Only Coral I saw was Crack's old lady. He's built like a wall & mean as a snake.'* This was true, and Jack didn't like the asshole, but he seemed to treat Coral well.

Heat building in his head, Jack did not waste another second. He handed Keys' phone back, hit Lindi's number on his phone and waited.

"Um … hi?" she said, her voice hesitant.

"What the ever-loving fuck, Lindi?" Jack demanded. "I been gone three days and you're up to your old tricks. You maybe think of askin' me who I'm with or not with?"

"And you're up to your old tricks too, Jack," she fired back, her voice rising. "Did you wake me up to say goodbye before you left? *No.* Did you call me every evening to tell me about your day, and say you missed me? *No.* Did you hang up on me when another woman was cooing in your ear? *Yes!*" She was breathing hard by the time she finished, and he could picture her eyes narrowed, her mouth prissy, one hand on her hip.

Grinning at this picture in his mind, Jack relaxed a little, because he guessed maybe he saw her point.

"You want the truth? Yeah, I was with Coral once or twice. We had us some good times, but she's with Crack now, and when I say *with*, I mean that dude will rip my head off if I do more'n kiss her on the cheek."

"Good," Lindi muttered.

"Which I don't wanna do anyway," Jack went on. "Far as that other shit, would've called you to *chat*, but didn't have the brain cells left the first couple of days, or any privacy. Keys and I rode hard to get here, then had to hunt down the guys we wanted to see. Got right to business negotiations. After that …" he shook his head. "Never done this couple's shit before. Guess I can learn, though. With the right incentive, that is."

"And that incentive would be?" Lindi demanded, her voice full of suspicion.

He chuckled. "I call you, talk about my day and shit. Then I get phone sex."

"*Jack*!"

Keys chuckled, and Jack met his friend's gaze and laughed with him for the first time all day. It felt good.

"You are impossible," Lindi said, but now there was a smile in her soft voice. "And so's your buddy—I hear him laughing."

"Me? I'm all yours, honey. An' when I call you back later, I'll prove it."

He shoved his phone back in his pocket with a smile, looking forward to later.

"You two gonna make a go of it, you think?" Keys asked.

Jack watched a pair of seals chasing each other through the shallows just off the beach, spray flashing silver in the late sun. He'd bet anything the one chasing was the male, trying to get him some.

"I think so," he said. "Never thought I'd be sayin' this, but I think she's the woman for me. She's got her business and goals, and they mesh with some ideas I got. And she's ... I dunno, just the right combination of sweet and hot."

He grinned. "She's funny as hell—man never knows what's gonna come out of her mouth. Y'know, bro, I've known women I enjoyed shootin' the shit with, and women who were the hottest fucks ever. Lindi's the first woman I ever met that I wanted to talk to *and* fuck and I ain't sure which I like the best."

Keys nodded. "Sounds good. I like her—hope maybe I find one that good for myself one of these days."

Jack held out his bottle and they toasted that.

And later, he proved to Lindi that he was all hers, even on the road. With their phones on speaker, he lay in his hotel bed and worked his cock with his hand while she employed one hand between her legs and the other on her nipple as he instructed. She whimpered his name when she came, and he let go and came hard, his cum pulsing onto his bare belly and abs. He swiped it off with a hand towel.

"Now that," he said, his voice lazy, "was phone sex. Although next time I'm gonna want video too."

She gasped. "*Jack.* You're not getting it, mister."

He gave a low, dirty chuckle, but then he yawned deeply, relaxed as a man only is after release. "Damn, I gotta get some sleep. We're out early tomorrow mornin'. One more deal to finish." And thank God it was Keys', so all Jack had to do was hang with his friend.

"And then you can come back to Coeur d'Alene?" she asked, a wistful note in her voice.

"Don't say it that way," he corrected her, frowning at the ceiling.

"Um, what?"

"Last time you asked, 'when are you comin' home'. I like it like that." He did. Now that they had their little tiff settled, he could not wait to get back there.

"Okay," she agreed, her voice soft as velvet. "When are you coming home, Jack?"

Warmth flowed up through him, settling deep in his chest. "Soon, honey," he promised. "Soon. And by the way, no more little misunderstandings like this one, okay? 'Cause I don't do that cheating on the road shit. I'm with you, I'm *with you*. You get that?"

"Yes, Jack. I get that."

"Good."

Fabric rustled as she moved, and she yawned. "Oh, I miss you. Phone sex is fun, but it's not as good as the real thing."

"That's for damn sure. Night, honey."

"Night, Jack."

He snapped off the bedside light and was about to set his phone on the bedside table when it pinged. He grinned when he saw she'd sent him an emoticon of a smiling honeybee.

He texted one back that said 'Zzz', and then added, 'Go to sleep, woman.'

And then he went to sleep himself, and slept better than he had in days.

Chapter Twenty-Three

Wednesday

Jack and Keys rolled back into Coeur d'Alene late on a warm spring afternoon that had the whole town out of doors, including Lindi's coed neighbors, giggling as they washed one girl's car, clad in bikini tops and shorts, despite the fact it was only in the low seventies.

Lindi sat on her front porch, enjoying the warm sun on face and her bare arms—she wore her new jeans with black lace trim, the black tank and her short-sleeved black cardi that dipped just under her breasts. She'd fixed her hair and makeup with extra care, because her biker man was due at any moment.

She alternated between admiring her newly painted hot pink toes in her black sandals, and checking the clock on her phone every few moments, because Jack had promised to be home by three o'clock at the latest.

Home. Each time she remembered Jack's insistence that she ask him when he was coming home, instead of merely when he was coming back to town, Lindi felt a shiver of pleasure followed by a cold niggle of uncertainty. She'd been so sure that Jack would leave soon—her, if not the area.

So what were they doing now? Playing house, or on the way to something more permanent? She'd shared her difficulty with trusting a man to keep his word, and he'd shared his anger at not being taken at his word ... so where did that leave them?

The coeds squealed as one of them splashed the other with cold water from the hose. Lindi turned her head to watch the victim splash back, and both of them gave exaggerated shrieks, flapping their arms and giggling. She smiled to herself, remembering playing that way with friends ... although she'd been in high school. It seemed college was a kind of emotional extension of that carefree time. Must be nice.

Herself, she'd begun working in high school, as had Cissie. And Lindi had never stopped. Her waitressing jobs had segued into cooking part time, where she'd learned to run a grill and a kitchen. And then she'd found the BeeHive. But looking back, she realized with surprise that she wouldn't change her path, not at all.

She was only twenty-six and already owned her own business. Not bad for a high-school grad. And now, with her inheritance from Dave, she was independent. She wanted Jack, but she didn't need him to take care of her.

The deep growl of big motors rumbled, scattering her thoughts like the spray coming from the girls' hose.

Her heart leaping with excitement, Lindi sat up straight as two big, gleaming Harleys rolled up the street, and slowed to a stop at her curb. The lead rider dropped both booted feet to the pavement, cut his motor, and reached up to push his sunglasses onto his bandanna-wrapped head. Then he gave her a hard look.

"Woman, get your ass over here and gimme some honey," Jack ordered in a deep, rough voice.

Behind him, Keys grinned.

Lindi rose, dusted off the back of her jeans and sauntered across the few feet of sidewalk and grass as Jack lifted one leg over his bike and stood, looking big and dangerous and bad-ass in his black leather jacket and chaps over faded jeans, his too-long, sandy hair curling from under the bandanna. Then, as he gave her that heavy-lidded look, his eyes gleaming, she let her smile of welcome loose, and leapt into his arms, wrapping her arms around his neck and her legs around his hips.

His scruff of beard scraped her skin as he grabbed her, one arm under her ass, the other around her back, and kissed her, long and deep and wet. When they finally parted just enough to breathe, she pressed kisses to his cheek, the corner of his mouth. She wanted to eat him up, even sweaty and covered in the remnants of sunscreen.

"Oh, Jack, I missed you so much."

He kissed her again and flexed his burgeoning erection into her center, demonstrating wordlessly that he felt the same.

"Hey, you two, take it inside," Keys called. "Although, you get the neighbor girls steamed up a little more, maybe I can get lucky too."

Jack looked over her shoulder and grinned at the coeds. "Give it a go, bro. We'll see you later."

"Later. Bye, Lindi."

"Bye, Keys," she called, her gaze on Jack as he carried her across the grass and up onto her porch. She caught one glimpse of the coeds, wide-eyed gazes moving from her and Jack to Keys, who still sat his bike, watching the girls. With a bandanna wrapped around his long, silver hair, his eyes blue against his tanned skin, he as usual rocked the biker look.

Sheesh, he might get lucky.

She totally had to keep Kit away from him.

Then Jack carried her into her apartment, set her down in the living room and stepped back just far enough to unzip his leather jacket and haul it off. Lindi forgot everyone but him.

"Strip those jeans off," he said, his voice rough. "I need inside you now."

"I need you inside me too." With a shiver of excitement, Lindi unfastened her jeans and shoved them down, along with her

Victoria's Secret panties. Jack watched, his face taut and hungry, and she watched just as hungrily as he yanked his own long-sleeved tee up and off, and unfastened his jeans.

His bandanna fell off, and he ran one hand through his hair, leaving it standing on end. Lindi's fingers itched to run through the unruly waves.

She started to pull her tank up, but had it no farther than her breasts when he swooped, lifting her up against his hot, bare torso and carried her the few feet to the kitchen counter. He set her down just long enough to pull a condom from his pocket and rip it open with his teeth.

"There's that pretty little blonde pussy," he said as he sheathed himself. "You wet for me?"

"Yes, Jack." Lindi ran her hands greedily down his hot, smooth skin, over corded abs and the grooves that pointed the way to his cock, spring out thick and long from the dark thatch of curls at his groin.

She reached for him, but he took over, moving close to stroke the broad head of his cock into her wet furrow. "Hang on, honey, this is gonna be fast and hard."

His words sent her flying up the steep slope of need. "Yes. Hurry," she urged, delving her hands into his jeans to grab his ass. The taut swells of muscle tensed in her grasp, and he shoved deep inside her on the first thrust. It hurt a little, but still she nearly came just from finally having him inside her.

"That's right," he approved, his hands holding her open on the edge of the counter while he began to move, taking her with swift, driving strokes. "Grab me and hold me tight, honey. Take it the way I wanna give it to you."

Lindi complied, and Jack stiffened, his head falling back as he shuddered with completion. Nearly there herself, she bit back a whine of dismay as he pulled her against his chest, his face in her hair and sighed deeply.

"So sweet," he muttered. "My woman's good to me when I come home."

She smiled up at him as he lifted his head and gave her a gleaming look, his face flushed and relaxed. "I like being good to you, Jack."

"I know, honey. Also I fired too fast, and you didn't get there. Gonna fix that now."

He slid one big, calloused hand between them, and found her swollen clitoris. He circled it with his thumb, and bent to kiss her. "Come for me, Lindi. Let me feel it."

With his cock still heavy inside her, and the slippery caress of his big thumb, Lindi came for him, whimpering into his mouth as her pussy convulsed with pleasure.

"Mm-mm," he approved. " I feel that … sweet."

He pulled out of her, but stayed her with his hands on her open thighs when she would have slipped to the floor. "This time, you come on my mouth. Been waitin' days to get another taste of you."

And then her bad biker man dropped to his knees and buried his face between her thighs, inhaling deeply. "Fuckin' love the way you smell, honey," he growled. "Jesus fuck. Sweetest pussy ever."

Then he raked his tongue up through her swollen labia. As Lindi watched, her hands in his hair, he teased her by thrusting it as deep as he could into her pussy a few times, and laughing when she gasped, "Jack."

"Take off your top," he ordered. "Wanna see your tits while I eat you."

Eagerly, Lindi complied, although he didn't make it easy, giving her clit teasing flicks of his tongue and then going back to fucking her with his tongue. By the time she had her bra off, she was quivering with need again.

"Jack, please," she breathed.

"You need to come again, honey?" He pressed a kiss to her inner thigh, and carefully thrust one, then two long, rough fingers inside her.

She nodded quickly, her hair flicking her bare shoulders.

"Good. Play with your tits for me, and tell me where you want my tongue."

Lindi froze for an instant, self-consciousness niggling through her sexual heat. But Jack kissed her thigh again, and pressed his fingers against her G-spot, and she melted.

With Jack, there were no rules, no restrictions. She was free to show him her need and want, free to let him see all of her. She could take care of herself in the ways that mattered. And realizing this freed her like never before. It was better to be vulnerable and alive than to be barricaded against the stings of life.

She cupped the heavy weight of her breasts in her hands, enjoying the silkiness of her own skin. Then she took her erect nipples in her fingertips, and squeezed them, rolling them between her thumbs and forefingers.

"Jesus fuck," Jack growled. "So pretty." He surveyed her from his fingers in her pussy to her breasts, and up to her face. His eyes blazed at her. "Fuckin' perfect for me, Lindi."

"Jack," she breathed, joy filling her until she felt as light as air. "Please—I need your mouth on me."

He caressed her G-spot again. "Where, honey?"

"On my-my clit," she managed, heat suffusing her face and chest, even as her pussy clenched around his fingers.

He didn't miss either, his grin widening. "You want my tongue on your sweet little clit? Want me to lick up your honey till you scream for me?"

She nearly came right then. "Uh-huh," she breathed.

Then she watched as he leaned in and put out his tongue to caress her there where she was most sensitive, and her world narrowed down to the man between her knees and what he was doing with his rough fingers and his wet butterfly tongue.

She opened her mouth to say his name, but only a moan came from her throat, then another, rising in intensity and volume as she came again, this time so long and hard she could finally sit up no more and fell back, banging her head against a cupboard door, her hands still in his hair.

Afterward, Jack rose, picked her up and bore her into her bedroom, where he set her on the bed and then followed her down, and proceeded to fuck her again.

As her old bed creaked under them, more loudly with the increasing intensity of his thrusts, Jack—without pausing in what he was doing—lifted his head.

"We gotta get you a new bed."

Since Lindi was scaldingly aware her neighbors on both sides and upstairs no doubt could tell exactly what was transpiring in her bedroom, she could not argue.

"Fuck, honey, I'm comin'," Jack groaned. At this, Lindi forgot everything but the joy of him in her arms. This time they cried out together their mingled pleasure.

As Jack collapsed in her arms, a damp, heavy weight of exhausted man, Lindi wrapped her arms and legs around him and smiled to herself in the late afternoon dimness of her bedroom.

Jack roused himself to roll off of her. He rubbed his thumb over the corner of her mouth, and chuckled. "I know that smile. Says you pleased me and you like that."

Lindi sat up and reached for the quilt folded at the end of the bed, and pulled it up over both of them. "It also says I just got three orgasms, courtesy of a bad-ass biker. Now why don't you take a nap? You look like you're about to crash."

Jack grunted, his eyes already slipping shut. "Just a short one. Then I'm takin' you out to supper."

After sleeping for an hour, Jack went out to unload his bike. Lindi fretted that there was nowhere for him to stow his things in her tiny apartment, but he tossed his duffel in one corner by the bed, gave her a lazy grin and told her not to worry about it.

They never made it out to supper, but as Lindi had a well-stocked refrigerator this time, she happily cooked for them. And Jack told her she was right, her meatloaf and twice-baked potatoes were to die for.

Sunday

Lindi's alarm went off at five. Before she could move, a heavy hand pressed down on her back, and Jack rolled to her in the bed, all sleep-warmed naked man and a hard cock pressing into the crease of her ass.

She groaned into her pillow. "Can't. Gotta get up."

"Not until I get my morning pussy," he rasped in her ear, already getting busy with a condom.

"Jack," she whined, because of course she'd rather stay in bed with him than get up and step into a shower and rush off into the chilly dawn, "I don't have time."

His hand worked between her thighs, and he stroked her. "Yeah, you do. I set your alarm fifteen minutes earlier while you were washin' up last night. Fuck, I love how you wake up wet for me."

Since he pressed kisses across her back, his lips soft and whiskers rough on her sensitive skin as he petted her, Lindi decided to forgive him for messing with her phone.

Then he slid a pillow under her hips and fucked her thoroughly, his fingers on her clit, and she decided he could do anything he wanted with her phone. She may have said this aloud, because after he groaned his release, he dropped his head onto her shoulder and laughed into her hair. "Fuck, woman, only you could make me laugh when I'm comin'."

Then he slapped her ass and pulled back the covers. "Up. You got a café to run."

"Bossy," she grumbled as she curled to a sitting position on the edge of the bed, but when he pulled her back for a slow, thorough kiss, she participated with so much enthusiasm he released her with reluctance.

"Get up now, or I'll have you under me again, and Remi'll have to run the place himself."

Remi probably could do this with one hand tied behind his back, but it was her café, so Lindi got up.

Chapter Twenty-Four

That afternoon, Jack took Lindi for the promised ride on his motorcycle.

Clad in her biker chick apparel, Lindi donned her new helmet and sashayed out to climb on the back of Jack's big silver Harley behind him, careful to put her feet where he told her and keep her leg away from the tailpipe, which he informed her could give third degree burns—which was one reason bikers wore heavy boots and leathers.

He showed her how to hang on to him, and then revved up the big bike. Nerves and excitement jumped in Lindi's middle like popcorn as the vibrations of the big motor reverberated up through her legs, her ass and her torso.

She nearly squealed like a teenager. However, she didn't think Jack would appreciate hearing that in his ear, so she contained herself.

They rolled down her street past quiet homes, a few joggers and cyclists, swung left toward Sherman, and braked at the stop sign.

"Lean with me on the turns," Jack called, "otherwise you're fighting me and the bike."

"Okay."

He lifted his chin and grinned, and then accelerated out onto Sherman. A few blocks later, they took the exit up to the highway, and roared eastward up a long hill and over the Centennial Bridge, the lake gleaming far below them.

That was the beginning of what was for Lindi, who had never been much for speed sports, a magical journey.

She felt as if she and Jack were part of the landscape, one with the road as they glided south, twisting and turning along the eastern shore of the big lake, through forest lands, past cabins and fancy lake homes, with the blue waters of the lake sparkling in the spring sun.

Once, as they slowed to admire a view of the lake below, Jack turned his head enough to smile back at her. Lindi squeezed him with her arms and smiled back.

They rode south to Carlin Bay, a winding journey of about thirty miles, and slowed to cruise into the parking lot of a small gas station and store, with a bar near the docks.

"Well, what d'ya think?" he asked her as he parked the bike and waited for her to step down.

Lindi hung onto his arm for a moment, waiting for her legs to stop feeling so lax and rubbery. Then she lifted her helmet off and smiled at him. "I love it! Can we ride every day?"

Jack grinned back at her, a slash of white in his tanned face. "Nah, but I'll take you on a road trip soon. Go see some new country."

She nodded eagerly. "Okay."

Jack bought them each a soda, which they drank wandering the docks.

"I might get a boat," he said, looking around at the pleasure craft moored in the small marina.

"Kind of like a motorcycle on the water, huh?" Lindi asked.

He laughed. "Yeah, only you'll be in a bikini."

"And you'll be in swim trunks," she agreed. Picturing this nearly gave her a mini-orgasm.

Then she squinted up at him, tipping her head to hide from the bright sun pouring over his shoulder. "So ... does that mean you're staying around here?" she asked, her heart beating double-time. Buying a boat implied staying here in lake country.

Jack shifted so the sun wasn't in her eyes. He gave her a quiz-zical look and shook his head, grinning crookedly. "Fuck me, I'm sorry, honey. Guess I haven't exactly shared my plans, have I?"

She shook her head uncertainly.

He pulled her to him, his hands on the small of her back the way he liked, and smiled down at her.

"I'm stayin', Lindi. I've cut all my ties to Cali, and I've had enough ramblin' around. I like this place, like the lakes, the people, and the open spaces. I'm gonna look around, find a business to buy, or invest in. Prob'ly even rent a house, or buy one. What d'ya think of that?"

"I like it," she breathed.

"Good, 'cause my plans involve spendin' my nights in your bed, or you in mine," he told her. "And us figurin' out where this is goin' with you and me."

"You've had enough Corals too?" she blurted.

He pulled her closer, his gaze going hot, but with a new edge of tenderness that made her heart flutter.

"Yeah, I have. Knew the minute I saw you lookin' at me, I could have you. But then I realized, spendin' time with you, honey … that went both ways. Knew you could have me, too, anytime you wanted me."

"Oh, Jack," she whispered. Good thing he was holding on to her, or she'd float right up off this dock.

He kissed her, a deep, hot kiss that tasted of sunshine and Jack, and then they climbed back on his bike and rode home.

They met Keys for dinner and drinks at a small brewpub on Sherman.

He was staying at a small motel on East Sherman, within walking distance of bars and restaurants and the lake.

"Don't like fancy shit," he told Lindi. "I'm a simple man."

Lindi looked into his twinkling blue eyes. He might not like fancy, but she had her suspicions that Jack's friend was far from being a simple man. Still waters ran deep, as her mama always said.

Jack chuckled over his glass of amber ale. "Don't think she's buyin' your country boy shit, Keys."

Keys lifted his own glass of dark stout to Lindi. "Got yourself a smart one, Jack."

"And she can hear you both," Lindi said, poking her finger into Jack's ribs. She took another sip of her own beer, a light wheat brew that she was still trying to decide if she liked. She just wasn't a beer drinker.

She was saved from more teasing by the arrival of their supper, a huge, aromatic artisan pizza loaded with a selection of smoked meats, olives, onions, artichokes and other veggies, along with, according to the menu, five cheeses.

She'd been pleasantly surprised by Jack and Keys agreement to try the brewpub's most complex pizza. Dave, bless his home-town boy heart, had refused to eat anything but pepperoni on his, Kit was just as picky, and Sara always wanted the lowest calorie version.

Lindi guessed living in California had broadened Jack's tastes. As for Keys, God only knew.

Jack ordered another round of beers for the men, and a glass of chardonnay for her.

"Because it's too fuckin' painful watchin' you make that face every time you take a drink of beer," he told her, screwing up his own face to mimic her distaste.

She poked him in the ribs again, and he laughed and grabbed her, pulling her in for a kiss.

"You get her on the back of your bike yet?" Keys asked.

"I did," Jack said. "And after she loosened up, she did good."

Lindi beamed. "It was fabulous," she told Keys. "We rode south all the way to Carlin Bay. That's what, thirty or forty miles?" she asked Jack. She leaned from one side to the other in her chair snaked her hand through the air to show the winding road. "I loved it."

Jack gave her a squeeze. "And when we got back, she showed me how much. The perfect woman."

Lindi blushed. She had, and it had been hard and fast. Evidently the big engine purring between their legs turned Jack on as much as it had her. And later, she'd also showed him how much she appreciated his plans to stay here with her. Jack had enjoyed that, a lot. And she'd loved pleasing him so much she'd come with her hand between her legs and her mouth full of him.

Keys sat back in his chair, grinning at them, like he had a pretty good idea why they were both so pleased with life. With his lean frame, ponytail, leather vest and silver pendants, along with the silver rings on each hand, and light eyes, he reminded Lindi of the picture of a wolf she'd seen, relaxing with its pack, nearly looking as if it were laughing at the camera.

And Jack, big and broad in his usual tee, this one brown with a copper and silver Indian cycle logo, the long sleeves pushed up over his brawny forearms, his sandy blond hair mussed as always, laughing down at her with his heavy arm hanging around her shoulders, well, he was simply the sexiest man in the place, and possibly on the planet.

A trio of thirty-ish women walked by on their way out, and Lindi did not miss their sidelong looks at Jack and Keys, and finally at her. She smiled to herself. They were trying to figure what she had that they didn't, to be with not one, but two hot bikers.

"What're you smilin' at?" Jack asked, picking up his piece of pizza with his free hand to take a big bite.

"I'm happy," she said. And as she picked up her own pizza and took a hot, cheesy, flavorful bite, she realized that this was truer than it had ever been. Her life was like this pizza—it had gone from plain and sparse to loaded.

Dave had been her first love, but she'd lost him. And then Jack had roared into her world, daring her to open up the deepest parts of herself to him. It had taken all her courage to do so, but now she was learning that only this kind of daring brought true happiness.

"You're happy," he repeated. "That's good, honey. Gonna do everything I can to keep you that way."

Lindi smiled at him. "I know."

When she surfaced from her Jack-induced haze of contentment, Lindi noticed Jack tilting his head at Keys, as if encouraging him to speak. Keys nodded, and she waited.

"So, babe," Keys said to her. "Got a proposition for you. You contacted a Realtor yet about the property?"

"Yes. Why, do you know someone who might want to buy in?"

"Yep," he said. "Me. Not all of it, but the chunk that includes the shop and home site, and enough acreage around it to keep neighbors out of my hair."

"Oh," she said. "Um, why do you want it?"

Keys wanted to stay here too? Her mind reeled. He was Jack's best friend of course, but he was also his MC brother. If he stayed, did that mean he and Jack would be off with the club all the time, partying and doing mysterious and probably illegal activities that Jack would refuse to share with her?

Keys grinned at her. "'Cause that's what I do, babe. Work on vehicles. It runs with a motor and tires, I can fix it, rebuild it, etceter-ah."

He leaned forward. "I want twenty acres, to include the road in. That'll give me some privacy when you sell the other chunks, and ensure I never lose the right-of-way."

"Well, okay," Lindi said slowly. How could she say no? He was Jack's best friend.

Jack chuckled, but Keys raised his brows. "Okay? That's it? You don't wanna hear my offer, and maybe talk to your Realtor, counter it?"

"I don't need to," she said, and it was true. "You're Jack's best friend, which means he's in favor. I'd rather have you up there than some stranger. And I also know you won't try to cheat Jack, so you won't lowball me. I just have one, um, condition."

"What's that?" Jack asked curiously.

She looked from him to his friend. "No … overtly illegal activities going on up there, and no huge ass MC parties with bonfires and women and all that implies. I plan to sell the other parcels too, and people who can afford to buy out here don't want, you know, that kind of commotion."

She felt a little sick as she finished speaking, because what if Keys shook his head and told her she was a hardass bitch, and then Jack got mad at her for dissing his friend?

Instead, Keys gave her a look of approval, his blue eyes kindling with warmth. "Knew it. You are a sharp woman as well as a sweetheart, Lindi Carson. No, I won't try to lowball you, and while I reserve the right to party at my place, you and

Jack will likely be there for most of 'em, and we'll keep the commotion to a redneck level, not MC crazy-ass."

"Thank you," she said, sagging with relief.

Jack burst out laughing and pulled her over into a hug, pressing a kiss to her temple.

"You're right, bro," he said. "She's one in a million, sweet and feisty. You weren't even surprised, were you?" he asked her.

"Not really. I saw the way Keys looked that shop over, and the vehicles in it. And when he hauled my Caprice up there to work on it himself instead of taking it to another shop ..." she shrugged.

"Wasn't gonna give it to another shop where they'd over-charge you for simple tune-up," Keys said in clear disgust. "Although I gotta tell you, babe, you need to unload that car on the local craigslist and get you something more reliable. Your engine is showing deep wear, and the carburetor needs rebuilt. Not to mention it has no style."

"It's fine for now," she said.

"We'll get her somethin' else, don't you worry," Jack said over her.

She gave him a look and he returned it with interest. "You really think I'm lettin' my woman drive an unreliable POS when I can get her somethin' better?"

"Stop being sweet when I'm trying to economize," she told him.

"False economy," he shot back. "You're only as safe as your vehicle, whether it's a bike or a car. Gotta be able to depend on it to get you there, especially when you're a woman."

"Got a choice vintage Blazer sittin' up there in that shop," Keys put in.

Lindi shuddered. "You know what? You can have that Blazer—if you'll either repaint it or sell it out of state, somewhere I don't have to look at it and remember Darrell stalking me in it—and maybe running his own brother off the road with it."

"Deal," he said, raising his beer to her, his face solemn. "Agree, you shouldn't have to see that. I'll make it my first sale, but you'll get half the profits, and you can donate 'em to the local shelter for all I care."

Lindi raised her wineglass in return. "Deal. The Union Gospel Mission has a women and children's' center here." Then she giggled. "Can you imagine the look on Darrell's face if he knew his precious Blazer was being sold, half for the women's shelter?"

Keys exchanged a look of amusement with Jack. "Damn, I like that. And for giving us that fine picture, let's make it one hundred percent of the profits to the shelter."

They all toasted this.

"Now," Keys said, "I just gotta get me a woman. Lindi, you have any friends as pretty and sweet as you?"

Uh-oh. Lindi nearly chugged her wine in one go. "I do, but ... Sara works for the DA's office, and Kit ... I'm not sure she's your type either."

"Is she the redhead or the blonde?" Jack asked.

Lindi looked at him.

"You got a photo of you and two other women in that digital photo frame on your dresser," he said. "Not your mom and sis, they're in different shots. So, is Kit the redhead? I'm bettin' she is."

"If she's a redhead, she's my type," Keys said, his eyes twinkling.

Lindi bit her lip, not sure how to inform Jack's tough, biker best friend that if he hurt Kit, Lindi would find a way to hurt him. And it wouldn't do any good to warn Kit against his love 'em and leave 'em ways, because with Kit's background, that's all she knew.

She sighed to herself. "I'll introduce you." She just hoped she was being a good friend by doing so.

Chapter Twenty-Five

Monday

Lindi woke slowly, wincing as a shaft of spring sunlight hit her in the eyes.

Ugh, déjà vu, the blinds were crooked again. She reached for her phone and squinted at the time. Seven thirty, oh crap! She needed to get up two hours ago!

Then she remembered that she'd asked Remi to open the Bee-Hive this morning, and sagged back into her pillow with relief. She closed her eyes and considered pleasurably the idea that she could just go back to sleep if she wanted to.

She'd been kept up late by her lover, who'd been in a randy mood when they got back from their dinner with Keys.

She smiled to herself as she remembered the naughty twinkle in Jack's eye as he claimed it was her fault for being so hot in her biker mama attire, and the way he'd demonstrated his approval.

Jack shifted behind her in the bed, his hard, hairy knee connecting with her hip. Lindi moved away—carefully, as she was already on the edge of the bed. He liked to fall asleep holding her, but she was learning that at some point, he always turned into a total bed hog. He was the reason king-sized beds had been invented.

She turned over, away from the sunlight, gave Jack's leg a shove and yawned, her eyes drifting shut again. It had only been two weeks ago that he walked into her café and her life, and proceeded to scare the daylights out of her. It had been a bumpy ride, but worth every minute to get to where they were now.

Which meant Jack was right ... love's sweetness was worth the sting.

Lindi jolted awake, her eyes flying open. Love? Wait a minute, when she'd gone to him and apologized, he'd said her sweetness was worth her sting, but he hadn't said anything about *love*.

And again, when he'd told her yesterday that he was staying, and wanted to be with her, still nothing about love.

Her heart pounding as if she'd been running, she pushed herself up onto her elbow and stared down at her lover. Sprawled out across the rumpled sheets, his big, muscular body taking up most of her old bed, his hair mussed in all directions by her hands, his eyes closed, mouth open slightly as he slumbered, he was the picture of male decadence.

He smacked his lips, and one of his eyes cracked open. "What?" he grunted. "Somethin' wrong?"

Lindi made a sound that veered between a whimper and a squeak. "Oh, my God," she blurted. "This wasn't supposed to happen. *I'm in love with you*!"

Then, realizing what she'd revealed, she bolted for the edge of the bed. But even barely awake, Jack was too fast for her. Like the big predator he was, he reacted instantly. He clamped his arm around her waist, levered one leg around hers and rolled with her, pinning her under him in the middle of the big bed.

She stared up at him, panic stopping her breath, shoving ineffectually at his broad, hairy chest. What if he said something kind, like, 'Look, babe, I really like you, but I'm not down with this love shit,' or what if he laughed at her, like she was sweet but clueless, because all they had was great sex and some fun times going for them?

"Let me go," she mumbled. "I—I have to pee."

"Nuh-uh." Jack kissed her, hard and swift, then lifted his head just far enough to give her a look blazing with heat and passion and tenderness. "You gotta do nothin' except settle, and listen to me."

He framed her face with his big hands. "Love you too, Lindi."

She drew a hiccupping breath and stared up at him, shock reverberating through her.

"Y-you do?"

He laughed, deep in his chest, and kissed her again, this time slow and tenderly. "I do," he whispered against her lips. "But I'll point out, you're doin' it again, doubtin' what I say."

"Oh, my God," Lindi breathed, happiness swelling inside her till she felt incandescent. "Jack." She slipped her arms around him, holding on to him. "Sorry. I … I believe you."

"Say it again," he ordered, his nose brushing hers, his gaze locked with hers.

"I love you," she said. "I do. But ... it's just so fast." Along with the happiness, nerves popped, those bees buzzing around in her middle.

He gave her a squeeze, calming and soothing. "Sometimes it's slow, sometimes fast. Still real, honey."

Her biker man philosopher. Lindi nodded. "Okay."

He flexed his big body, pressing her into the soft mattress, and she felt something else real prodding her. His cock, hot and hard and swollen all over again.

He shifted, tugging the thong to one side and making a place for himself between her thighs, and then slid into her, gazing into her eyes as he did so. "Been around, honey, a lot. But I'm yours now. All of me. For good."

Lindi's heart nearly burst with happiness, and she gave a shiver of sheer pleasure as he prodded deep inside her. "And I'm yours, Jack. All of me, for good." She lifted her legs to wrap them around his lean hips, and drew him even deeper, a croon of satisfaction in her throat as he nudged against her womb.

He shuddered, and groaned, dropping his forehead to hers. "Jesus fuck, so sweet, the way you respond to me. Wanna stay right here, all day and all night, with you holdin' me so tight."

Her pussy clenched around his hot, silken girth. "Oh, Jack."

"Fuck," he muttered, and kissed her, deep and wet. Then he slid his arms around her and lifted her up with him so he sat on his heels in the bed, Lindi in his lap, wrapped around him like a vine. He tugged her nightie off so her bare breasts were against his chest.

Slowly, he began to move inside her, every stroke so deep it was nearly painful, but also sending pleasure streaking through her pussy, and up through the rest of her body.

In this position, he controlled every move, how fast and how deep.

"Give me your tit, honey," he urged.

She let go of him to lift her breasts in her hands, and he lifted her higher with his arm under her bottom and bent to suck one nipple deep into his mouth. The hot, wet suction combined with his cock inside her drove her wild.

"Jack," she whimpered, holding his head to her. "Oh, my God. Harder."

He gave it to her harder with his mouth, and then switched to the other breast. Lindi screamed as she began to come helplessly around him. "Jack. I love you."

When she was finished, he lifted his head and kissed her mouth again. "Good girl. Now take me with you, yeah?"

"Yes," she breathed, kissing him back. "Anything you want."

"I know, honey. Fuck, the things I'm gonna teach you. But for now, ride me. Ride me sweet and hard and wild. Wanna see your tits bounce while you take me there."

He rolled back in the bed, with Lindi astride him, and she rode him, loving the way he watched her, the way he stiffened, and then went rigid, his cock pulsing inside her when he lost control.

His big hands clamped on her hips, and she felt heat flood her. Suffused with delight, Lindi came again with her man, taking in all that was him and giving it all to him.

Afterward, Jack pulled her down onto his hot, damp chest, his arms tight around her, his breath hard in her hair. Their hearts thundered together.

He stroked her back, fondled her bottom, and pressed a kiss to her temple. "Forgot the fuckin' condom," he muttered.

"I noticed," she whispered. And although the realization they'd had unprotected sex struck a note of fear into her heart, it was also incredibly sexy to know she'd had him in the raw.

"First time I've done that since I was a teenager," he said. "You got me so hot, lost all control. Gotta say, though, I'm not sorry."

She raised her head far enough to eye him curiously. "You're not?"

He dipped his chin and looked up at her, smoothing her hair back from her face. "Nope. I want kids with you. Maybe not right away, but I want 'em. Want a family, Lindi. A home. I'm done wanderin', wanna put down roots right here, with you. When you asked me, that night on the road, when I was comin' home? I realized that here, with you, it feels like that. Like home."

Lindi's heart and body spasmed at this, and Jack gave her a slow, beautiful, smile. "That mean you want that too, honey?"

She nodded, and then dipped her head to his chest again as tears flooded her eyes. "Yes," she said thickly. "Oh, I do. So much. But I want to run the BeeHive too."

"'Course you do," he said. "You got some help now, and you can hire more if you need to. We'll make it work."

Lindi's heart swelled even more. "Oh, Jack. I … I never dared hope for a family of my own and my café, too. I guess I thought I'd have to choose one or the other."

"Nah. Look around you. There's people with families runnin' businesses everywhere you turn. We'll make it work, honey."

Lindi pictured big, rough Jack holding a blonde baby in one arm, an equally blonde toddler by the hand, all of three of them smiling at her as they walked into her café, and had to blink back more tears of sheer joy.

He kissed her wet cheeks. "We'll be careful from now on, get you on the Pill if you can tolerate it, 'cause I got plans too, that'll keep us extra busy for a while. But in a year or two, I'll plant a baby in here, and watch you get round and sassy."

"Oh, Jack. What big plans?"

"C'mere, honey. Let's get cleaned up first, then we'll talk."

Cozily ensconced in the pillows, the covers tucked around her, he shared his ideas.

"I'm settling down once and for all, no doubts. But I need somethin' to do. I'm thinkin' the restaurant business is a good one," he said. "And the north shore could use a supper club."

"This is true," she agreed. "There used to be one closer to town, but it closed down. But where would you build it?"

"Well, since your property runs all the way down to the lake, there's room to build one next to the BeeHive. Not a fancy place, just a top-notch steak & rib house. Place with good food, good beer and drinks where folks can eat and then stick around to get a little rowdy to some live music. We could even build a dock on the shore, so folks could come up the lake by boat to eat if they want."

He looked at her. "Whaddya think?"

Lindi pressed her face into his shoulder and giggled.

"What?" Jack demanded, stiffening, his brows lowering. "I'm not without experience, woman—owned half interest in a supper club in Cali. That's one of the sales I finalized while I was down there."

"No, I l-love it," she managed. "It's a wonderful idea. I just thought of the perfect name. You can c-call it 'The Stinger'."

Jack relaxed and let loose his deep, raucous belly laugh, his body shaking under hers. "Damn—just might have to do that."

When their laughter had quieted, Lindi gave him a grave look. "Jack, what about the club? The Devil's Flyers—are you going to join, or whatever, and start hanging out with them?"

He considered this. "Nah, I been independent for years, since I left Redding, and it's what I'm used to. Stick knows Keys and I won't stir shit if we're here but not patched in locally. We'll have to stay solid with the chapter, help out when needed. But I'll tell you this—I won't be off partyin' and raisin' hell with the brothers all the time. And I won't be goin' on the road more than once or twice a year."

"And when you do, I get payback," she decided. "Girl's weekend at the casino and spa."

"Sounds fair enough."

"And you'll wear a wedding ring," she told him. "So those club women know you are taken."

He grinned at her. "Damn, woman. Next thing you'll have a ring through my nose so you can yank on it if I don't come runnin' fast enough."

"Euww," she protested. Then she had a wicked idea. "But maybe you could get one of those apra-hoohahs, you know. Penis piercings. I hear they're really fun for the woman."

Jack gave her a look of horror. "An apradavya? Oh, no, woman. Don't even go there. I ain't getting' no metal stuck through my cock. You'll take me big and hard and natural and like it."

She sighed wistfully, but then gave it up and tipped her head down, giggling against his chest. "I love your cock just the way it is, Jack Moran."

"That's good." He tugged on her hair, tipping her face up to his, his gaze soft. "I know your daddy left scars on your heart, honey. You sure you're ready to gamble on a ramblin' man like me?"

Lindi smiled at him. "Yes, Jack. If you're willing to gamble on a woman who jumps to conclusions first and remembers to ask her man for an explanation second."

He chuckled. "Oh, yeah. I'll take the sting, because I know you'll always show me the honey."

The End

More Red Hot Romance by Cathryn Cade

Dear Readers,

I hope you enjoyed reading about Jack and Lindi as much as I loved writing about them!

Please consider leaving a review to express your thoughts, good and bad, to help other readers like you—because you are cool—find the books.

Come by my Website
www.cathryncade.com

And hey, you! While you're there,
Leave me an email
Subscribe to My Newsletter
So you'll be the first to know about upcoming releases,
exclusive excerpts, giveaways, swag and more!

You can also find me on
Facebook.com/CathrynCade.Author

And for more

Sweet & Dirty BBW Romance

turn the page ...

Book Two
Honey for Nothin'
featuring Keys, Kit and Remi
in a red hot MMF ménage romance

Kit hates making choices—life has taught her she makes all the wrong ones. So what's a BBW redhead to do when she must choose between two hot bikers?

Book Three
The Man With All the Honey
featuring Sara and Stick

She's a cool, BBW blonde who works for law & order. He's the hot, dangerous president of the Devil's Flyers MC. When they end up neighbors, what could possibly go wrong?

Book Four
Follow the Honey
featuring Lesa and Pete

After she's fired unjustly for embezzling from a brewpub owned by the Devil's Flyers MC, revenge is the worst idea this bubbly, BBW brunette ever had. But when she's caught in a childish prank by her former boss, he has a very adult punishment in mind—starting with holding her captive.

Book Five
Honey in the Rock *(coming in 2017)*
Featuring Rocker & Billie

A tough biker saves a shy, BBW game designer from the local thugs and sets out to teach her self-defense skills, only to learn she can teach him a thing or two ... about opening up to love.

Book Six
Take the Honey and Run (*coming in 2017*)
featuring T-Bear and Coral

A lonely biker hires a pretty BBW strawberry blonde for the night, only to learn she has no idea he paid for her charms. If he wants her for more, he'll have to rescue her from some very bad dudes ... but the hardest part may be convincing her to believe in him.

Book Seven
Hawaiian Honey (*coming in 2017*)
Featuring Moke & Shelle

She ran all the way to Hawaii to hide from her past. He came to regain his—and this biker is willing to ride into the heart of the volcano to get what he wants ... including her.

*... and for more Sexy Contemporary Romance,
turn the page*

**Oh, Look! Here's more
Sexy Contemporary Romance**

Hawaiian Heroes
Walking in Fire
Rolling in the Deep
Blooming in the Wild
Burning Up the Rain
Maui Moon (*coming in 2017*)

Club 3
She's All In
She's All Tied Up
She's All That
She's Worth It All

(Barely) Married
Show Me I'm Yours (*coming in 2017*)
Show Me You're Mine (*coming in 2017*)
Show Me You Mean It (*coming in 2018*)
Just Show Me (*coming in 2018*)

Chasing Wild
Cougar's Bride (*coming in 2017*)
and doubtless more big cat tracks to follow …

About the Author

Cathryn Cade lives and writes in the beautiful lake country of North Idaho. When she's not tossing hot alpha heroes together with feisty heroines, she loves to quilt with colors as wild as her characters, read, and chat on Facebook.

She and her own alpha male enjoy bicycling, hiking, gardening, trying new brew pubs and spending time on their boat. Then she sends him out to play in his huge, backyard workshop so she can write some more.

Copper, the incredibly patient golden retriever, keeps her company as she writes. He tried critiquing for her, but he was too kind, so she gave him a dog treat and fired him.

* * *

Made in the USA
Coppell, TX
22 September 2020